RESIDENT EVIL

NEMESIS

RESIDENT EVIL™

NEMESIS

S.D. PERRY

TITAN BOOKS

RESIDENT EVIL: NEMESIS
Print edition ISBN: 9781781161814
E-book edition ISBN: 9781781161876

Published by Titan Books
A division of Titan Publishing Group Ltd
144 Southwark Street, London SE1 0UP

First edition November 2012
3 5 7 9 10 8 6 4

A CIP catalogue record for this title is available
from the British Library.

Printed and bound in India by Thomson Press India Ltd.

Did you enjoy this book? We love to hear from our readers.
Please email us at readerfeedback@titanemail.com or write to
us at Reader Feedback at the above address.

To receive advance information, news, competitions, and
exclusive offers online, please sign up for the Titan newsletter
on our website: **www.titanbooks.com**

FOR THE READERS, WHO KEEP THIS THING GOING. AND FOR CURT SHULZ, WHO DIDN'T THINK I'D DEDICATE A BOOK TO HIM.

"Yield not to evils, but attack all the more boldly."

VIRGIL

AUTHOR'S NOTE

Faithful readers of this series may notice time and/ or character discrepancies between the books and the games (or the books and the books, for that matter). With the games and novelizations being written, revised, and produced at different times and by different people, complete consistency is nearly impossible. I can only apologize on behalf of us all, and hope that in spite of chronological errors, you will continue to enjoy the mix of corporate zombies and hapless heroes that makes *Resident Evil* so much fun.

PROLOGUE

Carlos was just getting out of the shower when the phone rang. He wrapped a towel around his waist and stumbled out into the cramped living room, nearly tripping over a still unopened box of books in his haste to get to the bleating phone; he hadn't had time to get an answering machine since moving to the city, and only the new field office had his number. It wouldn't pay to miss any calls, particularly since Umbrella was footing his bills.

He snatched up the receiver with one dripping hand and tried not to sound too out of breath.

"Hello?"

"Carlos, it's Mitch Hirami."

Unconsciously, Carlos stood up a little straighter, still clutching the damp towel. "Yes, sir."

Hirami was his squad leader. Carlos had only met him twice, not enough time to get a solid read on him, but he seemed competent enough—as did the other guys in the squad.

Competent, if not exactly up-front... Like Carlos, no one talked much about their past, although he knew for a fact that Hirami had been involved in gunrunning through South America a few years back before he'd started to work for Umbrella. It seemed that everyone he'd met on the U.B.C.S. had a secret or two—most of them involving activities not strictly legal.

"Orders just came down on a developing situation. We're calling everyone in on this, ASAP. You got an hour to report, and we leave in two, that's 1500 hours, *comprende*?"

"*Si*—uh, yes, sir." Carlos had been fluent in English for years, but he was still getting used to speaking it full-time. "Is there any info on what kind of situation?"

"Negative. You'll be briefed along with the rest of us when you come in."

Hirami's tone of voice suggested that he had more to say. Carlos waited, starting to feel chilled by the water drying on his body.

"Word is, it's a chemical spill," Hirami said, and Carlos thought he could hear a thread of unease in the squad leader's voice. "Something that's making people... making them act differently."

Carlos frowned. "Differently how?"

Hirami sighed. "They don't pay us to ask questions, Oliveira, do they? Now you know as much as I do. Just get here."

"Yes, sir," Carlos said, but Hirami had already hung up.

Carlos dropped the receiver into its cradle, not sure if he should feel excited or nervous about his first U.B.C.S. operation. Umbrella Bio-Hazard Countermeasure Service: an impressive title for a group of hired ex-mercenaries and ex-military, most with combat experience and shady backgrounds. The recruiter in Honduras had said that they'd be called upon to "deal" with situations that Umbrella needed handled quickly and aggressively—and legally. After three years of fighting in private little wars between rival gangs and revolutionaries, of living in mud shacks and eating out of cans, the promise of real employment—and at an astonishingly good wage—was like an answered prayer.

Too good to be true, that's what I thought... and what if it turns out that I was right?

Carlos shook his head. He wasn't going to find out standing around in a towel. In any case, it couldn't possibly be worse than shooting it out with a bunch of coked-up *pendejos* in some anonymous jungle, wondering if he'd hear the bullet that finally took him out.

He had an hour, and it was a twenty-minute walk to the office. He turned toward the bedroom, suddenly determined to show up early, to see if he could get any more out of Hirami about what was going on. Already, he could feel the warm build of nervous adrenaline in his gut, a feeling he'd grown up with and knew better than any other—part anticipation, part excitement, and a healthy dose of fear...

Carlos grinned as he finished toweling off, amused at himself. He'd spent too much time in the jungle. He was in the United States now, working for a legitimate pharmaceutical company—what was there to be afraid of?

"*Nada*," he said, and, still smiling, he went to find his fatigues.

*   *   *

Late September in the outskirts of the big city; it was a sunny day, but Carlos could feel the first whisper of autumn as he hurried toward the field office, a kind of thinning of the air, leaves beginning to wilt on the branches overhead. Not that there were very many trees; his apartment was at the edge of a sprawling industrial area—a few dingy fabrication plants, fenced lots overgrown with weeds, seeming acres of run-down storage facilities. The U.B.C.S. office was actually a renovated warehouse on an Umbrella-owned lot, surrounded by a fairly modern shipping complex complete with helipad and loading docks—a nice setup, although Carlos wondered again why they'd decided to build in such a crummy area. They could obviously afford much better.

Carlos checked his watch as he headed up Everett Street and started to walk a little faster. He wasn't going to be late, but he still wanted to get there before the briefing, see what the other guys were saying. Hirami had said they were calling in everyone—four platoons, three squads of ten in each platoon, 120 people all total. Carlos was a corporal in squad A of platoon D; ridiculous, how these things were set up, but he supposed it was necessary to keep track of everyone. Somebody had to know something...

He took a right where Everett met 374th, his thoughts wandering, vaguely curious about where they were being sent—

—when a man stepped out of an alley only a few meters in front of him, a well-dressed stranger wearing a wide smile. He stood there, hands jammed into the pockets of an expensive trench coat, apparently waiting for Carlos to reach him.

Carlos kept his expression carefully neutral, studying the man warily. Tall, thin, dark hair and eyes but definitely Caucasian, early to mid-40s—and grinning as though he meant to share an exceptionally funny joke.

Carlos prepared to walk past him, reminding himself of how many crazies lived in any decent-sized city, an unavoidable hazard of urban life.

He probably wants to tell me about the aliens monitoring his brain waves, maybe babble some conspiracy theory—

"Carlos Oliveira?" the man asked but it was more of a statement than a question.

Carlos stopped in his tracks, his whole body tensing, instinctively letting his right hand drop to where he wore a gun—except he wasn't carrying, hadn't since crossing the border, *carajo*—

As if sensing the upset he'd caused, the stranger took a step back, holding his hands up in the air. He seemed amused, but not especially threatening.

"Who's asking?" Carlos snapped. *And how the hell did you know my name?*

"My name is Trent, Mr. Oliveira," he said, his dark gaze glittering with barely suppressed mirth. "And I have some information for you."

ONE

In the dream, Jill didn't run fast enough.

It was the same dream she'd suffered every few days since the mission that had nearly killed them all that terrible, endless night in July. Back when only a few Raccoon citizens had been hurt by Umbrella's secret and the S.T.A.R.S. administration wasn't completely corrupt, back when she was still stupid enough to think that people would believe their story.

In the dream, she and the other survivors—Chris, Barry, and Rebecca—waited anxiously for rescue at the hidden laboratory's helipad, all of them exhausted, wounded, and very aware that the buildings around and beneath them were about to self-destruct. It was dawn, cool light coming in shafts through the trees that surrounded the Spencer estate, the stillness broken only by the welcome sound of the approaching 'copter. Six members of the Special Tactics and Rescue Service were dead, lost to the human and inhuman creatures that roamed the estate, and if Brad didn't set down quick, there wouldn't be any survivors. The lab was going to blow, destroying the proof of Umbrella's T-virus spill and killing them all.

Chris and Barry waved their arms, motioning for Brad to hurry. Jill checked her watch, dazed, her mind still trying to grasp all that had happened, to sort it all out. Umbrella Pharmaceutical, the single biggest contributor to Raccoon City's prosperity and a major force in the corporate world, had secretly created monsters in the name of bioweapons research—and in playing with fire had managed to burn themselves very badly.

That didn't matter now, all that mattered was getting the hell away—

* * *

—and we've got maybe three minutes, four max—

CRASH!

Jill whirled around, saw chunks of concrete and tar fly into the air and rain down over the northwest corner of the landing pad. A giant claw stretched up from the hole, fell across the jagged lip—

—and the pale, hulking monster, the one she and Barry had tried to kill in the lab, the Tyrant, leaped out onto the heliport. It rose smoothly from its agile crouch... and started toward them.

It was an abomination, at least eight feet tall, once human, perhaps, but no more. Its right hand, normal. Its left, a massive, chitinous grasp of claws. Its face had been horribly altered, its lips cut away so that it seemed to grin at them through sliced red tissue. Its naked body was sexless, the thick, bloody tumor that was its heart shuddering wetly outside of its chest.

Chris targeted the pulsing muscle with his Beretta and fired, five 9mm rounds tearing into its ghastly flesh; the Tyrant didn't even slow down. Barry screamed for them to scatter, and then they were running, Jill pulling Rebecca away, the thunder of Barry's .357 crashing behind them. Overhead, the 'copter circled and Jill could feel the seconds ticking away, almost believed she could feel the explosion building beneath their feet.

She and Rebecca pulled their weapons and started firing. Jill continued to pull the trigger even as she watched the creature knock Barry to the ground, slamming in a new clip as it went after Chris, firing and screaming, enveloped by a rising terror, why won't it go down?

From above, a shout, and something thrown out of the 'copter. Chris ran for it, and Jill saw nothing else—nothing but the Tyrant as it turned its attention to her and Rebecca, indifferent to the firepower that continued plugging bloody holes through its strange body. Jill turned and ran, saw the girl do the same, and knew—knew—that the monster was after her, the face of Jill Valentine embedded in its lizard brain.

Jill ran, ran, and suddenly there was no heliport, no crumbling mansion, only a million trees and the sounds: her boots slapping the earth, the pulse of blood in her ears, her ragged breath. The monster was

silent behind her, a mute and terrible force, relentless and as inevitable as death.

They were dead, Chris and Barry, Rebecca, even Brad, she knew it, everyone but her—and as she ran, she saw the Tyrant's shadow stretch out in front of her, burying her own, and the hiss of its monstrous talons slicing down, melting through her body, killing her, no—

* * *

No—

"No!"

Jill opened her eyes, the word still on her lips, the only sound in the stillness of her room. It wasn't the scream she imagined but the weak, strangled cry of a woman doomed, caught in a nightmare from which there was no escape.

Which I am. None of us were fast enough, after all.

She lay still for a moment, breathing deeply, moving her hand away from the loaded Beretta under her pillow; it had become a reflex, and one she wasn't sorry to have developed.

"Useless against nightmares, though," she muttered and sat up. She'd been talking to herself for days now; sometimes, she thought it was the only thing that kept her sane. Gray light crept in through the blinds, casting the small bedroom in shadow. The digital clock on the nightstand was still working; she supposed she should be glad that the power was still on, but it was later than she'd hoped—nearly three in the afternoon. She'd slept for almost six hours, the most she'd managed to get in the last three days. Considering what was going on outside, she couldn't help a flush of guilt. She should be out there, she should be doing more to save those who could still be saved...

Knock it off, you know better. You can't help anyone if you collapse. And those people you helped—

She wouldn't think about that, not yet. When she'd finally made it back to the suburbs this morning, after nearly forty-eight sleepless hours of "helping," she'd been on the verge of a breakdown, forced to face the reality of what had happened to Raccoon: The city was irretrievably lost to the T-virus, or some variant of it.

Like the researchers at the mansion. Like the Tyrant.

Jill closed her eyes, thinking about the recurring dream, about what it meant. It matched the real chain of events perfectly, except for the end—Brad Vickers, the S.T.A.R.S. Alpha pilot, *had* thrown something out of the 'copter, a grenade launcher, and Chris had blown up the Tyrant as it was going after her. They'd all gotten away in time... but in a way, that didn't matter. For all the good they'd been able to accomplish since then, they might as well have died.

It's not our fault, Jill thought angrily, aware that she wanted to believe that more than anything. *No one would listen—not the home office, not Chief Irons, not the press. If they'd listened, if they'd believed...*

Strange, that all of it had happened only six weeks ago; it felt like years. The city officials and the local papers had enjoyed a field day with the S.T.A.R.S.'s reputation—six dead, the rest babbling fantastic stories about a secret laboratory, about monsters and zombies and an Umbrella conspiracy. They had been suspended and ridiculed—but worst of all, nothing had been done to prevent the spread of the virus. She and the others had only been able to hope that the destruction of the spill site had put an end to the immediate danger.

In the weeks following, so much had happened. They'd uncovered the truth about the S.T.A.R.S., that Umbrella—technically, White Umbrella, the division in charge of bioweapons research—was either bribing or blackmailing key members nationally in order to continue their research unimpeded. They'd learned that several of Raccoon City's council members were on the Umbrella payroll, and that Umbrella probably had more than one research facility experimenting with man-made diseases. Their search for information about Trent, the stranger who'd contacted her before the disastrous mission as "a friend to the S.T.A.R.S.," had turned up nothing, but they'd come up with some extremely interesting background stuff on Chief Irons: it seemed that the chief had been in hot water at one point about a possible rape, and that Umbrella knew about it and had helped him get his position anyway. Perhaps most difficult of all, their team had been forced to split up, to make hard decisions about what needed to be done and about their own responsibilities to the truth.

Jill smiled faintly; the one thing she could feel good about in all of this was that at least her friends had made it out. Rebecca Chambers had joined up with another small group of S.T.A.R.S. dissidents who were checking out rumors of other Umbrella laboratories. Brad Vickers, true to his cowardly nature, had skipped town to avoid Umbrella's wrath. Chris Redfield was already in Europe, scoping out the company's headquarters and waiting for Barry Burton and Rebecca's team to join him... and for Jill, who was going to wrap up her investigation of Umbrella's local offices before hooking up with the others.

Except five days ago, something terrible had happened in Raccoon. It was still happening, unfolding like some poisonous flower, and the only hope now was to wait for someone outside to take notice.

When the first few cases had been reported, no one had connected them with the S.T.A.R.S. stories about the Spencer estate. Several people had been attacked in the late spring and early summer— surely the work of some deranged killer, after all; the RPD would catch him in no time. It wasn't until the Raccoon Police Department had put up roadblocks on Umbrella orders, three days earlier, that people had started paying attention. Jill didn't know how they were managing to keep people out of the city, but they were—nothing shipped in, no mail service, and the outside lines were cut. Citizens trying to leave town were turned back, told nothing about why.

It all seemed so surreal now, those first hours after Jill had found out about the attacks, about the blockades. She'd gone to the RPD building to see Chief Irons, but he had refused to talk to her. Jill had known that some of the cops would listen, that not everyone was as blind or corrupt as Irons—but even with the bizarre nature of the assaults they'd witnessed, they hadn't been ready to accept the truth.

And who could blame them? "Listen up, officers— Umbrella, the company that's responsible for building up our fair city, has been experimenting with a designer virus in their own backyard. They've been breeding and growing unnatural creatures in secret laboratories, then injecting them with something that makes them incredibly strong and extremely violent. When humans are exposed to this stuff, they become zombies, for lack of a better term. Flesh-eating, mindless, decaying-on-the-hoof zombies, who feel no pain and try to eat other people. They're not really dead, but they're pretty close. So, let's work together, okay? Let's go out there and start mowing down unarmed citizens in the streets, your friends and neighbors, because if we don't, you could be next."

Sitting on the edge of the bed, Jill sighed. She'd been a little more tactful, but no matter how well worded, it was still an insane story. Of course they hadn't believed her, not then, not in the light of day and in the safety of their uniforms. It hadn't been until after dark, when the screaming had begun...

That had been the 25th of September, and today was the 28th, and the police were almost certainly all dead; she'd last heard gunshots... yesterday? Last night? It could have been the rioters, she supposed, but it didn't matter anymore. Raccoon was dead, except for the brain-dead virus carriers that roamed the streets, looking for a meal.

Between no sleep and a near constant pump of adrenaline, the days had blurred together for her. After the police force had been destroyed, Jill had spent her time looking for survivors, endless hours ducking down alleys, knocking on doors, combing buildings for those who'd managed to hide. She'd found dozens, and with some help from a few of them, they'd made it to a safe place, a high school that they had barricaded. Jill had made sure they were secure before going back out into the city, searching for others.

She'd found no one. And this morning, when she'd gone back to the high school...

She didn't want to think about it, but some part of her knew that she had to, that she couldn't afford to forget. This morning, she'd gone back and the barricade had been gone. Torn down by zombies, or perhaps taken down by someone inside, someone who looked out and thought they saw a brother or uncle or daughter in the crowd of flesh-eaters. Someone who thought that they were saving the life of a loved one, not realizing that it was too late.

It had been a slaughterhouse, the air fetid with the stink of shit and vomit, the walls decorated with great smears of blood. Jill had nearly given up, then, more tired than she'd ever been, unable to see anything but the bodies of those who'd been lucky enough to die before the virus could amplify in their systems. As she'd walked through the almost empty halls, killing the handful of carriers that had still been stumbling around—people she'd found, people who had cried with relief when they'd seen her only hours before— whatever hope she'd held on to was gone, lost with the realization that everything she'd been through was worthless. Knowing the truth about Umbrella hadn't saved anyone, and the citizens she thought she'd led to safety—over seventy men, women, and children— were gone.

She couldn't really remember how she'd made it home. She hadn't been able to think straight, and had barely been able to see through eyes swollen from crying. Outside of how it affected her, *thousands* had died; it was a tragedy so vast it was nearly incomprehensible.

It could have been prevented. And it was Umbrella's fault.

Jill pulled the Beretta out from under her pillow, allowing herself to feel for the first time the immensity of what Umbrella had done. For the last few days, she'd kept her emotions in check—there had been people to lead, to help, and there'd been no place for any personal feelings.

Now, though...

She was ready to get out of Raccoon and make the

bastards who'd let this happen know how she felt. They had stolen her hope, but they couldn't stop her from surviving.

Jill chambered a round and set her jaw, the stirrings of true hatred in her gut. It was time to leave.

TWO

They would be in Raccoon city in just under an hour.

Nicholai Ginovaef was prepared, and he believed his squad would do well—better than the rest, anyway. The nine others that made up squad B respected him; he had seen it in their eyes, and although they would almost certainly die, their performance would be noteworthy. After all, he had practically trained them himself.

There was no talking in the helicopter that carried platoon D through the late afternoon, not even among the squad leaders, the only personnel who wore headsets. It was too loud for the troops to hear one another, and Nicholai had nothing to say to either Hirami or Cryan—or Mikhail Victor, for that matter. Victor was their superior, the commander of the entire platoon. It was a job that should have belonged to Nicholai; Victor lacked the qualities that made up a true leader.

I possess them, though. I was chosen for Watchdog, and when this is all over, I'm the one Umbrella will have to deal with, whether they like it or not.

Nicholai kept his face as stone, but he smiled inside. When the time came, "they," the men who controlled Umbrella from behind the scenes, would realize that they'd underestimated him.

He sat near the A and C squad leaders against one wall of the cabin, soothed by the steady and familiar throb of the transport. The very air was charged with tension and heavy with the scent of masculine sweat; again, familiar. He had led men into battle before—although if everything went as planned, he would never have to again.

He let his gaze wander over the taut faces of the troops, wondering if any of them would survive more than an hour or two. It was possible, he supposed. There was the scarred man from South Africa, in Cryan's group... and on his own squad, John Wersbowski, who had taken part in an ethnic cleansing a few years back, Nicholai couldn't remember which one. Both men had the combination of deep suspicion and self-possession that might conceivably allow them to escape Raccoon, however unlikely—and it *was* unlikely. The briefing hadn't prepared any of them for what was ahead...

Nicholai's own private briefing, two days earlier, had been a different matter; Operation Watchdog, they called it. He knew the projected numbers, had been told what to expect and how to most effectively dispatch the unclean, the walking diseased. They'd told him about the Tyrant-like seeker units that were going to be sent in, and how to avoid them. He knew more than anyone on the transport.

But I'm also readier than Umbrella can possibly imagine... because I know the names of the other "dogs."

Again, he suppressed a smile. He possessed additional information that Umbrella didn't know he had, that was worth a great deal of money—or would be, soon enough. On the surface, the U.B.C.S. was being sent in to rescue civilians; that was what they'd been told, anyway. But he was one of the ten who'd been chosen to gather and record data on the T-virus carriers, human and otherwise, and on how they fared against trained soldiers—the real reason the U.B.C.S. were being sent in, aka Watchdog. In the helicopter that carried platoon A were two others, disguised as U.B.C.S.; there were six already planted in Raccoon—three scientists, two Umbrella paper pushers, and a woman who worked for the city. The tenth was a police officer, a personal assistant to the chief himself. Each of them probably knew one or two of the others that Umbrella had handpicked as information collectors—but thanks to his well-developed computer skills and a few "borrowed" passwords, he was the only one who knew about all of them, as well as where each was supposed to be to file their reports.

Wouldn't their contacts be surprised when they failed to report in? Wouldn't it be amusing if only one

Watchdog survived and was able to name his price for the information that had been gathered? And wasn't it amazing to think that a man could become a multimillionaire if he was willing to expend thought, a bit of effort, and a few bullets?

Nine people. He was nine people away from being the only Umbrella employee to have the information they wanted. Most, if not all, of the U.B.C.S. would die quickly, and then he'd be free to find the other Watchdogs, to take their data and end their miserable lives.

This time he couldn't help it; Nicholai grinned. The mission that lay ahead promised to be an exciting one, a true test of his many skills... and when it was over, he was going to be a very wealthy man.

* * *

In spite of the cramped seating and the dull roar of the 'copter's engines, Carlos was only faintly aware of his surroundings. He couldn't get his mind off of Trent and the decidedly weird conversation they'd had only a couple of hours ago, and he found that he kept replaying it, trying to decide if any of it was useful.

To begin with, Carlos had trusted the guy about as far as he could toss him. The man had been way too happy; not outwardly so much, but Carlos had gotten the definite impression that Trent was laughing about something just beneath the surface. His dark eyes had fairly danced with humor as he'd told Carlos that he had information for him, stepping back into the alley he'd emerged from as if there had been no question Carlos would follow.

There hadn't been really. Carlos had learned to be very careful in his line of work, but he also knew a few things about reading people—and Trent, though obviously strange, hadn't been particularly threatening.

The alley had been cool and dark and had smelled faintly of urine. "What kind of information?" Carlos had asked.

Trent had acted as though he hadn't heard the question. "In the shopping district downtown, you'll find a diner called Grill 13; it's just up the street from the fountain and right next to the theater, you can't miss it. If you can manage to get there by"—he'd glanced at his watch—"say, 1900 hours, I'll see what can be done to help you."

Carlos hadn't even known where to start. "Hey, no offense, but what the hell are you talking about?"

Trent had smiled. "Raccoon City. It's where you're going."

Carlos had stared at him, waiting for more, but Trent had seemed to be finished.

God knows how he got my name, but this bato *ain't playing with a full deck.*

"Uh, listen, Mr. Trent—"

"Just Trent," he'd cut in, still smiling.

Carlos had started to get irritated. "Whatever. I

think you might have the wrong Oliveira... and while I appreciate your, uh, *concern,* I've really got to get going."

"Ah, yes, duty calls," Trent had said, his smile fading. "Understand, they won't tell you all you need to know. It will be far, far worse. The hours ahead may be dark ones, Mr. Oliveira, but I have faith in your abilities. Just remember—Grill 13, seven o'clock. Northeast corner of the city proper."

"Yeah, sure," Carlos had said, nodding, backing away into the daylight, wearing a somewhat forced grin of his own. "Good deal. I'll make a note of it."

Trent had smiled again, stepping out after him. "Be very careful who you trust, Mr. Oliveira. And good luck."

Carlos had turned and started to walk quickly away, throwing a glance back at Trent. The man had watched him, hands in his pockets again, his stance casual and relaxed. For a nutbag, he sure didn't *seem* crazy...

...and he seems a lot less crazy now, eh?

Carlos had still made it to the office a little early, but nobody seemed to have heard anything off the grapevine about what was up. At the short briefing presented by the U.B.C.S. platoon leaders, they'd all been told what few facts there were: a toxic chemical spill had occurred earlier in the week in an isolated community, causing hallucinations that bred violence. The chemicals had dissipated, but regular civilians continued to be harassed by those who'd been affected; there was evidence that the damage could be permanent, and the local police hadn't been able to get things under control. The U.B.C.S. was being sent in to help evacuate the citizens who hadn't been affected, and to use force, if necessary, to protect them from harm. Top secret all the way.

In Raccoon City. Which meant that maybe Trent knew something, after all... and what did *that* mean?

If he was right about where we're going, what about the rest of it? What didn't they tell us that we need to know? And what could possibly be far, far worse than a mob of deranged and violent people?

He didn't know, and he didn't like not knowing. He'd first picked up a gun at the age of twelve to help defend his family from a band of terrorists, and had gone pro at seventeen—for four years now, he'd been paid to put his life in danger for one cause or another. But he'd always known what the stakes were, and what he was up against. This was not at all cool, the thought of going in blind. The only consolation was that he was going in with over a hundred experienced soldiers; whatever it was, they'd be able to handle it.

Carlos looked around, thinking that he was with a good group. Not good men, necessarily, but adept fighters, way more important in combat. They even *looked* ready, their eyes hard and watchful, their faces determined—

—except for the B squad leader, who was staring off into space and grinning like a shark. Like a predator. Carlos was suddenly uneasy, looking at the guy, Nicholai something-or-other, cropped white hair, built like a weight lifter. He'd never seen anyone smile quite like that...

The Russian met his gaze, and his grin widened for just a moment, in a way that made Carlos want to sit with his back to a wall, a gun in hand—

—and then the moment was over, and Nicholai nodded absently at him and looked away. Just another soldier acknowledging a comrade, nothing more. He was being paranoid, that meeting with Trent had him on edge, and he was always a little skitchy before a fight...

Grill 13, next to the theater.

He wouldn't forget. Just in case.

THREE

Jill's plan was to skirt the town to the southeast, sticking to side streets and cutting through buildings as much as possible; the main streets weren't safe, and many of them had been blocked off in an attempt to corral the zombies, before things got too bad. If she could make it far enough south, she should be able to cut across farmland to Route 71, one of the feeders to the main highway.

So far, so good. At this rate, I'll make it to 71 before it gets completely dark.

It had taken less than an hour to make it from the suburbs to the apparently empty apartment building where she now stood, shivering a little from the damp chill that pervaded the poorly lit hallway. She'd dressed for ease of movement rather than protection from the elements—a tight shirt, a miniskirt, and boots, as well as a fanny pack to hold extra magazines. The body-hugging outfit clung to her like a second skin and would allow her to move quickly. She'd also brought a plain white sweatshirt for when she made it out of the city, which she now wore tied around her waist—for the time being, she'd rather suffer the chill and have her arms free.

The Imperial was a slightly run-down apartment building at the southern edge of uptown Raccoon. Jill had discovered from her earlier excursions that once infected, the T-virus zombies went in search of food as soon as they could, abandoning their homes and taking to the streets. Not all of them, of course, but enough so that cutting through buildings was generally safer than being out in the open.

A noise. A soft moan coming from behind one of the apartment doors farther down the hall. Jill froze, gun in hand, straining to hear which side it came from, and realized in the same moment that she could smell gas.

"Shit," she whispered, trying to recall the layout of the building as the oily, pungent scent filled her nostrils. A right turn where the corridor T-ed ahead, and...

...and, another right? Or is the lobby right there? Think, you were here two days ago, Jesus, that's gotta be a massive leak—

There was another groan from up ahead, definitely coming from the apartment on the left. It was the mindless, empty sound that the zombies made, the only sound they *could* make as far as she knew. The door was cracked open, and Jill almost imagined she could see the shimmering waves of gas-thick air pouring out into the hall.

She gripped the Beretta tighter and took a step backwards. She'd have to go back the way she'd come, she didn't dare risk firing and she didn't particularly want to fend off one of the carriers bare-handed; a single bite from one of them would pass the infection on to her. Another step backwards, and—

Creak.

Jill spun around, instinctively raising her weapon as a door swung open perhaps five meters back. A shuffling, stoop-shouldered man lurched out into the gloom, cutting her off from the back entrance. He had the sallow skin and dead eyes of a virus carrier, as if the fact that one of his cheeks had been ripped off wasn't proof enough; zombies felt no pain. As this one opened its mouth to moan hungrily at her, she could see the base of its gray, swollen tongue, and even the reek of gas couldn't entirely overwhelm the sickly sweet odor of its decaying flesh.

Jill turned, saw that the hallway ahead was still clear; she had no choice but to run past the apartment with the gas leak and hope that its resident was too slow to try for her.

Go. Now.

She took off, staying as close to the right side of the hall as she could, feeling the effects of the gas as she pumped her arms for more speed—a soft distortion of light, a sense of dizziness, an ugly taste at the back of her throat. She ran past the cracked door, distantly relieved that it opened no wider, suddenly remembering that the lobby was directly to the right. She rounded the corner—

—and *bam*, collided with a woman, knocking her down. Jill careened off her, hitting the stucco wall with her right shoulder hard enough that a light powder settled over them. She barely noticed, too intent on the fallen woman and on the three figures still standing in the small foyer, shifting their dumb attention to Jill. All of them were virus carriers.

The woman, dressed in the tatters of a once white nightgown, gurgled incoherently and tried to sit up. One of her eyes was gone, the red, raw socket shining in the overhead light. The three others, all male, started toward Jill, moaning, their gangrenous arms raising slowly; two of them were blocking the metal and glass wall that led into the street—her way out.

Three on foot, one crawling, reaching for her legs, at least two behind her. Jill scuttled sideways toward the security door, weapon pointed at the peeling forehead of the closest, less than two meters away. The wall of mailboxes behind him were made of metal, but she had no choice, she could only hope that the gas fumes were weaker here.

The creature lunged and Jill fired, simultaneously leaping for the door as the semi-jacketed round tore into his skull—

—and she felt as much as heard the explosion, *sssssh-BOOM*, a displacement of fiery air that shoved her in the direction she'd jumped, hard, everything moving too fast to separate, to understand chronologically—her body, aching, the door dissolving, the world blotted out in shades of strobing white. She tucked and rolled, hard asphalt biting into her shoulder, the horrific smells of flash-fried meat and burning hair washing over her as shards of blackened glass peppered the street.

Jill scrambled to her feet, ignoring all of it as she spun around, ready to fire again as flames began to eat the remains of the Imperial. She blinked her watering eyes, widening them, trying to see past the swimming flash spots that covered everything around her.

At least two of the zombies were down, probably dead, but two others stumbled around in the burning wreckage, their clothes and hair on fire. To Jill's right and rear were the remnants of a police blockade, barrier rails and parked cars; she could hear more of the human carriers on the other side, shuffling and moaning.

And there, to her left, already turning its slack and lolling head in her direction, was a single male, his ripped clothes slathered in drying blood. Jill took aim and squeezed the trigger, sending a bullet through its virus-riddled brain, walking toward it even as it crumpled; there was a Dumpster just past the dying body, and past that, several uptown blocks of shopping district, now her best choice for escape.

Have to head west, see if I can work around the blockades farther along...

With the immediate danger past, she took a few seconds to catalog her injuries—abrasions on both knees and a bruised shoulder speckled with grit; it could have been a hell of a lot worse. Her ears rang and her vision still suffered, but those would pass soon enough.

She reached the Dumpster and did her best to lean over it, to see down either side of the overcast north-south street in front of her. The bin was wedged between the side wall of a trendy clothes shop and a decidedly crunched car, limiting what she could see. Jill listened for a moment, for cries of hunger or the distinctive shuffling sounds of multiple carriers, but she heard nothing.

Probably wouldn't be able to hear a brass band at this point, she thought sourly and hoisted herself up. Straight across from the Dumpster was a door that she thought led through a back alley, but she was more interested in what lay to the left—with any luck, a straight shot out of town.

Jill jumped down, glanced to either side, and felt tendrils of real panic wrap around her brain. There were dozens of them, left and right, the closest already moving to cut her off from the Dumpster.

Move, Jilly!

Her father's voice. Jill didn't hesitate, took two running steps and threw her uninjured shoulder against the rusting door straight ahead. The door shuddered but didn't give.

"Come *on*," she said, unaware that she'd spoken, focusing herself on the door, *doesn't matter how close they are, gotta get through—*

She rammed the door again, the cloying scent of their rotting flesh enveloping her, and still the door held.

Focus! Do it, now! Again, the authoritative voice of her father, her first teacher. Jill gathered herself, leaned back, and felt the brush of cold fingers against the side of her neck, a rush of putrid, eager breath across her cheek.

Crash, the door flew open and slammed into the bricks behind, and Jill was through, running, remembering a warehouse ahead and to the right, her pulse racing. Behind her, rising wails of disappointment, of frustrated hunger, echoing through the alley that was her salvation. A door ahead.

Please be open, please—

Jill grabbed for the handle, pushed, and the metal door opened into silence, into a well-lit, open space, thank *God—*

—and she saw a man standing on the main floor, just below the landing she'd stepped onto; she raised the Beretta but didn't fire, quickly assessing him before lowering it again. In spite of his torn and blood-spattered clothes, she could tell by his desperate, fearful expression that he wasn't a carrier... or at least not one that had changed over yet.

Jill felt relief course through her at the sight of another person, and suddenly realized just how lonely she'd been. Even having an untrained civilian with her, someone to help who could help her in turn...

She smiled shakily, moving toward the steps that led down to the main floor, already making changes in her plans. They'd have to find him a weapon, she'd seen an old shotgun at the Bar Jack two days before, unloaded, but they could probably find shells and it was pretty close—

—and together, we can probably get through one of the barricades! She only needed someone to keep watch and to help her push some of the cars out of the way.

"We have to get out of here," she said, forcing as much hope as she could manage. "Help isn't going to be coming, at least not for a while, but between the two of us—"

"Are you crazy?" he interrupted, his fevered gaze darting around. "I'm not going anywhere, lady. My own daughter's out there somewhere, lost..."

He trailed off, staring at the door she'd come through as if he could see through it.

Jill nodded, reminding herself that he was probably in shock. "All the more reason to—"

Again, he cut her off, his panicky voice rising into a shout that reverberated through the open space. "She's out there, and she's probably *dead* like the rest of them, and if I won't go out there for *her*, you gotta be insane to think I'm going to go out there for *you*!"

Jill jammed the Beretta into the waist of her skirt, quickly holding up both hands, keeping her tone soothing. "Hey, I understand. I'm sorry about your daughter, really, but if we get out of the city, we can get help, we can come back—maybe she's hiding somewhere, and our best bet to find her is if we get some help."

He backed up a step, and she could see the terror

beneath his anger. She'd seen it before, the false fury that some people used to avoid being afraid, and she knew that she wasn't going to be able to get through to him.

But I have to try...

"I know you're scared," she said softly. "I am, too. But I'm—I was one of the members of the Special Tactics and Rescue Service; we were trained for dangerous operations, and I truly believe that I can get us out of this. You'll be safer if you come with me."

He backed up another step. "Go to hell, you, you *bitch*," he spat, then turned and ran, stumbling across the cement floor. There was a storage trailer at the far side of the warehouse. He crawled inside, panting as he pulled his legs in. Jill caught just a glimpse of his red and sweating face as he pulled the doors closed after him. She heard the metal *clink* of a lock, followed by a muffled shout that left no question as to his decision.

"Just go away! Leave me alone!"

Jill felt her own burst of anger, but knew it was useless, as useless as trying to reason with him any further. Sighing, she turned and walked back to the steps, carefully avoiding the depression that threatened to take over. She checked her watch—it was 4:30—and then sat down, going over her mental map of uptown Raccoon. If the rest of the streets out were as thoroughly overrun, she was going to have to veer back into town, try from another direction. She had five full magazines, fifteen rounds in each, but she'd need more firepower... like a shotgun, perhaps. If she couldn't find shells, she could at least club the bastards with it.

"The Bar Jack it is, then," she said quietly and pressed the heels of her hands into her eyes, wondering how she would ever make it.

FOUR

They reached the city in the late afternoon, 1650 by Carlos's check, and prepared to drop out over a deserted lot. Apparently there was an underground facility or somesuch nearby, owned by Umbrella; at least that's what they had been told at the briefing.

Carlos got in line with his squad, assault rifle slung over his shoulder as he hooked himself to the drop line and waited for Hirami to open the door. Directly in front of Carlos was Randy Thomas, one of the friendlier guys in A squad. Randy glanced back at him and pretend-growled, pointing his forefinger and thumb at Carlos, a mock-gun. Carlos grinned, then clutched his gut as if shot. Stupid shit, but Carlos found himself relaxing a little as their leader pulled the door open and the roar of multiple choppers filled the cabin.

Two by two, the men in front of Carlos slid down the dual rappelling lines anchored to the body of the helicopter. Carlos stepped closer to the opening, squinting against the whipping wind to see where they'd be landing. Their 'copter cast a long shadow in the late-day sun and he could see men from the other platoons on the ground, lining up by squad. Then it was his turn; he stepped out a second after Randy, the thrill of the practical free fall sending his stomach into his chest. A blur of passing sky, and he touched down, unhooking from the line and hurrying to where Hirami stood.

A few minutes later, they were all down. Almost in unison, the four transport 'copters swung west and buzzed away, their noise fading as dust settled around the assembled troops. Carlos felt alert and ready as the squad and platoon leaders started to point in different directions, assigning routes that had been plotted before they'd left the field office.

Finally, as the helicopters grew smaller, they could hear again—and Carlos was struck by the silence of their surroundings. No cars, no industrial sounds at all, and yet they were at the edge of a decent-sized city. Weird, how one took those noises for granted, not noticing them at all until they weren't there.

Mikhail Victor, platoon D's supervisor, stood quietly with Hirami and his other two squad leaders, Cryan and that creepy Russian, while the supervisors of A, B, and C platoons gave directions, the squads moving out briskly and with a minimum of noise. Their bootsteps seemed overly loud in the still air, and Carlos saw looks of vague unease on some of the passing faces, a look he knew he wore. Probably it was so quiet 'cause people were at home sick, or holed up somewhere, but it was kind of eerie anyway, the stillness...

"A squad, double-time!" Hirami called, and even his voice seemed oddly muted, but Carlos put it out of his mind as they started jogging after him. If his memory served from the briefing, they were all headed roughly west, into the heart of Raccoon City, the platoons fanning out to cover the greatest area. Within a hundred yards, squad A was on its own, thirty soldiers jogging through an industrial area not so different than the one that their field office was in; run-down lots strewn with trash, weedy patches of dirt, fenced storage units.

Carlos scowled, unable to keep quiet. "*Fuchi*," he said, half under his breath. Smelled like a fart in a bag full of fish.

Randy lagged back a few steps to run alongside Carlos. "You say something, bro?"

"I said something stinks," Carlos muttered. "You smell that?"

Randy nodded. "Yeah. Thought it was you."

"Ha, ha, you kill me, *cabrón*," Carlos smiled sweetly. "That means 'good friend,' by the way."

Randy grinned. "Yeah, I bet. And I bet—"

"Hold up! And shut up, back there!"

Hirami called a stop, holding one hand up to ensure silence. Faintly, Carlos could hear another squad a block or two north, the beat of their boots on pavement And after a second, he could hear something else.

Moans and groans, coming from somewhere ahead of them, faint at first but getting louder. Like a hospital population had been kicked out into the street. At the same time, the bad smell was getting stronger, worse—and familiar, like...

"Oh, shit," Randy whispered, his face paling, and Carlos knew at once what the smell was, just as Randy must know.

Not possible.

It was the smell of a human body rotting in the sun. It was death. Carlos knew it well enough, but never had it been so *huge*, so all-encompassing. In front of them, Mitch Hirami was lowering his hand uncertainly, a look of deep concern in his eyes. The distressed, wordless sounds of people in pain were getting louder. Hirami seemed about to speak—

—when gunfire erupted from nearby, from one of the other squads, and in between the blasts of automatic fire that ripped through the afternoon air, Carlos could hear men screaming.

"Line!" Hirami shouted, holding up both hands with the palms turned to the sky, his voice barely audible over the stutter of bullets.

Straight line, five men facing front, five back the way they'd come. Carlos ran to get in position, his mouth suddenly dry, his hands damp. The short bursts of automatic fire just north of their position were getting longer, drowning out whatever else there was to hear, but the stench was definitely getting worse. To cap his worries, he could hear distant fire, soft, clattering pops behind the closer blasts; whatever was going on, it sounded like all of the U.B.C.S. was engaged.

Carlos faced front, rifle ready, searching the empty street that stretched out in front of them and T-ed three blocks ahead. An M16 loaded with a thirty-round mag was nothing to scoff at, but he was afraid—of what, he didn't know yet.

Why are they still firing over there, what takes that many bullets? What is it—

Carlos saw the first one, then, a staggering figure that half-fell from behind a building two blocks in front of them. A second lurched out from across the street, followed by a third, a fourth—suddenly, at least a dozen plodding, stumbling people were in the street, coming their way. They seemed to be drunk.

"Christ, what's *wrong* with them, why are they walking like that?"

The speaker was next to Carlos, Olson his name was, and he was facing the direction they'd come from. Carlos shot a look back and saw at least ten more reeling toward them, appearing as if out of nowhere, and he realized in the same moment that the gunfire north of them was dying out, the intermittent bursts fewer and further apart.

Carlos faced front again and felt his jaw drop at what he saw and heard; they were close enough that he could make out individual features, their strange cries clearly audible now. Tattered, blood-stained clothing, although a few were partially naked; pallid faces stained red, with eyes that saw nothing; the way that several held their arms out, as if reaching for the line of soldiers, still a block away. And the disfigurations—missing limbs, great hunks of skin and muscle torn off, body parts bloated and wet with putrefaction.

Carlos had seen the movies. These people weren't sick. They were zombies, the walking dead, and for a moment, all he could do was watch as they tottered closer. Not possible, *chale*, and as his brain wrestled to accept what he was seeing, he remembered what Trent had said, about dark hours ahead.

"*Fire, fire!...*" Hirami was screaming as if from a great distance, and the sudden, violent chatter of automatic weapons to either side snapped Carlos back to reality. He aimed at the swollen belly of a fat man wearing ripped pajama bottoms, and he fired.

Three bursts, at least nine rounds smacked into the man's corpulent gut, punching a rough line across his lower belly. Dark blood splashed out, soaking the front of his pants. The man staggered but didn't fall. If anything, he seemed more eager to reach them, as if the smell of his own blood incited him.

A few of the zombies had gone down, but they continued to crawl forward on what was left of their stomachs, scraping broken fingers across the asphalt in their single-minded purpose.

The brain, gotta get the brain, in the movies shooting them in the head is the only way—

The closest was perhaps twenty feet away now, a gaunt woman who seemed untouched except for the dull glint of bone beneath her matted hair. Carlos sighted the exposed skull and fired, feeling crazy relief when she went down and stayed there.

"The head, aim for the head—" Carlos shouted, but already, Hirami was screaming, wordless howls of terror that were quickly joined by some of the others as their line began to dissolve.

—*oh, no*—

From behind, the zombies had reached them.

* * *

Nicholai and Wersbowski were the only two from B to make it, and only then because they'd both taken advantage where they could—Nicholai had pushed Brett Mathis into the arms of one of the creatures when it had gotten too close, gaining a precious few seconds that had allowed him to escape. He'd seen Wersbowski shoot Li's left leg for the same reason, crippling the soldier and leaving him to distract the closest virus carriers.

Together, they made it to an apartment building's fire escape some two blocks from where the others had fallen. Gunfire tatted erratically as they climbed the rusty steps, but already the hoarse screams of dying men were fading to silence, becoming lost in the cries of the hungry damned.

Nicholai weighed his options carefully as they scaled

the fire escape. As he'd predicted, John Wersbowski was a survivor and obviously had no problem doing whatever was necessary to remain one; with as bad as things were in Raccoon—worse, in fact, than Nicholai had been led to believe—it might pay to have such a man watching his back.

And if we're surrounded, there would be someone to sacrifice so that I might get away...

Nicholai frowned as they reached the rooftop, as Wersbowski stared out at what they could see from three stories up. Unfortunately, the sacrifice element worked both ways. Besides, Wersbowski wasn't an idiot or as trusting as Mathis and Li had been; getting the drop on him could be difficult.

"Zombies," Wersbowski muttered, clutching his rifle. Standing beside him, Nicholai followed his gaze to where squad B had made its last stand, at the broken bodies that littered the pavement and the creatures that continued to feed. Nicholai couldn't help feeling a bit disappointed; they'd died in minutes, hardly putting up a fight...

"So, what's the plan, *sir*?"

The sarcasm was obvious, both in tone and in the half amused, half disgusted expression he turned to Nicholai. Obviously, Wersbowski had seen him offer up Mathis. Nicholai sighed, shaking his head, the M16 loose in his hands; he had no choice, really.

"I don't know," he said softly, and when Wersbowski looked back at where they'd fought, Nicholai squeezed the assault rifle's trigger.

A trio of rounds hammered Wersbowski's abdomen, knocking him sprawling against the low cement ledge. Nicholai immediately raised the weapon and aimed at one of Wersbowski's shocked eyes, firing even as comprehension flooded the soldier's flushed face, an awareness that he'd made the fatal mistake of letting his guard down.

In under a second it was over, and Nicholai was alone on the rooftop. He stared blankly at the oozing body, wondering—and not for the first time—why he felt no guilt when he killed. He'd heard the term *sociopathic* before and thought that it probably applied... although why people continued to see that as a negative, he didn't understand. It was the empathy thing, he supposed, the bulk of humanity acting as though the inability to "relate" was somehow wrong.

But nothing bothers me, and I never hesitate to do what needs to be done, no matter how it is perceived by others; what's so terrible about that?

True, he was a man who knew how to control himself. Discipline, that was the trick. Once he'd decided to leave his homeland, within a year he didn't even *think* in Russian anymore. When he'd become a mercenary, he'd trained night and day with every manner of weapon and tested his skills against the very best in the field; he'd always won, because no matter how vicious his opponent, Nicholai knew that having no conscience set him free, just as having one hindered his enemies. This was an asset, was it not?

Wersbowski's corpse had no answer. Nicholai checked his watch, already bored with his philosophical wanderings. The sun was low in the sky and it was only 1700 hours; he still had much to do if he meant to leave Raccoon with everything he needed. First, he needed to pick up a laptop and access the files he'd created only the night before, maps and names; there was supposed to be one locked up and waiting for him in the RPD building, although he'd have to be extremely careful in the area, as the two new Tyrant seekers would surely be there at some point. One was programmed to find some chemical sample, and Nicholai knew there was an Umbrella lab not far from the building. The other unit, the more technologically advanced creation, would be set to take out renegade S.T.A.R.S., assuming there were any still in Raccoon, and the S.T.A.R.S. office was inside the RPD. He wouldn't be in any danger as long as he stayed out of the way, but he'd hate to get between any series of Tyrant and its target if even half of what he'd heard was true. Umbrella was taking full advantage of the Raccoon situation, taking proactive steps—using the new Tyrant models, if that's what they were, exactly—in addition to data gathering; Nicholai admired their efficiency.

Nicholai heard a fresh burst of gunfire and reflexively stepped back from the edge of the roof, looking down to see two soldiers run past a moment later. One was injured, a ripped, bloody patch near his right ankle, and he leaned heavily against the other for support. Nicholai couldn't identify the wounded man, but his helper was the Hispanic who'd been watching him on the helicopter.

Nicholai smiled as the two stumbled past and out of sight; a few of the soldiers would have survived, of course, but they would probably suffer the same fate as the injured man, who'd almost certainly been bitten by one of the diseased.

Or the fate that surely awaits the Hispanic. I wonder, what will he do when his friend starts to get sick? When he starts to change?

Probably try to save him in some pathetic tribute to honor; it would be his undoing. Really, they were all as good as dead. Amazed by how predictable they were, Nicholai shook his head and went to get Wersbowski's ammo pack.

FIVE

On her way to the Bar Jack, Jill thought she heard gunfire.

She paused in the alley that would eventually lead her to the tavern's back entrance, head cocked to one side. It sounded like shots, like an automatic, but it was too far away for her to be sure. Still, her spirits lifted a little at the thought that she might not be fighting alone, that help might be on the way...

...right. A hundred good guys have landed with bazookas, inoculations, and a can of whoop ass, maybe a steak dinner with my name on it to boot. They're all attractive, straight, and single, with college degrees and perfect teeth...

"Let's try to stick to reality, how 'bout," she said softly and was relieved that she sounded fairly normal, even in the dank and shadowy quiet of the back alley. She'd been feeling pretty bleak back in the warehouse, even after finding a thermos of still-warm coffee in the upstairs office; the idea of trekking through the dead city one more time, alone—

—*is what I have to do*, she thought firmly, *so I'm doing it.* As her dear, incarcerated father was fond of saying, wishing that things were different didn't make it so.

She took a few steps forward, pausing when she was about five feet from where the alley branched. To her right was a series of streets and alleys that would lead her further into town; left would take her past a tiny courtyard, with a path straight to the bar—assuming that she knew this area as well as she thought she did.

Jill edged closer to the junction, moving as silently as she knew how, her back to the south wall. It was quiet enough for her to risk a quick look down the alley to the right, her weapon preceding her; all clear. She shifted position, stepping sideways across the empty path to look in the direction she meant to go—

—and heard it, *uunnh*, the soft, pining cry of a male carrier, half hidden by shadow perhaps four meters away. Jill targeted the darkest part of the shadow and waited sadly for it to step into view, reminding herself that it wasn't really human, not anymore. She knew that, had known it since what had happened at the Spencer estate, but she encouraged the feelings of pity and sorrow that she felt each time she had to put one of them down. Having to tell herself that each zombie was beyond hope allowed her to feel compassion for them.

Even the shambling, decomposing mess that now swayed into view had once been a person. She didn't, couldn't let herself get overly emotional about it, but if she ever forgot that they were victims rather than monsters, she would lose some essential element of her own humanity.

A single shot to its right temple, and the zombie collapsed into a puddle of its own fetid fluids. He was pretty far gone, his eyes cataracted, his gray-green flesh sliding from his softening bones; Jill had to breathe through her mouth as she stepped over him, careful to avoid getting him on her boots.

Another step and she was looking down on the courtyard—

—and she saw two more zombies standing below, but also a flash of movement disappearing into the alley, heading toward the bar. It was too fast to be one of the carriers. Jill only caught a glimpse of camo pants and a black combat boot, but it was enough to confirm what she'd hoped—a person. It was a living person.

From the small set of steps that led down into the yard, Jill quickly dispatched both carriers, her heart pounding with hope. Camouflage gear. He or she was military, maybe someone sent in on reconnaissance; perhaps her little fantasy wasn't so far-fetched after all. She hurried past the fallen creatures, running as soon as she hit the alley, up a few steps, ten meters of brick, and she was at the back door.

Jill took a deep breath and opened the door

carefully, not wanting to surprise anyone who might be packing a gun—

—and saw a zombie lurching across the tiled floor of the small bar, moaning hungrily as it reached out for a man in a tan vest, a man who pointed what looked like a small-caliber handgun at the closing creature and opened fire.

Jill immediately joined him, accomplishing in two shots what he was unable to do in five; the carrier fell to its knees, and, with a final, desperate groan, it died, settling to the floor like liquid. Jill couldn't tell if it had been male or female, and at the moment, she didn't give a rat's ass.

She turned her eager attention to the soldier, an introduction rising to her lips, and realized that it was Brad Vickers, Alpha team pilot for the disbanded S.T.A.R.S. Brad, whose nickname had been Chicken-heart Vickers, who'd stranded the Alpha team at the Spencer estate when he'd been too afraid to stay, who'd crept out of town when he'd realized that Umbrella knew their names. A good pilot and a genius computer hacker, but when push came to shove, Brad Vickers was a grade-A weasel.

And I'm glad to see him, regardless.

"Brad, what are you doing here? Are you okay?" She did her best to keep from asking how he'd managed to survive, though she had to wonder—especially since he only seemed to be armed with a cheap .32 semi and had been the worst shot in the S.T.A.R.S. As it was, he didn't look good—there were splatters of dried blood on his vest and his eyes were haunted, wide and rolling with barely controlled panic.

"Jill! I didn't know you were still alive!" If he was glad to see her, he was hiding it well, and he still hadn't answered her question.

"Yeah, well, I could say the same," she said, working not to sound too accusatory. He might have information she could use. "When did you get here? Do you know anything about what's going on outside of town?"

It was as though every word she said compounded his fear. His posture was tense, wound up, and he had the shakes. He opened his mouth to answer, but nothing came out.

"Brad, what is it? What's wrong?" she asked, but he was already backing toward the front door of the bar, shaking his head from side to side.

"It's coming for us," he breathed. "For the S.T.A.R.S. The police are dead, they can't do anything to stop it, just like they couldn't stop this—" Brad waved one trembling hand at the bloody creature on the floor. "You'll see."

He was on the edge of hysteria, his brown hair slick with sweat, his jaw clenched. Jill moved toward him, not sure what to do. His fear was contagious.

"What's coming, Brad?"

"You'll see!"

With that, Brad turned and snatched the door open, blind panic tripping him as he stumbled out into the street and took off running without looking back. Jill took one step toward the closing door and stopped, suddenly thinking that maybe there were worse things than being alone. Trying to take care of anyone as she made her way out of Raccoon—particularly a hysterical man with a history of cowardice who was too scared to be reasonable—was probably a bad idea.

She felt a chill thinking about what he'd said, though. *What* was coming, specifically for the S.T.A.R.S.?

He seems to think I'll find out.

Unsettled, Jill mentally wished him luck and turned toward the polished bar, hoping that the ancient Remington was still tucked under the register—and wondering what the hell Chickenheart Vickers was doing in Raccoon, and what, exactly, had him so terrified.

* * *

Mitch Hirami was dead. So were Sean Olson, and Deets, Bjorklund, and Waller, and Tommy, and the two new guys, who Carlos couldn't remember except one of them was always cracking his knuckles and the other one had freckles—

Stop it, just knock it off! It doesn't matter now, all that matters is getting us out of here.

The wails had fallen far enough behind for Carlos to feel they could stop for a minute, after running for what felt like forever. Randy's limp seemed to be getting worse with every step, and Carlos desperately needed to catch his breath, just to think—

—*about how they died, about the woman who bit into Olson's throat and the blood that ran down her chin, and the way that Waller started to laugh, high and crazy, just before he threw his weapon away and let himself be taken, and the sound of somebody screaming prayers at the uncaring sky—*

Stop it!

They leaned against the back wall of a convenience store, a fenced recycling area with only one way in and a clear view of the street. There was no sound except the faraway singing of birds, wafting over them on a cooling, late afternoon breeze that smelled faintly of rot. Randy had slid into a sitting position, pulling his right boot off to take a look at his wound. His lower pant leg was shiny wet with blood, as was the collar of his shirt.

He and Randy were the only two that had made it, and just barely; already, it seemed like some impossible dream.

The others in the squad had already gone down, and there were at least six of the cannibal zombies still coming at him and Randy. Carlos had fired again and again, the smells of burning gunpowder and blood combining with the stench of decay, all of it making him dizzy with adrenaline-driven horror, so disoriented that he hadn't seen Randy fall, hadn't realized it until he'd heard the sound of Randy's skull smacking into the pavement, loud even over the cries of the dead.

A crawling one had grabbed Randy and bitten through the leather of his boot; Carlos had slammed the butt of his M16 down, breaking its neck, his mind screaming uselessly that it had been *eating* Randy's ankle, and he'd scooped up the half-conscious soldier with a strength he didn't know he possessed. And they had run, Carlos dragging his injured comrade away from the slaughter, his thoughts incoherent and wild and, in their own way, as terrifying to him as the rest of it. For a few minutes, he'd been *loco*, unable to understand what had happened, what was still happening—

"Aw, Jesus, man..."

Carlos looked down at the sound of Randy's voice, noticing with some alarm that his words were a little slurred, and saw the ragged edges of a deep bite maybe two inches above the top of his foot. Thick blood oozed steadily out, the inside of Randy's boot drenched with it.

"Bit me, goddamn thing bit right in. But it was dead, Carlos. They were all dead... weren't they?" Randy looked up at him, his eyes dazed with pain and something more, something that neither of them could afford—confusion, bad enough that Randy could barely focus.

Concussion, maybe. Whatever it was, Randy needed a hospital. Carlos crouched next to him, his heart sick as he tore off a piece of Randy's shirt and quickly folded it into a compress.

We're screwed, there were no cops out there, no

paramedics, this city is dying or already dead. If we want help, we're going to have to find it ourselves, and he's in no shape to fight.

"This may hurt a little, *'mano*, but we gotta stop you from getting your boot all wet," Carlos said, trying to sound relaxed as he pressed the folded material against Randy's bleeding ankle. There was no point in scaring him, especially if he was as whacked out as Carlos thought. "Hold it down tight, okay?"

Randy clenched his jaw, a violent tremor running through him, but he did as Carlos asked and held the makeshift bandage in place. As Randy leaned forward, Carlos studied the back of his head, wincing inwardly at the bloody, slightly misshapen spot beneath his tangled black curls. It didn't seem to be bleeding anymore, at least.

"We gotta get outta here, Carlos," Randy said. "Let's go home, okay? I want to go home."

"Soon," Carlos said softly. "Let's just sit here and rest for another minute, and then we'll go."

He thought about all of the wrecked cars they'd run past, the piles of broken furniture and wood and brick in the streets, hastily assembled blockades. Assuming they could even find a car with keys in it, just about every street was impassable. Carlos didn't have a pilot's license, but he had flown a helicopter a few times—fine, if they happened to stumble across an airport.

We'll never make it on foot, though. Even if Randy wasn't hurt, the entire U.B.C.S. was taken out, or damn near close. There's gotta be hundreds, maybe thousands of those things out there.

If they could find other survivors, group together... but tracking anyone down in this nightmare would be a nightmare all its own. The thought of Trent's restaurant occurred to him briefly, but he ignored it; to hell with that crazy shit, they needed to get out of town, and they needed help to do it. The squad leaders were the only ones who'd known the plan for pickup, or had radios, and there was no way Carlos was going to go back—

—but I don't have to, do I?

He closed his eyes for a minute, realizing that he'd missed the obvious; maybe he was more freaked than he thought. There was more than one radio in the world; all he had to do was find one. Send out a call to the transports—hell, to anyone listening—and wait for somebody to show up.

"I don't feel so good," Randy said, so quietly that Carlos almost didn't hear him, the slur of his words more pronounced than before. "Itches, it itches."

Carlos squeezed his shoulder lightly, the heat from Randy's feverish skin radiating out from beneath his T-shirt. "You're going to be okay, bro, just hang on, I'm going to get us out of here."

He sounded confident enough. Carlos only wished that he could convince himself.

S I X

Ted Martin, a thin man in his late 30s, had been shot several times in the head. Nicholai couldn't tell if he'd been murdered or if he'd been put down after contracting the virus, and he didn't care; what mattered was that Martin, whose official title was Personal and Political Liaison to the Chief of Police, had saved Nicholai the time it would have taken to track him down.

"Most kind of you," Nicholai said, smiling down at the very dead Watchdog. He'd also had the courtesy to die near where he was supposed to be, in the detective squadroom's office of the RPD's east wing.

An excellent start to my adventure; if they're all this easy, it will be a very short night.

Nicholai stepped over the body and crouched down next to the floor safe in the corner, quickly dialing in the simple four-digit combination given to him by his Umbrella contact: 2236. The steel door swung open, revealing a few papers—one looked like a map for the police station—a box of shotgun shells, and what would surely become Nicholai's best friend until he left Raccoon: a state-of-the-art cellular modem, designed to look like a piece of shit but more advanced than anything on the market. Grinning, he lifted out the PC laptop and carried it to the desk, the safe door closing itself behind him.

His trip to the station had been reasonably uneventful, except for the seven undead he'd dispatched point-blank to avoid too much noise; they were embarrassingly easy to kill, as long as one paid attention to one's surroundings. He hadn't yet come across any of Umbrella's pets, the only real challenge he expected to face; there was one nicknamed "brain sucker" that he was very much looking forward to meeting, a multi-legged crawler with killing claws...

One thing at a time; right now, you need information.

He'd already committed the names and faces of his victims to memory and had a general idea of where each one was supposed to make contact, if not necessarily when; all of the Watchdogs were on different schedules, subject to change but mostly accurate. Martin, for instance, was due to report to Umbrella from a computer terminal at the RPD building's front desk at 1750 hours, about twenty minutes from now; his last report should have been just after noon.

"Let's see if you succeeded, Officer Martin," Nicholai said, quickly punching in the codes he'd acquired to access Umbrella's updated progress reports. "Martin, Martin... ah, there you are!"

The policeman had missed his last two assigned windows, suggesting that he'd been dead or incapacitated for at least nine hours now. No information to collect there. Nicholai carefully read the numbers on the other Watchdogs, pleased with what he saw. Of the eight Watchdogs left after Martin, three others had failed to make their last assigned reports—one of the scientists, one Umbrella worker, and the woman who worked for the city's water department. Assuming they were dead—and Nicholai was willing to bet that they were—that left only five.

Two soldiers, two scientists, and the other Umbrella man...

Nicholai frowned, looking at the designated contact points for each of them. One scientist, Janice Thomlinson, would be in the underground laboratory facility, the other at the hospital near the city park; the Umbrella worker was to report in from an allegedly abandoned water treatment facility on the outskirts of town, a cover for its use as an Umbrella chemical testing site. Nicholai didn't foresee any problems finding them... but both of the soldier Watchdogs had been taken off the map.

"Where are you going to be, men..." Nicholai said absently, tapping at the keys, his frustration growing. At his last check only the night before, they had both been assigned to call in from the St. Michael Clock Tower...

Shit!

There they were, their names listed next to his; both men had been moved to portable status, just like him. They'd report in from Umbrella laptops or wherever was most convenient, and were only required to file once a day—which meant that they could be anywhere in Raccoon City, anywhere at all.

A seething haze of red enveloped him, tearing at him. Without thinking, Nicholai charged across the office and kicked Martin's body as hard as he could, once, twice, venting his rage, feeling a deep satisfaction at the wet sounds his boot made, the jerking movement of the body and the crunch of ribs giving way—

—and then it was over, and he was himself once again, still frustrated but in control. He exhaled sharply and moved back to the desk, ready to revise his plans. It was simply going to take longer to find them, that was all; it wasn't the end of the world. And perhaps they would fail to report in, conveniently dying just like Martin and the other three.

He could hope but wouldn't count on it. What he could count on was his own perseverance and skill. Umbrella wouldn't send in their pickup for nearly a week—the longest, they believed, that they could keep the disaster quiet—unless the Watchdogs called in with complete results, unlikely at best. With six days to find only five people, Nicholai was certain that he would be the only one left to pick up.

"I won't even need all six," Nicholai said, nodding

firmly at Martin's sprawled, lumpy corpse. "Three days, I'm sure I can do it in three."

With that, Nicholai leaned forward and started to call up the maps he would need, happy again.

* * *

Jill hadn't been able to find any shells for the 12-gauge, but she took it anyway, aware that her ammo wouldn't last forever; it would make a good club, and she might find shells for it later. She'd just about decided to try climbing over one of the western blockades when she saw something that changed her mind, something she had fervently hoped never to see again.

A Hunter. Like the ones at the estate, in the tunnels.

She'd stood on the fire escape outside of an uptown boutique, seen it in the street just past one of the vans that blocked the fire escape's alley. It didn't see her; she watched it lope by and out of sight, a little different than the ones from before, but close enough—the same strangely graceful, malignant carriage, the heavy, curved talons, the dark mud green color. She held her breath, her stomach in knots, remembering...

...hunched over so that its impossibly long arms almost touched the stone floor of the tunnel, both its hands and feet tipped with thick, brutal claws. Tiny, light-colored eyes peering out at her from a flat reptilian skull, its tremendous, high-pitched screech echoing

through the dark underground just before it sprang...

She'd killed it, but it had taken her fifteen 9mm rounds to do it, an entire magazine. Later, Barry had told her that he'd heard them referred to as Hunters, one of Umbrella's bio-organic weapons. There had been other kinds on the estate—feral, skinned-looking dogs; a kind of giant, flesh-eating plant that Chris and Rebecca had destroyed; spiders the size of small cattle; and the dark, mutant things with bladed hooks for hands, the ones that hung from the ceiling of the estate's boiler room, skittering overhead like spined monkeys.

And the Tyrant, somehow the worst because you could see that it had been human once; before the surgeries, before the genetic tampering and the T-virus.

So it wasn't just the T-virus loose in Raccoon. As awful as the realization was, it wasn't exactly shocking; Umbrella had been messing around with some very dangerous stuff, breeding slaughtering, nightmare children like some aberrant God without preparing for the inevitable consequences; sometimes, nightmares didn't just go away.

Unless—unless they did this on purpose.

No. If they'd meant to destroy Raccoon City, they would have evacuated their own people... wouldn't they?

It was a question that haunted her on her journey to the police station. Seeing the Hunter had made up her mind for her about what to do next; she simply had to have more ammo, and she knew there'd be some in the S.T.A.R.S. office, in the gun safe—9mm, probably shotgun shells, maybe even one of Barry's old revolvers.

The station wasn't too far away, at least. She stuck to the growing shadows, easily dodging the few zombies she passed; many of them had decayed too much to move any faster than a slow walk. One of the gates she had to pass through to get to the station had been heavily roped and knotted, the knots soaked with oil. She gave herself a mental kick for forgetting to bring a knife; lucky for her she'd picked up a lighter at the Bar Jack, although she worried some about the smoke drawing attention to her position—until she got through the gate and saw the heap of burning debris farther ahead, just in front of Umbrella's medical sales offices. Damage left over from the riots, she guessed. She thought about stopping to put out the flames, but there didn't seem to be any danger of their spreading in the cement and brick alleyway.

So, here she was, standing at the gates to the RPD courtyard. The rioting had been bad here. Trashed cars, broken barricades, and orange emergency cones littered the street, though there were no bodies amidst the rubble. To her right, a fire hydrant spewed a fountain of hissing water into the air. The gentle sound of splashing water might even have been pleasant in another circumstance—a hot summer day, children laughing and playing. Knowing that no fireman or city worker would be coming to fix the gushing hydrant made her ache inside, and the thought of children...

it was too much; she blocked it out, determined not to let herself start thinking about things she couldn't fix. She had enough to worry about.

Such as stocking up on supplies... so what are you waiting for, anyway? A written invitation?

Jill took a deep breath and pushed the gates open, wincing at the squeal of rusty metal. A quick scan told her the small, fenced yard was empty; she lowered her weapon, relieved, and carefully closed the gates before moving toward the heavy wooden doors of the RPD building. A lot of cops had died out in the streets, which would make this easier for her, as terrible as that was; not as many carriers to deal with once she got inside—

Sqreeak!

Behind her, the gates swung open. Jill spun, almost firing at the figure that crashed into the yard, until she realized who it was.

"Brad!"

He stumbled toward the sound of her voice, and she saw that he was badly wounded. He clutched his right side, blood dripping over his fingers, a look of complete terror on his face as he reached toward her with his free hand, gasping.

"Juh—Jill!"

She stepped toward him, so focused on him that when he suddenly disappeared, she didn't understand what had happened. A wall of black had sprung up between them, a blackness that emitted a deep, rumbling howl of fury, that started toward Brad and shook the ground with each massive step.

"*Sstaarrss*," it clearly said, the word nearly hidden beneath a wavering growl like that of a wild animal, and Jill knew what it was without seeing its face; she knew it like she knew her own dreams.

Tyrant.

Brad fell backwards, shaking his head as if to deny the approaching creature, staggering in a half circle and stopping when his back hit brick. In the split second before it reached him, Jill could see it in profile; time seemed to stop for that instant, allowing her to really *see* it, to see that it wasn't her nightmare Tyrant, but no less horrible for that; in fact, it was worse.

Between seven and eight feet tall, humanoid, its shoulders impossibly broad, its arms longer than they should have been. Only its hands and head were visible, the rest of its strangely proportioned body clothed in black, except for what appeared to be tentacles, slightly pulsing ropes of flesh that were only half tucked under its collar, their points of origin unseen. Its hairless skin was the color and texture of badly healed scar tissue, and its face looked as though whoever had designed the creature had decided not to bother, instead pulling a too-tight sack of torn leather over its rudimentary skull. Misshapen white slits for eyes were set too low and separated by an irregular line of thick surgical staples. Its nose was barely formed, but the dominant feature by far was its mouth, or lack thereof; the lower half of its face *was* teeth, giant and square, lipless, set against dark red gums.

Time started again when the creature reached out and covered Brad's entire face with one hand, still growling as Brad tried to say something, panting in high, wheezing gasps beneath its palm—

—and there was an awful, wet *squishing* sound, heavy but slick, like someone punching a hole in meat. Jill saw a flesh tentacle sticking out from the back of Brad's neck and understood that he was dead, that he would bleed out in seconds. Numbly, she saw that the ropelike appendage was moving, swaying like a blind snake, droplets of blood falling from its muscular length. The Tyrant-thing grasped Brad's skull, and in a single, fluid motion, it lifted the dead pilot and tossed him aside, retracting the killing tentacle back into its sleeve before Brad hit the ground.

"*Sstaarrss,*" it said again, turning to face her, and as it focused its attention to her, Jill felt a fear greater than any she'd ever known.

The Beretta would be useless. She turned and sprinted, barreling through the doors to the RPD, slamming and dead-bolting them behind her, all on instinct; she was too frightened to think about what she was doing, too frightened to do anything but back away from the double doors as the monster slammed into them, rattling them on their hinges.

They held. Jill was very still, listening to the pound of blood in her ears, waiting for the next blow. Long seconds dragged by, and nothing happened—but full minutes passed before she dared to look away, and even the realization that it had stopped for the moment brought her no relief.

Brad had been right, it *was* coming for them—and now that he was dead, it would be coming for her.

SEVEN

God help me, I've finally seen it for myself; God help us all.

They lied to us. Dr. Robison and the Umbrella people held a press conference at the hospital just this morning, and they damn near insisted that there's no need to panic—that the cases being called in were isolated events, that the victims were suffering from the flu; not, according to them, the so-called cannibal disease that the S.T.A.R.S. were going on about in July, in spite of what a few "paranoid" citizens are now saying. Chief Irons was there, too, he backed the docs up and reiterated his views on the defunct S.T.A.R.S.'s incompetence; case closed, right? Nothing to worry about.

We were on our way back to the office from the press conference, south on Cole Street, and there was a commotion holding up traffic, a couple of stopped cars and a gathering crowd. No cops on the scene.

I thought it was some minor accident and started to back up, but Dave wanted to get a few shots; he still had two rolls of film left from the hospital, what the hell. We got out and suddenly people were running, screaming for help, and we saw three pedestrians down in the middle of the street, and there was blood everywhere. The attacker was young, barely twenty, white male—he was straddling an older man, and...

My hands are shaking, I don't know how to say it, I don't want to say it but it's my job. People have to know. I can't let this get to me.

He was eating one of the older man's eyes. The other two victims were dead, slaughtered, an elderly woman and a younger one, both of them with bloody throats and faces. The younger woman's abdomen had been ripped open.

It was chaos, total hysteria—crying, shouting, even some crazy laughter. Dave snapped two pics and then threw up on himself. I wanted to do something, I did, but those people were already dead and I was afraid. The young man slurped away, digging his fingers into the man's other eye, seemingly oblivious to everything else; he was actually moaning like he couldn't get enough, gore all over him.

We heard the sirens and backed off along with everyone else. Most people left, but a few stayed, pale and sick and frightened. I got the story from a chubby shopkeeper who couldn't stop wringing his hands, though there wasn't much else to tell—the kid apparently just wandered onto the street and grabbed a woman, started biting her. The shopkeeper said the woman's name was Joelle something-or-other, and she was walking with her mother, a Mrs. Murray (the shopkeeper didn't know her first name). Mrs. Murray tried to stop the attack, and the kid turned on her. A couple of men tried to help, jumping the kid, and he managed to get one of them, too. After that, nobody tried to help anymore.

The cops showed up and before they even looked at the mess in the street—at the freakshow kid lunching on his fellow man—they cleared and secured the scene. Three squad cars surrounded the attacker, blocking him from view. The shopkeeper was actually told to close up and go home, along with the rest of us. When I told one of the officers that Dave and I were with the press, he confiscated Dave's camera; said it was evidence, which is total and utter bullshit, like they have a right...

Listen to me, worried about freedom of the press at this point. It doesn't matter. At four o'clock this afternoon, one hour ago, Mayor Harris declared martial law; blockades have been set up all over the place, and we've been cut off from the outside. According to Harris, the city's been quarantined so that the "unfortunate illness that is plaguing some of our citizens" won't spread. He wouldn't call it the cannibal disease, but there's obviously no question— and according to our police-scanner, the attacks are multiplying exponentially.

I believe that it may already be too late for all of

us. The disease isn't airborne or we'd all have it, but the evidence strongly suggests that you get it when you're bitten by one of them, just like in the movies I used to watch on the Double Creature Feature when I was a boy. That would explain the incredible growth rate of the attacks—but it also tells me that unless the cavalry comes in very soon, we're all going to die, one way or another. The cops have closed down the press, but I'm going to try to get the word out anyway, even if I have to go door-to-door. Dave, Tom, Kathy, Mr. Bradson—everyone else has gone home to be with their families. They don't care about letting the people know anymore, but it's all I have left. I don't want to—

I just heard glass breaking downstairs. Somebody's coming.

* * *

There wasn't any more. Carlos lowered the crumpled sheets he'd found, placing them on the reporter's desk, his mouth a grim line. He'd killed two zombies in the hallway... maybe one of them had been the writer, a distressing thought made all the worse by its application—how long had it taken for the writer to change?

And if he's right about the disease, how long does Randy have?

A police scanner and some kind of handheld radio sat on a countertop across the room, but suddenly all he could think of was Randy, downstairs and getting sicker, waiting for Carlos to come back. He'd held up pretty well so far, managing to crawl through two of the blockades with only a little help, but by the time they'd reached the Raccoon Press building, he'd hardly been able to stand up on his own. Carlos had left him propped up beneath a dead pay phone on the first floor, not wanting to drag him up the stairs; a few small fires were smoldering on the lower landing, and Carlos had been afraid that Randy might trip and get burned...

...*which might be the least of his worries right now. Puta, what a balls-up. Why didn't they tell us what we were getting into?*

Carlos choked down the despair that question raised; it was something he could take up with the proper authorities once they got out of here. He'd probably end up being deported, since he was only in the country through Umbrella, but so what? At the moment, going back to his old life sounded like a picnic.

He hurried to the radio equipment and switched the scanner on, not sure what to do next; he'd never used one, and his only experience with two-way radios was a set of walkie-talkies he'd once played with as a kid. 200 CHANNEL MULTI-BAND was written on top of the scanner, and there was actually a scan button. He pushed it and watched a small digital readout flash meaningless numbers at him. Except for a few static bursts and clicks, nothing happened.

Great. That's real helpful.

The radio was what he wanted, anyway, and it at least *looked* like a walkie-talkie, though it said, AM/SSB TRANSCEIVER on the side. He picked it up, wondering if there were channels, or if there was some memory control button—

—and heard footsteps out in the hall. Slow, dragging footsteps.

He dropped the radio on the counter and hefted his assault rifle, turning toward the door that opened into the hallway, already recognizing the shuffling, aimless steps of a zombie. The large newspaper office was the only room on the second floor; unless he wanted to jump out a window, the hall and stairs were the only way out. He'd have to kill it to get back to...

Oh, shit, it had to go past Randy, what if it got to him? What if—

What if it *was* Randy?

"Please, no," he whispered, but once the possibility occurred to him, he couldn't *not* think about it. He backed across the room, feeling sweat slide down the back of his neck. The footsteps continued, getting closer—and was that a limp he heard, the sound of one foot dragging?

Please, don't be, I don't want to have to kill him!

The footsteps paused just outside the door—and then Randy Thomas stepped, *lurched* into view, his expression blank and free of pain, strings of drool hanging from his lower lip.

"Randy? Stop there, *'mano*, okay?" Carlos heard

his voice break with dismal fear. "Say something, okay? Randy?"

A kind of dread acceptance filled Carlos as Randy tilted his head toward him and continued forward, raising his arms. A low, gurgling moan erupted from his throat, and it was the loneliest sound Carlos thought he'd ever heard. Randy didn't really see him, didn't understand what he was saying; Carlos had become food, nothing more.

"*Lo siento mucho*," he said, and again in English, in case there was any part of Randy left, "I'm sorry. Sleep now, Randy."

Carlos aimed carefully and fired, looking away as soon as he saw the grouping of holes appear just above Randy's right eyebrow, hearing but not seeing his comrade's body hit the floor. For a long time he simply stood, shoulders slumped as he gazed at his own boots, wondering how he'd gotten so tired so fast... and telling himself there was nothing else he could have done.

At last, he walked over and picked up the radio, hitting the switch and thumbing the send control. "This is Carlos Oliveira, member of Umbrella's U.B.C.S. team, squad Alpha, Platoon Delta. I'm at the Raccoon City newspaper office. Can anyone hear me? We were cut off from the rest of the platoon, and now we—I need help. Request immediate assistance. If you can hear this, please respond."

Nothing but static; maybe he needed to try specific channels; he could go through them one by one and just keep repeating the message. He turned the radio over, looking at all of the buttons, and saw, stamped into the backing, RANGE FIVE MILES.

Which means I can call anybody in town, how useful—except nobody's gonna answer, because they're dead. Like Randy. Like me.

Carlos closed his eyes, trying to think, trying to feel anything like hope. And he remembered Trent. He checked his watch, realizing how crazy this was, thinking that it was the only thing that made sense anymore; Trent had *known*, he'd known what was going on and he'd told Carlos where to go when the shit came down. Without Randy to think about and with no clear path out of town...

Grill 13. Carlos had just over an hour to find it.

* * *

Jill had just reached the S.T.A.R.S. office when the communication console at the back of the room crackled to life. She slammed the door behind her and ran to it, words spitting out through a haze of static.

"... is Carlos... Raccoon... were cut off... platoon... help... assistance... if you can hear... respond..."

Jill snatched up the headset and hit the transmit switch. "This is Jill Valentine, Special Tactics and Rescue Service! You're not coming in very clear, please repeat—what's your location? Do you read me? Over!"

She strained to hear something, anything—and then saw that the light over the transmit relay switch wasn't on. She tapped several buttons and jiggled the switch, but the little green light refused to show itself.

"Damn it!" She knew dick about communications, too. Whatever was broken, she wasn't going to be the one to fix it.

Well, at least I'm not the only one up Shit Creek without a paddle...

Sighing, Jill dropped the headset and turned to look at the rest of the office. Other than a few loose papers scattered on the floor, it looked the same as always. A few desks cluttered with files, PCs, and personal items, some overloaded shelves, a fax machine—and behind the door, the tall, reinforced steel gun safe that she hoped to God wasn't empty.

That thing out there isn't going to die easy. That S.T.A.R.S. killer.

She shivered, feeling the knot of fear in her lower belly clench and grow heavier. Why it hadn't broken down the doors and killed her, she didn't know; it was easily strong enough. Just thinking about it made her want to crawl into a dark place somewhere and hide. It made the few zombies she'd passed on her way through the building seem as dangerous as infants. Not true, of course, but after seeing what the Tyrant-thing did to Brad...

Jill swallowed, hard, and pushed it out of her mind. Dwelling on it wasn't going to help.

Time to get to business. She stepped to her desk, randomly thinking that when she'd last sat there, she'd been a totally different person; it seemed like a lifetime had gone by since then. She opened the top drawer and started to dig—and there, behind a box of paper clips, was the set of tools she'd always kept at the office.

Yes! She lifted the small cloth bundle and unrolled it, looking over the picks and torsion bars with a practiced eye. Sometimes having grown up as the daughter of a professional thief paid off big. She'd been having to shoot at locks for the last few days, which wasn't nearly as easy or safe as people seemed to think; having a decent lockpick set along would be an enormous help.

Besides which, I don't have the key for the gun safe—but then, that never stopped me before. She'd practiced when no one was around just to see if she could do it and had experienced very little trouble; the safe was ancient.

Jill crouched in front of the door, inserted the bar and pick, and gently felt for the tumblers. In less than a minute, she was rewarded for her efforts; the heavy door swung open, and there, in plain sight, was the stainless steel answer to at least one of her recent prayers.

"Bless you, Barry Burton," she breathed, lifting the heavy revolver off the otherwise empty lower shelf. A Colt Python .357 Magnum, six-shot with a swing-out cylinder. Barry had been the weapons specialist for the Alpha team and was a total gun nut besides. He'd taken her shooting several times, always insisting that she try out one of his Colts; he had three that she knew of, all different calibers—but the .357 packed the biggest wallop. That he'd left it behind, either by mistake or on purpose, seemed like a miracle... as did the twenty-plus rounds in a box on the floor of the safe. There weren't any shotgun shells, but there was one magazine's worth of 9mm rounds loose in one of the drawers.

Worth the trip, at least—and with the picks I can go through the downstairs evidence room now, check for confiscated materials...

Things were looking up. Now all she had to do was sneak out of the city in the dark, avoiding zombies, violent, genetically altered animals, and a Tyrant-creature that had proclaimed itself nemesis to the S.T.A.R.S. A Nemesis made for her.

Amazingly, the thought made her smile. Add an impending explosion and some bad weather to the mix, she'd have herself a party.

"Whee," she said softly and started to load the Magnum with hands that weren't quite steady, and hadn't been for a long time.

EIGHT

As he slogged his way through the sewer system underneath the city streets, Nicholai found himself fascinated by the careful planning that had gone into Raccoon's design. He'd studied the maps, of course, but it was another thing entirely to actually wander through it, to experience the arrangement firsthand. Umbrella had built a perfect playground; how unfortunate that they'd ruined it for themselves.

There were several underground passages that connected key Umbrella-owned facilities to one another, some more obvious than others. From the basement of the RPD building, he'd entered the sewers that would lead him all the way to the multilevel underground laboratory where Umbrella had done its most serious research. Research had also been conducted at the Arklay/Spencer mansion lab in Raccoon Forest, and there were three "abandoned" factory or warehouse test sites on the outskirts of town, but the best scientists had worked in and under the city. It would certainly make his job much easier; moving from one area to another would be much less hazardous underground.

Not for much longer, though. In another ten or twelve hours, nowhere will be safe. The bio-organics that Umbrella worked with were kept sedated, grown in Raccoon but usually shipped elsewhere for field trials. With the operation in virtual ruin, they'd break out in order to find food; some had surely escaped already, and the majority would undoubtedly make an appearance once they'd missed a few injections.

And won't that be fun? A little target practice to clear my palate in between searches, and with the firepower to enjoy it.

Holding the assault rifle in the crook of his right arm, he reached down and patted the extra mags he'd taken from Wersbowski; he hadn't thought to check them before, but the quick look before he'd descended into the sewers had left him quite pleased. U.B.C.S. soldiers were issued magazines of fully jacketed .223s, designed to shoot cleanly through a target; Wersbowski had loaded up with hollow points, rounds that expanded and flattened on contact for maximum damage. Nicholai had already planned to raid the lab's small arsenal; with an additional sixty rounds of HP, he'd be walking easy...

...unlike now...

The cold, murky water that ran through the poorly lit tunnels came almost to his knees and smelled terrible, like urine and mold. He'd already come across several undead, most wearing Umbrella lab coats, though there were a few civilians—maintenance people, or perhaps just unlucky souls who'd ventured into the sewers thinking to escape the city. He dodged them, mostly, not wanting to waste bullets or alert anyone to his whereabouts.

He came to a T junction and hung a right after checking for movement in either direction. As with much of his journey so far, there was nothing but the soft lap of polluted water against gray stones, the ripple of sullen yellow light against the oily surface. It was a dank and miserable environment, and Nicholai couldn't help but think of the A334s, the sliding worms. At the Watchdog briefing, they'd been listed as something like giant leeches that traveled by water in groups, one of Umbrella's newest creations. He wasn't afraid so much as disgusted by the thought of running into them, and he hated surprises, hated the idea that even now a school of them could be slipping through the dark waters, jaws stretching wide, seeking warmth and sustenance from human blood.

When he saw the raised ledge at the end of the tunnel, he was ashamed at the relief he felt. He quickly blocked the feeling, preparing himself for his meeting; a look at his watch as he stepped out of the water told him he was right on time. Dr. Thomlinson would be filing her next report within ten minutes.

Nicholai hurried down the short corridor in front of him, annoyed by the faint squelching of his boots as he reached the door to the warehouse anteroom. He listened for a moment and heard nothing; he gave a soft push at the door and it opened, revealing an empty break room for city workers—table, a few chairs, lockers—and, bolted to the far wall, a descending ladder. He crept in, gently closing the door behind him.

The ladder went down into the small warehouse from which Dr. Thomlinson would report; a computer terminal was hidden behind some cleaning equipment on one of the shelves. Assuming Thomlinson would be coming from the lab, she'd enter via the small elevator platform in the corner of the room, if he'd read the map correctly. Nicholai sat down to wait, unhooking his shoulder bag and removing the laptop; he wanted to recheck his maps after the appointment with the good doctor.

Thomlinson was punctual, arriving a full four minutes before she was supposed to file. At the sound of the grinding lift motor, Nicholai trained the rifle's muzzle into the corner, resting his finger on the trigger. A tall, disheveled woman rose into view, a distracted look on her smudged face. She wore a stained lab coat and carried a handgun she kept pointed at the floor; obviously, she expected her checkpoint to be safe.

Nicholai didn't give her a chance to react to his presence. "Drop your weapon and step away from the lift. Now."

She was a cool one, he had to give her that. Except for a slight widening of her eyes, there was no visible sign of alarm across her even features. She did as he asked, the clatter of the semiautomatic loud as she warily moved a few paces into the still room.

"Anything new to report, Janice?"

She studied him, her light brown gaze searching his as she crossed her arms. "You're one of the Watchdogs," she said. It wasn't a question.

Nicholai nodded. "Empty your pockets onto the table, Doctor. Slowly."

Thomlinson smiled. "And if I won't?" Her voice was throaty, deep and alluring. "Will you... take it from me?"

Nicholai thought for a few seconds about what she was suggesting then pulled the trigger, obliterating her lovely smile in a sudden cough of fire. Really, he didn't have time to play that particular game; he should have shot her on sight, so as not to be tempted. Besides, his feet were cold and wet, which he detested; nothing like wet boots to make a man miserable.

Still, it was a shame; she was his type, tall and curved, obviously intelligent. He walked to her slumped body and fished a disk out of her breast pocket without looking at the blood and bone confusion that had been her face, reminding himself that this was business.

Only four to go. Nicholai slipped the disk into a plastic pouch, sealed it, and placed it in his bag. There'd be time to pore over its contents later, once he'd collected everything.

He turned on the portable and called up the sewer system map, frowning as he traced his next path. At least another half mile of wading through the dark before making it topside. He glanced at Dr. Thomlinson again and sighed; perhaps he'd made a mistake. A quick tussle would have warmed him up... though he disliked having to kill women after enjoying them, on any level; the last time, he'd experienced feelings of true regret.

No matter. She was dead, he had the information, and it was time to move on. Four left, and he could forget about business for the rest of his extremely wealthy life, concentrating instead on the kinds of pleasure that poor men could only dream about.

* * *

Carlos knew he was close. From the area near the newspaper building, where the street signs had all begun with north, he'd ended up lost in a series of alleys to the east—what had to be Trent's shopping district.

He said shopping district, northeast... so where's the theater? And he said something about a fountain, didn't he?

Carlos stood in front of a boarded-up barbershop at the intersection of two alleys, no longer sure which way to go. There weren't any street signs, and twilight had given its last gasp; it was full-on dark and he only had ten minutes left before the 1900 deadline, thanks to an initial blunder that had led him back toward the industrial part of town—not really what could be considered the city proper, as Trent put it. Ten minutes... and then what? Once he found the infamous Grill 13, what was supposed to happen? Trent had said something about helping... so if he blew the appointed time, would Trent be able to do anything for him?

Taking a left would lead him back to the newspaper office, he thought—or was that behind him? Straight ahead was a dead end and a door that he hadn't tried yet, might as well give that a shot—

He didn't see it coming, but he heard it.

He'd taken a single step when a door crashed open behind him—and the thing was so fast that he was still turning, raising the assault rifle in reaction to the sound of the door when it reached him.

What—

A wave of malodorous darkness, an impression of shining black claws and hard, ribbed body like the exoskeleton of some giant insect—

—and something *ripped* the air inches from his face, would have hit him if not for his stumbling step backwards. He tripped over his own feet and fell, watching in horrified amazement as some *thing* flew over his upturned face, leaping nimbly to the wall on his right, and continued to run, sideways, clinging to the brick in a skittering gallop. Awestruck, Carlos tracked it as far as he could turn his head, flat on his back, watching as it agilely pivoted on at least three of its legs and dropped to the ground.

He might have simply waited for it to come for him, unable to believe his eyes even as it slashed one of its six, long-bladed legs across his throat, except that it screamed—and the trumpeting, triumphant whine that erupted from its inhumanly curved and bloated face was enough to get him moving.

In a flash, Carlos rolled into a crouch and opened fire on the screeching, running thing, unaware that he was screaming, too, a low, raspy cry of terror and disbelief. The creature faltered as the rounds tore into its brittle flesh, its limbs flailing wildly, the quality of its shriek changing to a howl of furious pain. Carlos kept firing, spraying the creature with deadly hot metal, continuing even after it collapsed and was only moving because of him, the rounds jerking at its limp form. He knew it was dead but couldn't let himself stop, couldn't until the M16 ran dry and the alley was silent except for the sound of his own tortured breathing. He backed against a wall, slammed a fresh mag into the rifle, and desperately tried to understand what the hell had just happened.

At last he recovered enough of himself to approach the dead thing—it *was* dead; even a six-legged, wall-climbing bug the size of a man was dead when its brains were drooling out of its skull. It was one truth he could hold on to in the face of this madness.

"Deader than shit," he said, staring down at the twisted, bloody creature, and for just a second, he could feel part of his mind attempting to turn in on itself, to lock him away from what he was seeing. Zombies were bad enough, and he'd finally refused to accept the fact that Raccoon was overrun by the walking dead; they were just sick, that cannibal disease he'd read about, because there was no such thing as zombies except in the movies. Just like there were no real monsters, either, no giant killing bugs with claws that could walk on walls and scream like it had screamed—

"*No hay piri,*" he whispered, his one-time motto, this time spoken as a plea, his thoughts following in a kind of desperate litany, *Don't sweat it, hang loose, be cool.* And after a while, it took hold; his heart slowed to almost normal, and he started to feel like a person again, not some mindless, panicking animal.

So, there were monsters in Raccoon City. It shouldn't be a surprise, not after the day he'd had; besides, they died like anything else, didn't they? He wasn't going to survive if he lost it, and he'd already been through way too much to give up now.

With that, Carlos turned his back on the monster and headed down the alley, forcing himself not to look back. It was dead, and he was alive, and chances were good that there were more of them out there.

Trent might be my only way out, and now I've got ... shit! Three minutes, he had three goddamn minutes.

Carlos broke into a run, up a few steps to the single door at the end of the alley and through—and found himself standing in a spacious, well-lit kitchen. A restaurant's kitchen.

A quick look around; no one, and quiet except for a soft hiss from a large gas canister standing against the back wall. He took a deep breath but couldn't smell anything; maybe it was something else—

—and I wouldn't leave if it was toxic nerve gas. This has to be it, this is where he told me to go.

He walked through the kitchen, past shining metal counters and stoves, heading toward the dining area. There was a menu on one of the counters, GRILL 13 written across the front in gold script. It was unnerving, how relieved he felt; within a few hours, Trent had gone from being some creepy stranger to his best friend in the world.

I made it, and he said he could help—maybe a rescue team is already on its way, or he arranged for me to be picked up here... or maybe there are weapons stored in the front, not as good as an evac but I'll take what I can get.

There was an opening in the wall between the kitchen and the dining room, a counter where the chefs put the orders up. Carlos could see that the small, slightly darker restaurant was empty, although he took a moment to be certain; dancing light from a still-burning oil lamp wavered over the leatherette booths that lined the walls, casting jittery shadows.

He stepped around the serving counter and walked into the room, absently noting a faint scent of fried food lingering in the cool air as he stared around, searching. He wasn't sure what he expected, but he definitely didn't see it—no unmarked envelope propped up on a table, no mysterious packages, no trench-coated man waiting. There was a pay phone by the front door; Carlos walked over and picked up the receiver but got nothing, just like every other phone in town.

He checked his watch for what felt like the thousandth time in the past hour and saw that it was 1901—one minute after seven o'clock—and he felt a rush of anger, of frustration that only served to increase his unacknowledged fear. *I'm alone, no one knows I'm here and no one can help me.*

"I'm here," he said, turning to face the empty room, his voice rising. "I made it, I'm here on time and *goddamnit, where the hell are you?*"

As if on cue, the telephone rang, the shrill sound making him jump. Carlos fumbled for it, his heart thumping dully in his chest, his knees suddenly weak with hope.

"Trent? Is that you?"

A brief pause, and Trent's smooth, musical voice spilled into his ear. "*Hola*, Mr. Oliveira! I'm so pleased to hear your voice!"

"Man, not half as glad as I am to hear yours." Carlos sagged against the wall, gripping the receiver tightly. "This is some bad shit, *amigo*, everyone's dead and there are things out there, like—there are *monsters*, Trent. Can you get me out of here? Tell me you can get me out of here!"

There was another pause, and Trent sighed, a heavy sound. Carlos closed his eyes, already knowing what he would say.

"I'm very sorry, but that's simply out of the question. What I *can* do is give you information... but surviving, that's your job. And I'm afraid that things are going to get worse, much worse before they get any better."

Carlos took a deep breath and nodded to himself, knowing that this was what he'd been expecting all along. He was on his own.

"Okay," he said and opened his eyes, straightening his shoulders as he nodded again. "Tell me."

NINE

Two of the twelve faux gems that are an integral part of the "clock-lock" at the ornamental main gate of the municipal complex have been removed, between (approximately) 2100 hours yesterday (September 24) and 0500 hours this morning. With many local businesses boarded up at this time, looters have been defacing town property and attempting to take what they believe to be valuable. This officer believes that the perp thought the gems were real, and stopped after removing two (one blue, one green) when he/she realized they were only glass.

This gate (aka "City Hall" gate) is only one of several entrances/exits that lead to the municipal complex. The gate is now locked due to its complicated (and in this officer's opinion, ridiculous) design, which requires that all gems be present for the gate to be unlocked. Until the City Parks Department removes the gate, or until the two gems can be recovered and reinstalled, this entrance/exit will remain locked. Due to the lack of available manpower at this time, there is no choice but to suspend the investigation of this case.//reporting officer Marvin Branagh

ADDITIONAL COMMENTS, CASE 29-087, M. BRANAGH

Sept. 26—One of the missing gems (blue) has turned up inside the RPD building. It's 2000 hours. Bill Hansen, deceased owner of the restaurant Grill 13, was apparently carrying the fake gem when he came here seeking shelter earlier this evening. Mr. Hansen died shortly after arriving, killed by police fire after succumbing to the effects of the cannibal disease. The gem was found on his person, though this officer has no way of knowing if he stole it or where the other gem might be.

With the city now under martial law, no effort will be made to find the second gem or to put this one back—but with several of the streets surrounding the municipal complex now impassable, the need for these gems may at some point become relevant.

On a personal note: this will be my last written report until the current crisis has passed. Paperwork doesn't seem—at this time, the need to document misdemeanors seems secondary to the enforcement of martial law, nor do I believe myself to be alone in this assessment.

Marvin Branagh, RPD

* * *

Jill put the typed report and handwritten addendum back into the evidence drawer, sadly wondering if Marvin was still alive; it seemed unlikely, which was a thoroughly depressing thought. He was one of the best officers in the RPD, always nice as hell without sacrificing a professional demeanor.

Right up to the end, a real pro. Goddamn Umbrella.

She reached into the drawer and took out the diamond-shaped piece of blue glass, gazing at it thoughtfully. The rest of the evidence room had been a bust, the locked cabinets and drawers yielding nothing useful as far as weapons went; obviously, she wasn't the only one who'd thought to check it for guns and ammo. The gem, on the other hand...

Marvin was right about the streets being blocked all around the City Hall gate; she'd tried to get through the area once already and had found most of it barricaded. Not that there was much over there—the gate opened into a small garden with paved walkways, really a showcase for a rather boring statue of ex-mayor Michael Warren. Past that was City Hall, not used for much since the new courthouse had been built uptown, and a couple of paths that led north and west, respectively—an auto shop and a few used-car lots if you veered north, and to the west...

"Oh, shit, the trolley!"

Why hadn't she thought of it before? Jill felt a rush of excitement, hampered only slightly by the urge to slap her forehead. She'd totally forgotten about it. The old-fashioned two-car train's scenic route was a tourist thing, the city only ran it summers anymore, but it went all the way out to the westernmost suburbs, past City Park and through a few of the more expensive neighborhoods. There was an allegedly abandoned Umbrella facility out that way, too, where there might still be working cars and clear roads. Assuming it was in running condition, the trolley would be the easiest way out of the city, hands down.

Except with all the blockades, the only way to get to it is through that locked gate—and I've only got one of the jewels.

She didn't have the equipment to take the heavy, over-sized gate down by herself... but Marvin's report said that Bill Hansen had had the blue gem, and his restaurant was only three or four blocks away. There was no reason to assume he'd had the green one at some point, too, or that it was at the Grill, but it'd be worth checking out. If it wasn't there, she was no worse off—but if she *could* find it, she might be able to get out of the city much sooner than she'd expected. With the Nemesis running around out there, it couldn't be soon enough.

So, it was decided. Jill turned and walked toward the hall door, slipping the blue gem into her fanny pack. She wanted to check out the RPD's darkroom before she left, see if she could find one of the photographer's vests laying around; she didn't have any speed loaders for the Colt, and she wanted a few pockets to carry the loose rounds. While she was at it, she thought she might as well leave the shotgun behind. She'd rigged up an over-the-shoulder strap using a belt she'd taken off a dead man, so carrying it wasn't too bad, but without shells—and with the .357 as additional firepower—she didn't see the point in lugging it around anymore...

She stepped into the hall and took a left, deliberately not looking at the one slumped body beneath the windows that faced south. It was a young woman carrier she'd shot at from the stairs to the second floor, just around the corner, and she was pretty sure that she'd known the girl—a secretary/receptionist who worked at the front desk on weekends, Mary something. The darkroom faced the opening beneath the stairs; she'd have to pass within a few feet of the corpse, but she thought she could avoid looking too closely if she—

CRASH!

Two of the windows imploded, a driving rain of glass spraying over the receptionist's body, shards of it slicing at Jill's bare legs. In the same instant, a giant black mass was hurled inside, bigger than a man, as big as—

—*S.T.A.R.S. killer*—

It was all she had time to think. Jill sprinted back the way she'd come, slamming into the evidence room door, while behind her, she heard crunching glass as it rolled to its feet, heard the ugly opening note of its single-minded cry, "*SSst—*"

She ran, snatching the heavy revolver from beneath

her waist pack's strap, through the evidence room to the next door, through that into the patrol squadroom. A sharp left as soon as she was inside and desks blurred past, chairs and shelves and an overturned table spattered with the blood and fluids of at least two cops, their sprawled bodies reduced to obstacles in her path.

Jill leaped over the twisted legs, hearing the door open, no, *disintegrate* behind her, a roar of splinters and cracking wood that couldn't drown out the Nemesis's fury.

Gogogofaster—

She hit the door running, ignoring the dull blossom of pain that enveloped her bruised shoulder, twisting to the right as she pounded into the lobby.

Shhh-BOOM!

A flare of brilliant light and smoke jetted past her, blowing a jagged, burning hole in the floor not three feet to her left. Shards of blackened marble and ceramic tile flew, exploding up and outward in a fountain of noise and heat.

Jesus, it's armed!

She ran faster, down the ramp into the lower lobby, remembering that she'd dead-bolted the front doors, the realization like a punch in the stomach. She'd never get them open in time, no chance—

—and *BOOM*, another blast from what had to be a grenade launcher or bigger, close enough that she could feel the air part next to her right ear, could hear the whistle of incredible speed just before the front doors blasted open in front of her. They hung drunkenly on bent hinges, swaying and smoldering as she ran through, the night cool and dark.

"*Ssstaaarrrsss!*"

Close, too close. Instinctively Jill sacrificed a second of speed to leap to the side, kicking away from the ground, dimly aware that Brad's body was gone and not caring. Even as she landed, the Nemesis blew past her, barreling through the space she'd occupied an instant before. Its momentum carried it several giant steps away, it was fast but too heavy to stop, its monstrous size giving her the time she needed. A squeal of rust and she was through the gates, slamming them, scrabbling the shotgun off her back.

She turned and rammed the shotgun through the gates' hoop handles, both of them cracking against the barrel before she had time to let go, hard enough for her to realize that the gates wouldn't hold for very long. Behind the gates, the Nemesis screamed in animal rage, a demonic sound of bloodlust so strong that Jill shuddered convulsively. It was screaming for *her*, it was the nightmare all over again, she was marked for death.

She turned and ran, its howl fading into the dark behind her as she ran and ran.

* * *

When Nicholai saw Mikhail Victor, he knew he'd have to kill him. Technically, there was no reason, but the opportunity was too enticing to pass up. By some fluke, the leader of platoon D had managed to survive, an honor he didn't deserve.

We'll just see about that...

Nicholai was feeling good; he was ahead of the schedule he'd set for himself, and the rest of his journey through the sewers had been uneventful. His next goal was the hospital, which he could reach quickly enough if he took the cable car in Lonsdale Yard; he had more than enough time to relax for a few moments, take a break from his pursuit. Climbing back into the city and seeing Mikhail across the street, from the roof of one of Umbrella's buildings—the perfect sniper's roost—was like some cosmic reward for his work so far. Mikhail would never know what hit him.

The platoon leader was two stories below, his back to the wall of a wrecking yard's shack as he changed rifle magazines. A security light, its bright beam flickering with the erratic movement of nocturnal insects, clearly illuminated his position—and would make it impossible for him to see his killer.

Well, you can't have everything; his death will have to be enough.

Nicholai smiled and raised the M16, savoring the moment. A cool night breeze ruffled his hair as he studied his quarry, noting with no small satisfaction the fear on Mikhail's lined, unknowing face. A head shot? No; on the off chance that Mikhail had been infected, Nicholai wouldn't want to miss the resurrection. He had plenty of time to watch, too. He lowered the barrel a hair, sighting one of Mikhail's kneecaps. Very painful... but he would still have use of his arms and would probably fire blindly into the dark; Nicholai didn't want to risk getting hit.

Mikhail had finished his rifle inspection and was looking around as if to plot his next step. Nicholai took aim and fired, a single shot, extremely happy with his decision as the platoon leader doubled over, grabbing his gut—

—and suddenly, Mikhail was gone, around the corner of the building and into the night. Nicholai could hear the crunch of gravel fading away.

He cursed softly, clenching his jaw in frustration. He'd wanted to see the man squirm, see him suffer from the painful and probably lethal wound. It seemed that Mikhail's reflexes weren't as poor as he'd thought.

So, he dies in the dark somewhere instead of where I can see him. What is it to me? It's not as though I have nothing else to occupy my time...

It didn't work. Mikhail was badly injured, and Nicholai wanted to see him die. It would only take a few minutes to find the trail of blood and track him down—a child could do it.

Nicholai grinned. *And when I find him, I can offer my assistance, play the concerned comrade—who did this to you, Mikhail? Here, let me help you...*

He turned and hurried to the stairs, imagining the look on Mikhail's face when he realized who was responsible for his plight, when he understood his own failure as a leader and as a man.

Nicholai wondered what he'd done to deserve such happiness; so far, this had been the best night of his life.

* * *

When their conversation was over, the line went dead and Carlos walked to one of the booths and sat down, thinking hard about the things Trent had told him. If all he'd said was true—and Carlos believed that it probably was—then Umbrella had a lot to answer for.

"Why are you telling me all this?" Carlos had asked near the end, his head spinning. "Why me?"

"Because I've seen your records," Trent answered. "Carlos Oliveira, mercenary for hire—except you only ever fought the good fight, always on the side of the oppressed and abused. Twice you risked your life in assassinations, both successful—one a tyrannical drug lord and the other a child pornographer, if memory serves. And you never harmed a civilian, not once. Umbrella is involved in some extremely immoral practices, Mr. Oliveira, and you're exactly the kind of person who should be working to stop them."

According to Trent, Umbrella's T-virus—or G-virus, there were apparently two strains—was created and used on homemade monsters to turn them into living, breathing weapons. When humans were exposed to it, they got the cannibal disease. And Trent said that the U.B.C.S. administrators knew what they were sending their people into, and probably did it on purpose—all in the name of research.

"The eyes and ears of Umbrella are everywhere," Trent had said. "As I said before, be careful who you trust. Truly, no one is safe."

Carlos abruptly stood up from the table and walked toward the kitchen, lost in thought. Trent had refused to talk about his own reasons for undermining Umbrella, though Carlos had gotten the impression that Trent also worked for them in some capacity; it would explain why he was so secretive.

He's being careful, covering his ass—but how could he know so much? The things he told me...

A jumble of facts, some that seemed totally arbitrary —there was a fake green jewel in a cold storage locker underneath the restaurant; Trent had said that it was one of a pair but had refused to say where the other one was or why either of them was important.

"Just make sure they end up together," Trent had said—as if Carlos was going to just *happen* to come across the other one. "When you find out where the blue one is, you'll get your explanation."

For as cryptically useless as *that* seemed to be, Trent had also told him that Umbrella kept two helicopters at the abandoned water treatment plant west and north of the city. Perhaps most useful of all, Trent had said that there was a vaccine being worked on at the city hospital, and while it hadn't been synthesized yet, there was at least one sample there.

"Although there's a good chance the hospital may

not be there for much longer," he'd said, leaving Carlos to wonder again how Trent came by his information. What was supposed to happen to it? And how would Trent know that?

Trent seemed to think that Carlos's survival was important; he seemed convinced that Carlos was going to be a significant part of the fight against Umbrella, but Carlos still wasn't sure why, or if he even wanted to join up. At the moment, all he wanted was to get out of the city... but for whatever reason Trent had decided to offer up information, Carlos was glad for the help.

Although a little more would've been nice—keys to an armored getaway car, maybe, or some kind of antimonster spray.

Carlos stood in the kitchen, gazing down at the heavy-looking cover to what was, presumably, the basement ladder. Trent had told him that there were probably more weapons at a clock tower, not far from the hospital; that and the bit about the Umbrella helicopters, due north from the tower and hospital, definitely useful...

But why let me come here at all if I'm so goddamn important? He could've stopped me on the way to the field office.

A lot of it didn't make sense, and Carlos was willing to bet money that Trent hadn't told him everything. He had no choice but to trust him a little, but he was going to be very careful when it came to depending on Trent's information.

Carlos crouched next to the basement entrance, grabbed the handle to the cover, and pulled. It was heavy, but he could just manage it, leaning back and using his leg muscles for leverage. Unless the cooks were body builders, there was probably a crowbar around somewhere.

The front door to the restaurant opened and closed. Carlos gently, quietly put the cover aside and turned, still in a crouch, M16 aimed at the dining room entrance. He didn't think the zombies were coordinated enough to open doors, but he had no idea what the monsters were capable of, or who else might be wandering the city streets.

Slow, stealthy footsteps moved toward the kitchen. Carlos held his breath, thinking about Trent, wondering suddenly if he'd been set up—

—and about the last thing he expected to see was a .357 revolver come around the corner, held by an attractive and extremely serious-looking young woman who moved in fast and low and aimed at Carlos before he could blink.

For a beat they stared at each other, neither moving, and Carlos could see in the woman's eyes that she wouldn't hesitate to shoot him if she thought it necessary. Since he felt pretty much the same way, he decided it might be best to introduce himself.

"My name is Carlos," he said evenly. "I'm no zombie. Take it easy, huh?"

The girl studied him another moment, then nodded slowly, lowering the revolver. Carlos took his finger off the rifle's trigger and did the same as they both straightened up, moving carefully.

"Jill Valentine," she said, and seemed about to say something else when the back door to the restaurant crashed open, the thundering sound matched by a guttural, barely human scream that raised the hairs on the back of Carlos's neck.

"*Sstaarrsss!*" whatever it was howled, the cry echoing through the restaurant, giant footsteps pounding toward them, relentless and certain.

TEN

There was no time for questions, no time to wonder how it had found her so quickly. Jill motioned for the young guy to get behind her and backed into the dining room as he hurried past; she desperately looked around for something she could use to distract it long enough for them to escape. They ducked behind the service bar, Carlos moving as though he had some experience; he at least had the good sense to keep quiet as the S.T.A.R.S. killer charged into the kitchen, still screaming.

Fire! A guttering oil lamp sat on a cart next to the counter. Jill didn't hesitate; it would reach them in seconds if she didn't act immediately, and maybe a little burning oil would slow it down.

She motioned for Carlos to stay put, scooped up the lamp and stood, leaning over the counter and cocking her arm back. The hulking Nemesis had just started across the expansive kitchen when she threw the lamp at it, grunting with the effort it took to make the distance.

The lamp flew, and then everything slowed to a near stop, so much happening at once that her mind fed it to her one event at a time. The lamp shattered at the monster's feet, glass and oil splashing and puddling, a tiny lake of spreading fire; the creature raised its massive fists, screaming in anger; Carlos yelled something and grabbed her waist, pulling her down, the clumsy movement toppling them both to the floor—

—and there was a mighty clap of brilliance and sound that she'd suffered once already since waking up, a displacement of air that slapped at her eardrums, and Carlos was trying to shield her, holding her head down, saying something in rapid Spanish as time sped up to normal and something started to burn.

God, again? The whole city's going to blow up at this rate... The thought was vague, disoriented, her mind muddled until she remembered to breathe. A deep inhalation and Jill pushed Carlos's arm away and stood, needing to see.

The kitchen was blasted, blackened, utensils and cookware everywhere. She saw several canisters leaning against the back wall, one of them the obvious source of the explosion, its smoking metal sides peeled back like jagged petals. Rancid smoke curled up from the smoldering body on the floor, the Nemesis laid out like a fallen giant, its black clothes singed and burnt. It didn't move.

"No offense, but are you batshit?" Carlos asked, staring at her as though the question was rhetorical. "You could've barbecued us both!"

Jill watched the Nemesis, ignoring him, the .357 aimed at its still legs; its head and upper body were blocked by a low shelf. The blast had been powerful, but after all she'd been through, she knew better than to assume anything.

Shoot, shoot it while it's down, you may not have another chance—

The Nemesis twitched, a slight jerk of the fingers on the hand she could see, and Jill's nerve fled. She wanted out, she wanted to be far away before it sat up, before it shook off the effects of the explosion, as it surely would.

"We have to get out of here, now," she said, turning to Carlos. Young, good-looking, obviously unnerved by the blast, he hesitated, then nodded, holding his assault rifle tightly to his chest. It looked like an M16, military, and he was dressed for combat—a very good sign.

Hope there's more where you came from, Jill thought, heading for the door at a brisk pace, Carlos right behind her. She had a lot of questions for him and realized that he probably had a few for her, too... but they could talk somewhere else. Anywhere else.

As soon as they were outside, Jill couldn't stop herself; she broke into a run, the young soldier pacing her, hurrying through the cool dark of the dead city as she wondered if there was anyplace left where they could be safe.

* * *

The girl, Jill, ran a full block before slowing down. She seemed to know where they were going, and it was obvious that she'd had some kind of combat training; cop, maybe, though she sure as hell wasn't in uniform. Carlos was desperately curious but saved his breath, concentrating instead on keeping up with her.

From the restaurant they ran downhill, past the theater Trent had mentioned, taking a right at a decorative fountain at the end of the block; another half block and Jill signaled at a door on the left for a standard sweep. Carlos nodded, standing to one side of the door, rifle up.

Jill pulled the handle and Carlos stepped in, ready to fire at anything that moved, Jill covering him. They were in some kind of a warehouse, at the end of a walkway that T-ed some fifteen meters ahead. It seemed to be clear.

"It should be all right," Jill said quietly. "I came through this way a few minutes ago."

"Better safe than sorry, though, right?" Carlos said, keeping the rifle up but feeling some of the tension leave his body. She was definitely a pro.

They edged into the warehouse, carefully checking it out before saying another word. It was cold and not very well lit, but it didn't smell as bad as most of the rest of the city and by standing at the T junction in the middle of the warehouse, they'd be able to see anything coming well before it got to them. In all, it felt like the safest place he'd been since the helicopter.

"I'd like to ask you something, if you don't mind," Jill said, finally turning her full attention to him.

Carlos opened his mouth and the words just spilled out. "You want to ask me out, right? It's the accent, chicks love the accent. You hear it and you just can't help yourselves."

Jill stared at him, eyes wide, and for a moment he thought he'd made a mistake, that she wouldn't realize he was kidding. It was a stupid call, joking around in these circumstances. Just as he was about to apologize, one corner of her mouth lifted slightly.

"I thought you said you weren't a zombie," she said. "But if that's the best you can do, maybe we ought to reevaluate your situation."

Carlos grinned, delighted with her comeback—and suddenly thought of Randy, of him playing around just before they'd landed in Raccoon. His smile faded, and he saw the bright glitter of humor leave her face, too, as if she'd also remembered where they were and what had happened.

When she spoke again, her tone was much cooler. "I was going to ask if you were the same Carlos who sent out a message about an hour ago, hour and a half maybe."

"You heard that?" Carlos asked, surprised. "When no one answered, I didn't think—"

Be careful who you trust. Trent's words flashed through his mind, reminding him that he had no idea who Jill Valentine was. He trailed off, shrugging indifferently.

"I only caught part of it, and I couldn't transmit from where I was," Jill said. "You said something about a platoon, didn't you? Are there other, ah, soldiers here?"

Stick to the basics, and nothing about Trent. "There were, but I think they're all dead now. This whole operation's been a disaster from word go."

"What happened?" she asked, studying him intently. "And who are you with, anyway, National Guard? Are they sending backup?"

Carlos watched her in turn, wondering how careful he needed to be. "No reinforcements, I don't think. I mean, I'm sure they'll send someone in eventually, but I'm just a grunt, I don't really know anything— we set down, the zombies attacked. Maybe some of the other guys got away, but so far's I know, you're looking at the last surviving member of the U.B.C.S. That's Umbrella Bio-Hazard Countermea—"

She cut him off, the expression on her face close to disgust. "You're with *Umbrella*?"

Carlos nodded. "Yeah. They sent us in to rescue the civilians." He wanted to say more, to tell her what he suspected—anything to change the look on her face, like she'd just found out he was a rapist or something—but Trent's advice kept repeating, reminding him to be wary.

Jill's lips curled. "How 'bout you can the shit? Umbrella's responsible for what happened here, as if you didn't know—where do you get off lying? What are you really doing here? Tell the truth, Carlos, *if* that's your name."

She was definitely pissed, and Carlos felt a moment's uncertainty, wondering if she was an ally, someone who knew the truth about Umbrella—but it could also be a trap.

Maybe she works for them and is trying to feel me out, find out where my loyalties are...

Carlos allowed a touch of anger to creep into his own voice. "I'm just a grunt, like I said. I'm—all of us—are guns-for-hire. No politics, dig? They don't tell us shit. And at the moment, I'm not interested in what Umbrella is or isn't responsible for. If I see someone who needs help, I'm gonna do my job, but otherwise, I just want to get out."

He glared at her, determined to stay in character. "And speaking of who-what-why, what are *you* doing here?" he snapped. "What were you doing in that restaurant? And what was that thing that you blew up?"

Jill held his gaze for another second, then dropped her own, sighing. "I'm trying to get out, too. That *thing* is one of Umbrella's monsters, it's hunting me, and I doubt very much that it's dead, even now—which means I'm not safe. I thought there might be... I was looking for a kind of key, I thought it might be at the restaurant."

"What kind of key?" he asked, but somehow, he thought he already knew.

"It's this jewel, it's part of a locking mechanism to the City Hall gate. There are two jewels, actually, and I've got one already. If I can get the other one, get the gate open, there's a way out of town—a cable car that runs west, out to the suburbs."

Carlos kept his face neutral, but he was jumping beneath his skin. What had Trent said?

Go west, for one thing... and when I find out where the blue gem is, I'll understand their relevance... but what does this mean about Jill Valentine? Do I trust her now, or not? What does she know?

"No shit," he said, keeping his tone mild. "I saw something like that, in the basement at the restaurant. A green gem."

Jill's eyes widened. "Really? If we can get it... Carlos, we have to go back!"

"*If* that's my name," he said, caught somewhere between irritation and amusement. She seemed to leap from mood to mood, brisk then funny then angry then excited; it was kind of tiring, and he still wasn't sure whether or not he could turn his back on her. She *seemed* to be sincere...

"I'm sorry," she said, touching his arm lightly. "I shouldn't have said that, it's just—Umbrella and I aren't on the best of terms. There was a biohazardous incident at one of their labs, here, about six weeks ago. People died. And now this."

Carlos melted a little at the warmth of her hand. Jesus, but he was a sucker for *un primor*, and she was something to look at.

"Carlos Oliveira," he said, "at your service."

Down, boy. Head out of town, says Trent, but are you sure you want to travel with someone who might end up killing you? You want to clear your head before you take off with the cuero *Miss Valentine.*

Immediately he started arguing with himself. *Yeah, be careful, but are you going to leave her all alone? She said that monster was after her...*

He joked about it sometimes, but he wasn't truly a sexist; she could take care of herself, as she'd already proven. And if she *was* one of Umbrella's spies... well, she deserved what she got, then, didn't she?

"I—I wouldn't feel right about leaving without at least trying to find some of the others," he said, and now that he knew there was a way out, he realized it was true. Even an hour ago, the thought would have been ridiculous; now, armed with Trent's information, everything had changed. He was still scared, sure, but actually *knowing* something about the situation made him feel less vulnerable somehow. In spite of the risks, he wanted to walk a few more blocks before he left town, make some attempt to help *someone*. He wanted time to think, to make up his mind.

That... and knowing that she survived means that I can, too.

"I saw the gate you're talking about, the one over by the newspaper office, *sí*? Why don't I meet you there... or better yet, at the cable car."

Jill frowned, then nodded. "Okay. I'll go back to the restaurant while you look around, and I'll wait for you at the trolley. Once you go through the gate, just follow the path and keep to the left, you'll see signs for Lonsdale Yard."

For a few seconds, neither spoke, and Carlos saw, in the careful way she looked at him, that Jill had her own misgivings about him. Her leeriness made him trust her a little more; if she *was* anti-Umbrella, it made sense that she wouldn't be too hot on hanging out with one of their employees.

Stop debating it and just go, for Christ's sake!

"Don't leave without me," Carlos said, meaning for it to come out lightly. He sounded dead serious.

"Don't make me wait too long," she returned and smiled, and he thought that maybe she was okay after all. Then she turned and jogged lightly away, back down the walk they'd entered by.

Carlos watched her leave, wondering if he was crazy for not going with her—and after a moment, he turned and walked quickly toward the other exit before he could change his mind.

* * *

For someone who was bleeding like a stuck pig, Mikhail was surprisingly swift. For at least twenty minutes Nicholai had followed the trail of dark droplets through a blockade, over gravel and asphalt, grass and debris, and still he hadn't sighted the dying man.

Perhaps dying is too strong a word, considering...

Nicholai had planned to give up if he wasn't able

to find the platoon leader after a few minutes, but the longer he searched, the more determined he became. He found himself getting angry, too—how dare Mikhail run from his just punishment? Who did he think he was, wasting Nicholai's precious time? To frustrate him even further, Mikhail had covered quite a distance and was leading him back into town; another block or so and he'd be at the RPD building again.

Nicholai opened another door, scanned another room, sighed. Mikhail had to know that he was being followed—or he just didn't have the good sense to lay down and die. Either way, it wouldn't, *couldn't* be long now.

Nicholai walked through a small, orderly office, apparently attached to a parking garage, the erratic blood trail shining purple on the blue linoleum by the caged bare bulbs overhead. The splatters seemed to be thinning; either Mikhail was bleeding out—unlikely, it seemed—or he had found time to staunch his wound.

Nicholai gritted his teeth, reassuring himself. *He'll be weak, slowing down, perhaps looking for a place to rest. I saw the hit, he can't go on much longer.*

He stepped out into the dark, cavernous garage, the cold air thick with the smells of gasoline and grease— and something else. He stopped, breathed deeply. A weapon had been fired recently, he was sure of it.

He moved quickly and silently across the cement, edging around a white van that blocked one of the rows of cars, and saw what appeared to be a dog sprawled in a puddle of blood, its strange body curled in a fetal position.

He hurried toward it, disgusted and thrilled at once. They'd warned him about the dogs, how quickly they became infected, and he knew that research had been conducted on their viability as weapons at the Spencer estate...

...and they were deemed too dangerous when they turned on their handlers. Untrainable, and their decay rate higher than the other organics.

Truly, the half-skinned animal at his feet looked and smelled like a piece of raw meat that had sat in the sun for too long. Accustomed as he was to death, Nicholai still felt his gorge rise at the stench, but he continued to study the creature, certain that the canine had been the target of recent gunplay.

Sure enough. Two entry wounds below the torn flap of its left ear... but not from an M16, the holes were much too big. Nicholai backed away, frowning. Someone besides Mikhail Victor had come through the garage in the last half hour, and probably not a U.B.C.S. soldier, unless they'd brought their own weapon, probably a handgun—

Nicholai heard something. His head snapped up, his attention on the exit door, ahead at two o'clock. A soft sliding sound, an infected human brushing against the door, perhaps—or perhaps a wounded man, slumped and dying against the exit, too exhausted to press on.

Nicholai moved toward the door, hopeful—and grinned at the sound of Mikhail's voice, strained and weak, floating past the aging metal.

"No... get away!"

Nicholai eagerly pushed the door open, wiping the smile off his face as he assessed the situation. A vast wrecking yard, gated, vehicles piled in a useless barricade, two more dead dogs limp on the cold ground.

Mikhail lay next to the garage door, partially propped against the wall and trying desperately to lift his rifle. His pale face was beaded with sweat and his hands shook wildly. Five meters away, half of a person was pulling itself toward the downed man on shredded fingertips, its rot-sexless face corrupted into a leering perma-grin. Its progress was achingly slow but constant; it seemed that having no lower body—certainly not a complete digestive system—didn't stop the carrier from wanting to eat.

Do I play the hero, save my leader from being gnawed to death? Or do I enjoy the show?

"Nicholai, help me, please..." Mikhail rasped, rolling his head to look up at him, and Nicholai found he couldn't resist. The idea that Mikhail would be grateful to him for saving his life seemed extraordinarily... *funny*, for lack of a better term.

"Hang on, Mikhail," Nicholai said forcefully. "I'll take care of it!"

He dashed forward and jumped, slamming his boot heel into the carrier's skull, grimacing as a large section of its matted scalp sloughed wetly away from the bone.

He brought his heel down again, and a third time, and the once-human died in a thick, splintering *crunch*, its arms spasming, its fleshless fingertips dancing briefly on the asphalt.

Nicholai turned, hurrying back to kneel next to Mikhail.

"What happened?" he asked, voice heavy with concern as he gazed down at Mikhail's bloody stomach. "Did one of them get you?"

Mikhail shook his head, closing his eyes as if too exhausted to keep them open. "Somebody shot me."

"Who? Why?" Nicholai did his best to sound shocked.

"I don't know who, or why. I thought someone was following me, too, but—maybe they just thought I was one of *them*. A zombie."

Actually, that's not so far from the truth... Nicholai had to stifle another grin; he deserved an award for his performance.

"I saw... at least a few men got away," Mikhail whispered. "If we can get to the evac site, call in the transport..."

The St Michael Clock Tower was the alleged evacuation site, where the soldiers were supposed to take the civilian survivors. Nicholai knew the truth—that a reconnaissance team would put down first disguised as emergency medical, and no other helicopters would show unless Umbrella gave the word. Since the squad leaders were probably all dead, Nicholai had to wonder if any of the soldiers even knew about the "evacuation," though he supposed it wasn't important. It wouldn't affect his plans either way.

He found that he wasn't enjoying this game as much as he'd thought he would. Mikhail was too pathetically trusting, it was as much of a challenge as hunting a friendly dog. It was almost shameful to watch, too, the way he surrendered to his pain...

"I don't think you're in any shape to travel," Nicholai said coolly.

"It's not that bad. Hurts like hell, and I've lost some blood, but if I can just catch my breath, rest for a few minutes..."

"No, it looks very bad," Nicholai said. "Mortal. In fact, I think—"

Creeaak.

Nicholai shut up as the door to the garage opened next to them, a slow and even motion, and one of the U.B.C.S. soldiers stepped out, his eyes lighting up when he saw them, his assault rifle lowering—but only slightly.

"Sirs! Corporal Carlos Oliveira, A squad, Platoon Delta. I'm... shit, it's good to see you guys."

Nicholai nodded briskly, annoyed beyond measure as Carlos crouched next to them, checking Mikhail's wound, asking stupid questions. He was ninety-nine percent sure he could kill both of them before they realized what was happening, but even one percent was too great a risk considering what was at stake. He would have to wait... but perhaps he could find a way to use these new circumstances to his advantage.

And if not... well, people turned their backs on their friends all the time, didn't they? And neither of them had reason to believe Nicholai was anything but.

What was the saying, about how an obstacle was only a disguised opportunity? Things were going to be fine.

ELEVEN

Jill slid to a stop at the city hall gate, both gems held tightly in one sweaty hand. The area was clear, at least as far as she could see, but the restaurant had been empty, the Nemesis gone, and that meant she needed to hurry; she didn't know how, but it *was* tracking her, and she wanted to get gone.

Her blurred dash through the alleyways behind the restaurant had left her short of breath and not a little frightened. She'd nearly tripped over the body of some unlikely creature, one she'd been unable to see in the deepening blackness—but the dark silhouette of multiple claws hanging dead in the shadows had been more than enough to keep her moving. It didn't look like anything she'd seen before; that, and the threat of the Nemesis's inevitable pursuit had her in a mild panic. She used it to lend speed to her efforts, careful to maintain tight control. She knew from experience that keeping in touch with one's animal instincts was a vital part of surviving; a little fear was a good thing, it kept the adrenaline flowing.

The ornamental clock was set into a raised dais next to the gate. She fumbled the blue jewel into place, the diamond-shaped glass setting off a faint electrical hum, a circular chain of lights that bordered the jewels flickering on. The green diamond went in just as easily, turning the light chain into a complete circle. There was a heavy grinding sound and the gate's two sets of doors slid open, revealing a shadowy path surrounded by overgrown hedges.

It didn't look bad from where she stood. She eased into the silent walk, opening her senses. Cool, dark, a mild breeze promising rain the only thing that moved, rustling the trees, brushing leaves, chilling the sweat on her face and arms. She could hear the soft wailing of a distant virus-zombie drift through the air, and she saw the pale smudges of early moonlight on the path stones. Alert but sensing no immediate danger, she stepped further inside, her thoughts turning to Carlos Oliveira.

He was telling the truth about being one of Umbrella's hired hands and probably about not knowing what the company was really up to, but he was also holding something back. He wasn't as good a liar as he thought, and his apparent willingness to lie didn't bode well.

On the other hand, he didn't come across as devious in any way—a liar who meant well, perhaps, or at least who didn't mean any harm. He was probably just being careful—doing exactly what she was doing. Whatever the case, she didn't have time to do any major interpreting, so she was going with her first impression: he was one of the good guys. Whether or not that would be of any help to her was another story; for the moment, she was willing to settle for any ally who didn't have plans to kill her.

But should I be hooking up with anyone? What happens if he gets in the way of the Nemesis, and—

As if on cue she heard it, a malevolent coincidence that seemed unreal, like some deadly joke.

"Sstaarrss—"

Speak of the devil, oh, shit, where is it? Jill was almost at the center of the small park, where three trails intersected, and the sound came from somewhere ahead—or was it behind? The acoustics were strange, the tiny courtyard just in front of her making the low, hissing cry seem to come from everywhere. She spun, searching, but the path behind her and the two that stretched away from the open yard disappeared into shadow.

Which way... She stepped lightly into the open space, giving herself greater access to escape and room to maneuver, if it came to that.

A solid, heavy footstep. Another. Jill cocked her head—

—and there, ahead and to the left, the path that led to the trolley. A thickening darkness, still just out of clear sight.

Go back, newspaper office or back to the station,

no, no way I can outrun it but there's the gas station, it has a metal lock-down shutter and there's a shitload of cars, the better to hide—

Ahead and to the right. A simple plan was better than none, and she'd run out of time to consider her options any further.

Jill took off, the light patter of her boots lost beneath a sudden clash of motion, the rising howl and dense tread of semisynthetic feet bearing down on the courtyard. She was deeply conscious of herself, of her muscles contracting, of the sounds of her heart and breath as she flew over the stones. In an instant, she was at the small gate that led further north, that would take her down a block packed with abandoned cars, past a gas station/repair shop, toward—

She couldn't remember. If the street was clear, she could head through the industrial section of town, hope that she didn't run into any of the zombie packs. If blockades had been put up—

—then I'm screwed, and it's too late anyway.

She let her well-trained body do the rest of her thinking, nimbly slipping through the gate and into a crouching run, carrying her into the relative safety of a maze of gridlocked cars and trucks. She could feel it coming, and she allowed herself to flow into the shadows, to find in herself some primal understanding of her place in the hunt. She was the prey, she had to be as elusive as the Nemesis was determined; if she did it right, she would survive and the creature would go hungry. If not...

No time, no more thinking. The Nemesis was coming. Jill moved.

* * *

In the parking garage's office, Carlos found a half case of bottled water, some duct tape, and a men's dress shirt still in its package—as close to sterile supplies as they were going to get. He immediately set to doing what he could for Mikhail while Nicholai kept watch, staring out at the broken automobiles in the dark, rifle in hand. The courtyard was silent except for Mikhail's harsh breathing and the lonely cry of a distant crow.

Carlos didn't know much beyond simple triage, but he thought the wound wasn't too bad; the bullet had gone clean through Mikhail's side, not far above his left hip bone; an inch or two closer in and he would've been toast, a shot to the liver or kidneys his death warrant As it was, his lower intestine had probably been pierced; it would kill him eventually, but with prompt medical attention, he should be okay for now.

Carlos cleaned and dressed the wound, taping compresses on, wrapping strips of the shirt around Mikhail's torso to keep the pressure up. The platoon leader seemed to be managing the pain well enough, though he was nauseous and dizzy from loss of blood.

Out of the corner of his eye, Carlos noticed that Nicholai was moving. He finished layering tape over the bandages and looked up, saw that the squad leader had taken a laptop computer out of his shoulder bag and was tapping at keys, his face a study in concentration. He'd slung his rifle and was crouched next to a smashed pickup truck.

"Sir—ah, Nicholai, I'm done here," Carlos said, standing. Mikhail had insisted that they drop the formalities of rank, pointing out that their situation demanded flexibility. Carlos had agreed, though he hadn't gotten the impression that Nicholai liked it much; he seemed to be a by-the-book type.

Mikhail, pale and bleary-eyed, pushed himself up on his elbows. "Any way you can use that thing to call for evac?" His voice was weak.

Nicholai shook his head, sighing. He closed the laptop and returned it to his bag. "I found it at the police station and thought it might be of some use—lists of blockades, perhaps, or more information about this... disaster."

"No luck?" Mikhail asked.

Nicholai moved toward them, his expression resigned. "No. I think our best option is to try and make it to the clock tower."

Carlos frowned. Trent had told him there was supposed to be a supply of weapons at a clock tower, and that he should head north from there; between Jill's westbound cable car and this new information, he was starting to feel plagued by coincidences. "Why the clock tower?"

Mikhail answered, speaking softly. "Evacuation. It's where we were supposed to take the civilians and signal the transports to come in. The clock tower bells are scheduled to toll by computer, a system that emits a beacon signal when the program is being used. We ring the bells, the 'copters come. Cute, huh?"

Carlos wondered why no one had bothered to include *that* little nugget of information in their briefing but decided not to ask. It didn't really matter at this point; they had to get to the trolley. He didn't know Nicholai well, but Mikhail Victor was no threat, not in his condition, and he needed to get to a hospital. Trent had said there was one not far from the clock tower.

But Umbrella's eyes and ears—

No. Their stories were the same as his; they'd fought and watched their teammates die, gotten lost, looked for a way out and ended up here. It just felt weird, suddenly having two more people involved. Trent had him questioning everyone's motives now, wondering who might be involved in the alleged Umbrella conspiracy, worrying about what he could and couldn't say.

Besides, Umbrella screwed them over, too. Why would they want to help the bastards who landed us in this shit? Trent may be telling the truth, but he's not here. They are, and I need them. We need them. Jill couldn't possibly object to having a few soldiers on her side.

"There's a cable car we can use to get out there," Carlos said. "Right to the clock tower, I think. It's close, it runs west... and with all those things out there looking for fresh meat—"

"We could use a ride out of town," Nicholai broke in,

nodding. "Assuming the tracks are clear. Wonderful. Are you sure it's in operating condition?"

Carlos hesitated, then shrugged. "I haven't actually seen it. I ran into a—cop, I guess, a woman, she told me about it. She was on her way there, to see, she said she'd wait for me. I wanted to see if I could find anyone before we left." He felt almost guilty telling them about her, and abruptly he realized that he was letting all of Trent's crazy spy crap get to him. Why keep Jill a secret? Who cared?

Mikhail and Nicholai exchanged a look and then both nodded. Carlos was glad. At last, a real plan, a course of action. The only thing worse than being in deep shit was being in deep shit with no direction.

"Let's go," Nicholai said. "Mikhail, are you ready?"

Mikhail nodded, and together, Carlos and Nicholai lifted him, supporting his weight as evenly as they could. They edged into the parking garage and had almost made it back to the office when Nicholai let out a mild curse and stopped.

"What?" Mikhail closed his eyes, breathing deeply.

"The explosives," Nicholai said. "I can't believe I forgot why I even came back this way. After I found Mikhail, I just—"

"Explosives?" Carlos asked.

"Yes. Just after the zombies attacked, and my squad"—Nicholai swallowed, obviously struggling to maintain his composure—"after the zombies attacked, I ended up near a construction site, back in the industrial area. A building was being torn down, I think, and I saw a few discarded boxes with high explosive warnings. There was a locked trailer, I was going to break in but another wave of them came after me."

He met Carlos's gaze squarely. "They'd think twice about attacking in groups if we had a few RDX dynamite mixes to throw at them. Do you think you can make it to the trolley without me? I can meet you there."

"I don't think we should split up," Mikhail said. "We stand a better chance if—"

"If we have a way to keep them from getting too close," Nicholai interjected. "We can't afford to run out of ammo, not without something else to back us up. And there are the others to consider, the creatures..."

Carlos didn't think splitting up was such a good idea, either, but remembering that clawed thing from outside the restaurant—

—*and what about that big* feón *inside the restaurant? Jill said it would be coming after her again...*

"Yeah, okay," Carlos said. "We'll wait for you at the cable car."

"Good. I won't be long." Without another word, Nicholai turned and quickly walked away, out of the garage and into the night.

Carlos and the pale Mikhail struggled on in silence. They'd gone back through the office and out into the street before Carlos realized that Nicholai hadn't bothered asking for directions to the trolley.

* * *

Nicholai had to resist a powerful urge to check the computer again as soon as he was out of sight; he had wasted enough time playing the upstanding squad leader to the two idiot soldiers. It had already been nineteen minutes since Captain Davis Chan had filed a Watchdog status report from the Umbrella medical sales office—about two blocks from the parking garage—and if Nicholai was very lucky, he might catch Chan still in the act, checking updated memos or trying to get through to one of the administrators.

Nicholai jogged down a narrow alley plastered with flyers, hopping over several corpses strewn throughout, careful to avoid their upper bodies in case they weren't dead. Sure enough, one of the blasted-looking things near the end of the alley tried to reach around and grab his left boot. Nicholai jumped it with no trouble, smiling a little at its frustrated moan. Almost as pathetic as Mikhail.

Carlos Oliveira, though. Tougher than he looked, and definitely brighter—no match for *him*, of course, but Nicholai would want to get rid of him sooner rather than later...

...or not. I could bypass that charade entirely.

Nicholai pushed through a metal door to his right, into another alley littered with human remains, considering his options as he hurried along. He didn't need to go to the clock tower for any reason, just the hospital—and he didn't have to take the trolley.

Toying with Mikhail and now Carlos was enjoyable, but not a necessity. He could even let them live, if he chose...

He grinned, turning a corner in the winding alleyway. What fun would *that* be? No, he was looking forward to watching the trust in their eyes crumble, seeing them realize how stupid they'd been—

Tic tic tic.

Nicholai froze, understanding the sound instantly. Claws on rock, ahead of him, the almost gentle clatter coming from the shadows above and to the left. The only available light was behind him in the walkway's corner, one of those buzzing fluorescent security lamps that barely had the power to show itself; he backed toward it, the *tics* coming faster and closer, the creature still unseen.

"Show yourself, then," he growled, frustrated with yet another instance of bad timing. He had to get to the sales office before Chan disappeared, he didn't have time to battle one of Umbrella's freaks, much as he wanted to.

Tic tic tic.

Two of them! He could hear claws scratching cement to his right, where he'd just been, even as an unholy shriek sounded from the dark in front of him, a sound like madness, like souls being ripped apart—

—and there it was, screaming, leaping from the dark as the other joined in its monstrous song, moving black hell in stereo. Nicholai saw the raised hook claws of the one in front of him, the snapping, dripping mandibles, the gleaming insectile eyes, and knew the other was only a second behind its sibling, preparing to jump even as the first landed.

Nicholai opened up, the rattle of automatic fire lost beneath the twin howls, the rounds finding their mark on the first, its scream changing as it shuddered to a stop barely three meters away—and, still firing, Nicholai crouched and fell backwards, rolling up on his right side in a single fluid motion. The second charging animal was less than two meters away when he hit it, bloody divots appearing in its shining black exoskeleton like flowers in explosive bloom. Like the first, it twitched and spasmed to a halt before collapsing, its shrill cry becoming a gurgle, becoming silence.

Nicholai got to his feet, unnerved, not sure of the species—either brain sucker or the more amphibious *deimos*, another multi-legged breed. He'd expected the viciousness and the attack method, but hadn't understood how *fast* they were.

If I'd been even a second later...

No time to consider it, he was in a hurry. He edged forward, quickly stepping over the dark, oozing sprawl of limbs, breaking into a run as soon as he was past.

With each step away from the dead creatures he felt his composure returning, felt a flush of accomplishment warm him from the inside out. They were fast, but he was faster—and with such monsters loose in the city, he wouldn't have to worry about Mikhail or Carlos or *anyone* escaping what they were due. If he didn't get to enjoy the pleasure himself, he could revel in the knowledge that his comrades would certainly fall prey to any one of a dozen horrors, their inadequate reflexes failing them, their lack of skills ensuring their doom.

Nicholai tightened his grip on the M16, a rush of elation adding spring to each agile step. Raccoon was no place for the weak. He had nothing to fear.

TWELVE

The steel shutter that protected the front of the machine shop was down and locked, but Jill managed to get in through the garage, picking her way past a side door. The shop was sturdy enough, well protected from the average thief and certainly any zombie—but Jill had no doubt that if the Nemesis wanted to get in, it probably could. She'd just have to hope that it hadn't tracked her this far...

...however it does that, exactly.

Jill had no idea. Did it smell her? That didn't seem likely, considering her careful, breathless walk to the gas station; she'd dodged from shadow to shadow, hearing the Nemesis's thundering but clumsy progress as it searched for her amongst the crowd of abandoned cars. If it tracked her by scent, it would have caught her... though how did it know who she was, specifically? If another woman her size stumbled across its path, would it mistake that woman for Jill?

Jill walked through the well-lit garage, her boots making soft, wet noises against the oil-sticky floor, her thoughts wandering as she took in the layout and checked doors. She didn't know how the Nemesis had been programmed to find and kill S.T.A.R.S. or why it seemed to break off its pursuit from time to time, either; with Brad dead, she was the only S.T.A.R.S. member still in Raccoon.

Unless... Police Chief Irons had been a B team member, some twenty years back, and he was probably still in town...

Jill shook her head. Ridiculous. Chris had dug up enough information on Irons to make it a near certainty that he was working for Umbrella, just as they suspected their mysterious Mr. Trent was—the difference being that Trent seemed to want to help them, while Irons was a money-grubbing creep who didn't give a shit about anyone but himself. If Irons *was* on the Nemesis's hit list, Jill was pretty much okay with that.

From the garage, she stepped into a kind of combination office-break room—a soda machine, a small table with a couple of chairs, a cluttered desk. Jill tried the telephone on general principles, receiving the dead air she expected.

"Now I wait, I guess," she said to no one in particular, leaning against the counter. If the Nemesis didn't show up after a few moments, she'd slip out again, head back to the trolley. She wondered if Carlos was there yet, and if he'd found any survivors from his platoon—what was it? Umbrella Bio-Hazard something. Probably one of their semilegitimate branches; it would be good PR, once the news got out about Raccoon. Umbrella's admin would be able to point to their special task force, tell the media how quickly and decisively they'd acted when they'd realized there'd been an accident.

Except they won't call it an accident, because that could mean negligence on their part; no doubt they've already got a scapegoat lined up and ready to hang, some unlucky yes-man they can frame for the murder of thousands...

Not if she could help it, not if her friends could; one way or another, the truth was going to come out. It had to.

Jill noticed a few tools lying around—a set of socket wrenches, a couple of crowbars—and it occurred to her that it might be handy to pack a few things for the trolley. It'd suck to get there and end up needing a screwdriver or the like, something they'd have to come back for. She was a mechanical illiterate herself, but maybe Carlos had some experience—

Thump! Thump! Thump!

Jill dropped into a crouch behind the counter as soon as she heard the slow, heavy knocks at the garage's side door, insistent and steady.

Nemesis? No, the rappings were loud but not powerful, it was either a human or—

"Uuhh." The gently hungry cry filtered through the door, joined by another, then a third, then a chorus. Virus carriers, and it sounded like a large group of them. Any relief she felt upon realizing that it wasn't the Nemesis quickly faded; a dozen zombies hammering on the door was the equivalent of a flashing neon sign that read GOOD EATS.

And how exactly am I going to sneak out of here now?

Her simple plan, to hide until the Nemesis went away, had pretty much crapped out. She needed a new plan, preferably one she had more than a few seconds to map out.

So come up with something already. Unless you mean to go charging out there and start kicking ass.

Jill sighed, the low gnaw of dread in her stomach so constant that she no longer noticed it. Outside, the decaying carriers continued to shuffle and cry, beating helplessly against the door.

Might as well run through her options; she had a few minutes to kill.

* * *

They made it to the trolley without any trouble.

Carlos was feeling hopeful as they staggered into the station yard lit by an expanse of merrily burning debris to one side—no zombies, no monsters, and Mikhail didn't seem to be getting any worse. The City Hall gate had been open, a dozen jewels set into a kind of clock on a nearby pedestal, which meant Jill had already gone through. Carlos had expected her to make it, but it was still a relief.

"There it is," Mikhail said, and Carlos nodded, squinting as a gust of foul-smelling smoke washed over them. To their right was a grand old building, either the trolley station or the alleged City Hall. In front of them, past a stack of crates that blocked their path, was an old-fashioned trolley car, its red paint slightly faded. As they got closer, Carlos could see that a second car was attached, most of it hidden in the shadow of a building overhang.

Jill was probably waiting in one of them. Carlos shoved a few of the crates aside with one hip, Mikhail steadying himself against the station wall.

"Almost there," Carlos said.

Mikhail smiled weakly. "Bet you'll be glad to dump my ass into a seat."

"Be gladder to sit my own ass down. One-way ticket outta here."

Mikhail actually managed a laugh. "I hear that."

They moved beneath the overhang, Carlos searching the windows of both cars for movement. He didn't see anything; worse, he didn't *feel* anything. The place seemed totally deserted, still and lifeless.

Hope you're taking a nap in there, Jill Valentine.

The sliding side door of the first car they reached was locked; to their mutual relief, the second wasn't. After giving the car a once-over to be certain it was empty, Carlos helped Mikhail aboard, getting him settled into a window bench seat. As soon as the platoon leader was lying down, he seemed to fall into a half swoon.

"I'm going to check out the second car, then see what I can do to get a few lights on in here," Carlos said. Mikhail grunted in response.

Not surprisingly, Jill wasn't in the other car, either, but Carlos did find the electrical controls next to the driver's seat. At the touch of a button, a row of overhead lights switched on, illuminating an aging wood floor and red vinyl padded seats lining both walls.

"Where are you, Jill?" Carlos muttered, feeling real worry for her. If something had happened, he was going to feel at least partly responsible for not accompanying her back to the restaurant.

Mikhail was barely conscious when Carlos checked on him, but it was more like sleep than coma. Until a doctor looked at the wound, rest was probably the best thing for him.

There was an open control panel at the back of the car, which Carlos knelt to examine. His heart dropped when he saw that it was part of the primary power setup and that a few parts had been removed. He didn't know anything about cable cars, but it didn't take a genius to understand that you couldn't run a machine when the wires had been pulled, particularly on such an ancient system. It looked like there was a missing fuse, too.

"*Hijo de la chingada,*" he whispered and heard a feeble laugh behind him.

"I know just enough Spanish to know you shouldn't kiss your mother with that mouth," Mikhail said. "What's wrong?"

"There's a fuse missing," Carlos said. "And these circuits have got to be shorted out. We'll have to bypass them if we want to get this thing moving."

"Just northeast of here..." Mikhail started, but he had to pause for a few breaths before going on. "There's a gas station. Repair shop. It was one of the landmarks on... the city map, it's suburbs past that. Probably have equipment there."

Carlos thought about it. He didn't want to leave Mikhail alone, and Jill or Nicholai could show up any minute...

...but we ain't going no place without a power cable and a high amp fuse, and Mikhail's on a downhill slide; what choice have I got?

"Yeah, okay," Carlos said lightly, walking over to Mikhail. He gazed down at him, concerned about the high color of his cheeks, the waxy pallor of his brow. "Guess I'll go check that out—wanna come with?"

"Ha ha," Mikhail whispered. "Be careful."

Carlos nodded. "Try to get some sleep. If anyone shows up, tell them I'll be right back."

Mikhail was already slipping back into a doze. "Sure," he mumbled.

Carlos checked Mikhail's rifle to make sure it was loaded, and he placed it next to the padded bench, within easy reach. He hunted around for something else to say, some words of reassurance, and finally just turned and walked to the exit. Mikhail wasn't stupid, he knew what the stakes were.

His life, among other things.

Carlos took a deep breath and opened the door, praying that the gas station wasn't too far away.

* * *

Chan was gone, and not only was there no way to tell where he was headed but Nicholai had missed him by bare minutes. The computer he'd apparently made his report from was still warm, the glass of the monitor crackling with static electricity. Nicholai impulsively scooped up the monitor and threw it across the room, but wasn't satisfied with its mundane explosion of cheap plastic casing and glass. He wanted blood. If Chan came back to the office, Nicholai would beat him severely before ending his life.

He paced the small, heavily littered office, fuming.

He teases me with his ignorance. He is so stupid, so oblivious, how can he be so inferior and still be alive? Nicholai knew that the thought wasn't strictly rational, but he was furious with Chan. Davis Chan didn't deserve to be a Watchdog, he didn't deserve to *live*.

Gradually, Nicholai took hold of himself, breathing deeply, forcing himself to count to a hundred by twos. It was still early in the game. Besides, Nicholai's plan depended on having information that Umbrella wanted—and if he meant to steal that information, he had to allow *some* time for the other Watchdogs to collect it. The daily field reports were a bare summary of conditions and body count, used as much as a check-in as anything else; the real stuff was being stored on disk, transcribed from found documents or picked out of someone else's files, only downloaded by cell if the Watchdog considered it of critical importance.

And... while I'm waiting, I can check in with my comrades at the trolley.

Nicholai stopped pacing, struck by the realization that he had truly enjoyed his deception of Carlos and Mikhail. Somehow, that there were two of them had turned it into a more exciting game. Would they suspect him? What were they saying about his sudden departure? What did they *think* of him?

And what would it be like to witness Mikhail's slow, excruciating loss of life, watch him lose his capacity for reason as the young protagonist Carlos vainly struggles to beat the odds? Nicholai could disable the bell mechanism once they reached the clock tower... perhaps bravely volunteer to seek out the hospital, to bring back supplies—

Nicholai laughed suddenly, a harsh barking sound in the stillness of the room. He had to kill Dr. Aquino— the scientist who was supposed to report in from the hospital, the one working with the vaccine—anyway, and he knew that Aquino had been ordered to see to the hospital's destruction before leaving Raccoon, to eliminate trace evidence from his research. And there was also a specific species of organic stored at the hospital that Umbrella had decided to abandon, the Hunter Gamma series, so blowing up the hospital meant two objectives met for the price of one.

It seemed that the HGs weren't cost effective, although there had been serious disagreement within the administration about whether or not to destroy the prototypes. If Nicholai could lure Carlos into combat with one of them, he would have some valuable information of his own to sell... and he, too, would be meeting more than one objective with a single action.

It all came together, there was a kind of symmetry to it all. He'd drop the entire scheme if anything went wrong, of course, or if he found it wouldn't mesh with his plans. He wasn't an idiot—but having a project to fill his downtime would keep him from becoming overly frustrated.

Nicholai turned and started for the door, amused by his own indulgence. Raccoon City was like some haunted kingdom where he was ruler, able to do as he wished—*anything* he wished. Lie, murder, bathe in the glory of another man's defeat. It was all his for the taking, *and* with a payoff at the end.

He felt like himself again. It was time to play.

THIRTEEN

Jill had finally decided to open the metal shutter and make a break for it when she heard shots outside, the high-pitched chatter of an assault rifle. To say she was relieved was an understatement; the relentless thumping of the mostly dead outside had been eating at her nerves, almost tempting her to shoot herself, just so she wouldn't have to hear it anymore—and now, in a matter of seconds, it was quiet once again.

She moved quickly to the side door in the garage, ducking beneath a disemboweled red compact on a lift and pressing her ear to the cold metal. All was silent, the virus carriers surely dead—

Bam-bam-bam!

Jill jerked back as someone hammered on the door, her heart keeping time.

"Hey, is somebody in there? The zombies are dead, you can open up now!"

No mistaking the accent; it was Carlos Oliveira.

Relieved, Jill turned the lock, announcing herself as she threw the door open.

"Carlos, it's Jill Valentine."

She was happy to see him, but the look on his face was so sincerely elated that she felt almost shy suddenly. She moved back from the door so he could step inside.

"I'm so glad you're okay, when you weren't at the trolley, I thought..." Carlos trailed off, his "thought" obvious enough. "Anyway, it's really good to see you again."

His apparently serious concern for her was a surprise, and she was uncertain how to respond— irritation, that she was being patronized? She didn't *feel* irritated. Having someone interested in her well-being, particularly considering the kind of chaos they were in, was—well, kind of nice.

The fact that someone is tall, dark, and handsome isn't such a terrible thing, either, hmm? Jill instantly clamped down on the thought, cutting it short. True or not, they were in a survival situation; they could make eyes at each other later, *if* they made it out alive.

Carlos didn't seem to notice her slight discomfort. "So, what are you doing here?"

Jill gave him a half smile. "I got sidetracked. Don't suppose you saw Frankenstein's monster wandering around out there?"

Carlos frowned. "You saw him again?"

"Not him, it. It's called a Tyrant, if it's what I think it is—or some variation, anyway. Bio-synthetic, extremely strong, and very hard to kill. And it appears Umbrella figured out how to program it for a specific task—in this case, killing me."

Carlos gazed at her skeptically. "Why you?"

"Long story. The short answer is, I know too much. Anyway, I was hiding here, but—"

Carlos finished for her. "But a gang of zombies showed up, making it hard for you to leave. Gotcha."

Jill nodded. "What about you? You said you made it to the trolley, what you doing here?"

"I ran into two other U.B.C.S. guys. One of them got shot, he's still alive but not doing so great. Mikhail. Nicholai—that's the other one—thought he knew where to get some explosives, so Mikhail and I went to the trolley to wait for him. It turns out that there's an evac on standby, if we can get to the clock tower and ring the bells. We ring, helicopters come."

He noticed Jill's expression and shrugged, grinning. "Yeah, I know. It's some kind of computer signal, I don't know how it works. Great news, except to get the trolley running we're going to need a couple of things—a power cable and one of those old-fashioned electrical fuses, to start with. Mikhail told me there was a repair shop over here; he's one of the platoon leaders, he got a good look at a map before we landed..."

Carlos frowned, then nodded to himself as if he'd solved some puzzle. "Nicholai must have seen a map, too, that would explain why he didn't need directions."

"Carlos, Mikhail, Nicholai—Umbrella doesn't discriminate based on nationality, does it?" Jill made the joke offhandedly, mostly to cover a deepening sense of unease. She thought Carlos was decent at heart, but two more Umbrella soldiers, one of them a platoon leader—what were the odds that all three were stand-up guys who had been misled by their employer? Umbrella was the enemy, she couldn't lose focus of that.

Carlos was already walking away, his attention fixed on the raised red car. "If they were doing any electrical checks, there should be... there, that's what I'm looking for!"

It seemed that Carlos had seen the cable he wanted in the tangle of cords and wires spilling out from under the hood, some of them hooked to machines Jill didn't recognize, some just trailing on the oily cement.

"Careful," Jill said, moving to join him as he reached up and grabbed one of the cables, dark green. She had an instinctive mistrust of electrical equipment and vaguely believed that people who messed around with wires were just asking to be electrocuted.

"No problem," Carlos said easily. "Only a real *baboso* would leave any of these hooked up to the—"

Crack!

An orange-white spark spat out from one of the trailing wires, loud and bright and as explosive as a gunshot. Before Jill could draw breath, the cement floor was on fire—no gradual build, no sense of expansion, it was just suddenly and completely ablaze, the flames two, three feet high and rising.

"This way!" Jill shouted, running toward the open door that led into the office, the oil-fed fire blasting heat against her bare skin. *When it hits the car's gas tank it's going to blow, we gotta get out of here—*

Carlos was right behind her, and as they ran into the office, Jill felt her blood run cold. Screw the car, the car was nothing compared to what was going to happen when the fire got to the underground tanks in front of the station.

A chain pulley hung next to the steel shutter that blocked the front door. Jill ran for it, but Carlos was one step ahead. He snatched the chain and pulled, hand over hand, the shutter inching slowly upward in spite of the frantic rattle of metal links.

"Drop and crawl," Carlos said, raising his voice to be heard over the clanking, over the oceanlike rumble of spreading fire in the shop.

"Carlos, the tanks outside—"

"I know, now move!"

The bottom of the shutter was a foot and a half from the ground. Jill dropped, flattening herself against the cold floor, shouting up to Carlos before she belly-crawled outside.

"Leave it, it's good enough!"

Then she was through, stumbling to her feet, reaching around to grab Carlos's hand and pulling him up after her. Inside the shop, something exploded, a dull *whoomp* of sound, *maybe a gas can or that cabinet full of machine oil, Jesus I must be cursed, doomed, something, things keep blowing up around me—*

Carlos grabbed her arm, snapping her out of her wild-eyed freeze. "Come on!"

She didn't need to be told twice. With the rising light pouring from the machine shop's windows, illuminating in manic orange the heaped corpses of at least eight virus carriers, she ran, Carlos beside her.

The gridlock was bad, the street jammed, no clear path for them to make time. Jill could feel the seconds fly as they struggled through the maze of dead metal and blank, staring glass. The first real explosion and the sound of shattering windows behind them was too close, *we're not far enough yet*, but all they could do was what they were doing—that and pray that the fire would somehow miss the main tanks.

Maybe we should take cover, maybe we're out of the blast radius and—

Somehow, she didn't hear it—or rather, she heard a sudden, total absence of sound. Too focused on wending through the silent traffic in the dark, the rush of blood in her ears, the passing time, perhaps. All she knew was that she was running, and then there was a mammoth wave of pressure that boosted her from behind, lifting her up and forward at once, the side of a beaten panel truck rushing at her and Carlos screaming something—and then there was nothing but blackness, nothing but a distant sun that lapped at the edges of her dark, sending her dreams of angry light.

* * *

Mikhail was sinking, descending into the fevered delirium that would undoubtedly kill him. All Nicholai had been able to get out of the dying man was that Carlos had gone to get equipment to repair the trolley, and that he would be back soon. If there was any more, Nicholai would have to wait—until Mikhail's fever broke or Carlos returned, neither of which seemed likely. Mikhail was only going to get worse, and the deep, rumbling explosion that had quaked the ground beneath the trolley, that had preceded a lightening of the night sky to the north, suggested that there had been a fire at the gas station—not *necessarily* Carlos's fault, but Nicholai suspected that it probably was, and that Carlos Oliveira had burned to a crisp.

Which means I'll have to find a power cable myself if I want a ride to the hospital.

Irritating, but it couldn't be helped. Nicholai had found a box of spare fuses inside the station, as well as a five-gallon container of properly mixed machine oil, more than enough to get the cable car to the hospital—but no power cable, no wiring at all with which to bypass the shorted circuits. Nicholai wondered why Carlos hadn't thought to break into the station's maintenance room, and decided it was probably due to an absence of imagination.

"No... no, it can't—fire! Fire at will, I think... I think..."

Nicholai looked up from his inspection of the

trolley's control panel, curious, but whatever Mikhail thought was lost as he dropped back into a troubled slumber, the ancient bench creaking beneath his restless movements. Pathetic. He could at least babble out something interesting.

Nicholai stood and stretched, turning toward the door. He'd already added the oil to the engine's rudimentary tank system, but he'd taken the wrong kind of fuse. He'd get another one on his way back into town, probably all the way back to that same damned parking garage where he'd tracked Mikhail; he'd noticed some shelves of equipment there. All of the running back and forth was becoming tiresome, but at least most of the cannibals in the area had already been killed, so it wouldn't take too long—and when he returned, he could reward himself for his efforts by telling Mikhail who was responsible for his impending death.

He stepped out into the train's yard, thinking vaguely about where he might sleep for the night, when he saw two figures stumbling toward the trolley, their forms half hidden in the sparse light from a dying fire in the northwest corner of the yard. They drew closer, and he saw that Carlos had managed to escape death after all and had brought a woman with him, undoubtedly the same woman who'd told him about the trolley. Both were singed, their exposed skin reddened and grimy with ash; perhaps he hadn't been that far off the mark about who had started that fire...

...*and once again, let the games begin!*

"Carlos! Are you injured? Either of you?" He stepped forward so they could see him clearly, could see the deep concern on his face.

Carlos was obviously glad to see him. "No, I'm— we're both fine, just a little banged up. The gas station caught fire and blew. Jill blacked out for a minute or two, but she's..."

Carlos abruptly cleared his throat, nodding toward the woman. "Uh, Jill Valentine, this is Sergeant Nicholai Ginovaef, U.B.C.S."

"Nicholai, please," he offered, and she stared at him, her expression unreadable. It seemed that Ms. Valentine wasn't interested in making friends. That pleased him, though he wasn't sure why. She carried a .357 revolver and had what looked like a 9mm tucked into the waistband of an extremely snug skirt.

"We are indebted to you for telling Carlos about the trolley. You're with the police?" Nicholai asked.

Jill's gaze was fixed on his, and there was no mistaking the tone of challenge in her response: "The police are dead. I'm with the S.T.A.R.S., Special Tactics and Rescue Service."

Well, well, how ironic. I wonder if she's encountered Umbrella's little surprise yet... If she had, she probably wouldn't be standing in front of him; unless it was malfunctioning, a Tyrant could break a full-grown man in half without exerting even a quarter of its strength. Someone like Jill Valentine didn't stand a chance against something even more advanced, Umbrella's new toy that had been scheduled to appear.

Nicholai was pleased with the strange coincidence of meeting a S.T.A.R.S. member; it made him feel like everything was in order, that connections in his mind were reflected in the world around him...

"How's Mikhail?"

Nicholai looked away from Jill's unwavering stare to answer Carlos, not wanting to seem combative. "Not very well, I'm afraid. We should leave as soon as possible. Did you find anything useful? Mikhail said you were going to get repair equipment."

"It's all gone, burned up," Carlos said. "I guess we'll have to keep—"

"Did you get your explosives?" Jill interrupted, still watching him carefully. "Where were they?"

Not openly hostile, but very close; not surprising, considering. The inside line on the S.T.A.R.S. was that they had uncovered information about Umbrella's real research at the Spencer estate lab. They'd been discredited later, of course, but Umbrella had been trying to get rid of them ever since.

If they're all as suspicious as this one, it's no wonder Umbrella hasn't succeeded.

"There weren't any explosives," he said slowly, abruptly deciding to push her a little, see how forthright she was. "All I found were empty boxes. Ms. Valentine, is something bothering you? You seem... tense."

He deliberately shot a sharp glance at Carlos, as if angry that he'd brought the mistrustful woman along. Carlos flushed and quickly spoke up, trying to redirect the conversation.

"I think we're all on edge, but the important thing right now is Mikhail. We've got to get him out of here."

Nicholai held Jill's gaze a beat longer, then nodded and turned his attention to Carlos. "Agreed. If you can come up with a cable, I'll see what I can do about a fuse—there's a power station not too far from here, I'll look there. Back at the garage where we found Mikhail, I'm sure I saw battery cables, you should try there. Regardless of our success, we meet back here in a half hour."

Carlos nodded. Nicholai made a point of ignoring Jill's response, addressing Carlos instead. "Good. I'll check on Mikhail before I go. Move out."

He turned back toward the cable car as though everything was settled, silently congratulating himself as he climbed aboard. They would fetch the cable for him, while all he had to do was walk a dozen steps into the trolley station and reach into a box.

Which means I'll have plenty of time left over. I wonder what they'll talk about when I'm not around... Perhaps he'd arrange to meet them on their way back, watch them for a moment or two before revealing his presence.

Nicholai walked to where Mikhail was sleeping and grinned at him, well pleased. Things were getting interesting, finally. Carlos was working for him, Mikhail was at death's door, and the addition of the S.T.A.R.S. woman had thickened the plot, so to speak. He glanced out the trolley window and saw that the two of them had already gone, disappearing back into the dark. Jill Valentine was suspicious of him, but only because of what she knew about Umbrella; he was sure that she would warm to him, given a little time.

"And if she doesn't, I'll kill her along with the rest of you," he said softly.

Mikhail let out a soft sound of distress but slept on, and after a moment, Nicholai quietly left.

FOURTEEN

Although there was probably a lot they could talk about, Jill didn't feel like it and neither did Carlos. They had to get a power cable, get back to the trolley, and not get killed in the process—not exactly the time for small talk, even if the streets *did* seem to be clear. And after the near death experience they'd just shared running from the gas station, Carlos couldn't imagine chatting.

What would we talk about, anyway? The weather? How many of her friends are dead? How about whether or not that Tyrant-thing is going to pop up and kill her anytime soon, or maybe the top ten reasons she doesn't like Nicholai...

Jill was obviously uncomfortable with Nicholai—almost certainly because of her feelings about Umbrella—and Carlos thought Nicholai didn't like her much, either, though he wasn't sure why; the squad leader had been perfectly polite, if a little brisk. Carlos liked that Jill wasn't like that with him, suspicious and challenging, but the animosity between her and Nicholai made him a little nervous. As clichéd as it was, they needed to stick together if they meant to survive.

In any case, Jill wasn't volunteering to discuss her feelings on the topic, and Carlos was busy debating himself about whether or not to tell the others about Trent, and they both were watching their asses. They walked in silence from the trolley back into downtown and were almost back to the garage when Carlos saw someone he recognized.

The dead man was propped in the corner of a winding alley, not far from the grotesque bodies of two Umbrella creatures that Carlos had passed twice already in the past couple of hours, like the thing he'd killed by the restaurant; from the look of his corpse, he'd been there awhile—which meant Carlos had passed him by as well, never noticing. It was kind of distressing to realize he didn't even look at their faces anymore, but he was a little too surprised to hang on to the feeling.

"Hey, I've met this guy," he said, crouching next to him, trying to remember the name—Hennessy? Hennings, that was it. Tall, dark hair, a thin scar that ran from one corner of his mouth to his chin. Single gunshot wound to the head, no obvious signs of decay...

...*and what the hell is he doing here?*

Jill had been walking a few steps ahead of Carlos. She turned and walked back, surreptitiously checking her watch.

"I'm sorry about your friend, but we really have to get going," she said gently.

Carlos shook his head and started to pat the body down, searching for extra ammo or some ID. "No, we weren't friends. I met him at the field office right after I was hired, he worked for another U.B.C.S. branch, I think. The guy's a spook, ex-military, and he definitely didn't come to Raccoon with us... *hola*, what's this?"

Carlos pulled a small, leather-bound book about the size of a paperback out of Hennings's jacket lining and opened it. A journal. He flipped to the back and saw that the last entry was dated only the day before yesterday.

"This could be important," he said, standing up. "I'm sure Nicholai knew him, he'll want to see this."

Jill frowned. "If it's important, maybe *you* should look at it now. Maybe it... maybe he mentioned Nicholai or Mikhail."

The last was delivered lightly, but Carlos understood what she was getting at, and he didn't like it much. "Look, Nicholai's kind of standoffish, but you don't know him. He lost his entire squad today, men he's probably known and worked with for years, so why don't you give him a break?"

Jill didn't flinch. "Why don't *you* look through that book while I go get the power cable? You say this man's some kind of agent, that he works for Umbrella and that technically he shouldn't be here. I want to know what he had to say in his final hours, don't you?"

Carlos glared at her for another moment, then

nodded reluctantly, letting the tension go. She was right; if there was something definitive in Hennings's notes about what was happening in Raccoon, it might be of use to them.

"Fine. Just grab every cable you can find and hurry back, okay?"

Jill nodded and was gone a second later, disappearing into the shadows without a sound. Amazing, how quiet she was; that took serious training. Although he didn't know much about them, Carlos had heard of the S.T.A.R.S., heard they were supposed to be good; Jill Valentine certainly proved it.

"Let's see what you have to say for yourself, Hennings," Carlos muttered, flipped open the journal, and started to read the final entry.

I didn't know it was going to be like this. I owe them everything, but I would have turned this down if I had known. It's the screaming, I can't take it anymore and who gives a crap if my cover's blown? Everybody's going to die, it doesn't matter. The streets are filled with screaming and that doesn't matter, either.

When the company saved my ass two years ago, they told me that I was going to be working on the dark side, which was fine by me. I was about to be executed, I would have agreed to ten years of shit shoveling, and what the rep told me didn't sound too bad—me and some other cons were going to be trained as troubleshooters, dealing with illegal aspects of their research. They have their legit organizations already, couple of paramilitary units, the bio-hazard boys, a pretty decent environmental protection crew. Our job was going to be cleaning up messes before too many people noticed, and making sure the people who did notice never got a chance to talk about it.

Six months of intensive training and I was ready for anything. Our first assignment was to get rid of some test subjects who'd gone into hiding. These people wanted to go public about the drug they'd been injected with, it was supposed to slow down the aging process but it gave all of them cancer. It took awhile, but we got all of them. I'm not proud of myself for that, or for anything else I did in the last year and a half, but I learned to live with it.

I was specially selected for Operation Watchdog. They planted a bunch of us here right after the first spill, just in case, but not everyone was chosen to be a Watchdog. They said I was more committed than the others, that I wouldn't crumble watching others die. Hooray for me. I worked in a warehouse for two weeks as an inventory specialist, waiting for something to happen, bored out of my goddamn skull—and then everything happened at once, and I haven't slept for three days and everyone keeps screaming until the flesh eaters get to them, and then they either die or they also start to eat.

I tried to get hold of some of the others, the plants, but I can't find anyone. I only know a few of them anyway, four of the people selected as Watchdogs— Terry Foster, Martin, that spooky Russian, the hospital doc with the glasses. Maybe they're dead, maybe they escaped, maybe they have yet to be sent in. I don't care. I haven't made a report since day before yesterday, and Umbrella can blow it out their ass and burn in hell. I'm sure I'll see them there.

I've chosen to pull the trigger myself, a head shot so I won't come back. I wish they'd left me to be executed, I deserved that. Nobody deserves this.

I'm sorry. If anyone finds this, believe that much.

The rest of the pages were blank.

Carlos knelt next to Hennings in a kind of numb haze and examined his cold right hand for gunshot residue. It was there. Somebody must have taken the gun later—

"Carlos?"

He looked up and saw Jill holding a handful of cables, a look of curious concern on her dirty, pretty face.

That spooky Russian. How many could there possibly be? Carlos didn't know what a Watchdog was, but he thought that Nicholai had some explaining to do—and that it might be a good idea to get back to Mikhail as soon as possible.

"I think I owe you an apology," Carlos said, his stomach suddenly in knots. Nicholai had found Mikhail just after he'd been shot, allegedly by some random stranger...

"What for?" Jill asked.

Carlos tucked the journal into a vest pocket, taking

a last look at Hennings, feeling disgust and pity and a building anger—at Umbrella, at Nicholai, at himself for being so naive.

"I'll explain on the way back," he said, gripping his assault rifle so tightly that his hands started to tremble, the anger continuing to rise in him like a black flood. "Nicholai will be waiting for us."

* * *

After installing the new fuse in the trolley's control panel, Nicholai decided to wait inside the station for Carlos and Jill to return. Many of the first-floor windows were broken, and it was dark inside; he'd be able to hear any private, last-minute conversation between them as they entered the yard. Nicholai had no doubt that Jill would have a few words of warning for Carlos regarding Umbrella, perhaps about Nicholai directly, and the truth was, he just couldn't help himself; he wanted to know what the S.T.A.R.S. woman had to say, what paranoid drivel she'd spout, and how Carlos would react. He'd rejoin them a minute or so after they boarded the trolley, say he was checking the building for supplies or something, and see what developed from there.

Do we take a ride, or will I be traveling alone? Perhaps we'll stay together for the night, foraging for food, taking turns at standing guard. I could kill them in their sleep; I could entice both of them to accompany me to the hospital to engage the Hunters; I could disappear, and allow them to evacuate thinking that their dear friend had been lost.

Nicholai smiled, a cool night draft from a shattered pane breezing across his face. In a very real way, their lives were in his hands. It was a powerful feeling, even intoxicating, to have that kind of control. What had started out as a primarily financial venture had evolved into something new, something he had no words for—a game, but so much more. An understanding of human destiny like nothing he'd ever experienced. He'd always known that he was different, that societal boundaries didn't apply to him in the same way that others understood them; coming to Raccoon was an amplification of that, it was like an alternate reality in which *they* were the strangers, the outsiders, and he was the only one who really knew what was going on. For the first time in his life, he felt free to do as he liked.

Nicholai heard the gate from the alleyway creak open, slowly, stealthily, and he backed away from the window. A second later, the two young soldiers stepped into view, moving almost as silently as himself. He noted with some surprise that they were sweeping the yard, as if they expected trouble.

Perhaps they met up with the Tyrant-creature. That would certainly spice things up, if Jill was being tracked, although Nicholai meant to let the seeker have her if it showed up. It would kill anyone stupid enough to get in its way; Nicholai would happily step aside.

Jill was slightly ahead of Carlos, and as they cautiously edged forward, Nicholai saw that she carried several cables slung over one shoulder. Maybe he *would* keep them around awhile, they were proving to be successful at running errands.

"All clear," Carlos whispered, and Nicholai smiled to himself. He could hear them perfectly.

"He has to be back by now, if he didn't run into one of the creatures," Jill whispered.

Nicholai's smile faltered a little. It was impossible, but... were they sweeping for *him*?

"I say we approach like we don't know anything," Carlos said, keeping his voice low. "Get on board, get on either side of him, make him give up the rifle. He carries a knife, too."

What is this, what's changed? Nicholai was confused, uncertain. *What can they possibly know?*

Jill was nodding. "Let me ask the questions. I know more background on Umbrella, I think I have a better chance of convincing him that we know all about this Watchdog mission. If he thinks we already know—"

"—then he won't bother hiding anything," Carlos finished. "Okay. Let's do it. Keep your weapon ready, just in case he's planning a surprise party."

Jill nodded again, and they both straightened up, Carlos shouldering his rifle. They started toward the trolley, no longer bothering to keep quiet.

The fury that overtook Nicholai was so passionate, so all encompassing, that for a moment he was literally blinded by it. Flashes of red and black pounded through his brain, thoughtless and violent, and the only thing that kept him from running out into the yard and murdering them both was the distant awareness that they were prepared for his attack. He almost did it anyway, the urge, the *need* to hurt them so strong that the consequences seemed unimportant. It took all of his control to stand still, to stand and shake and not scream his rage.

After some indeterminate time, he heard the trolley's engine roar to life, the sound finally getting through to him. His mind began to work again, but he could only think simply, as though his anger was too great for complexity of thought.

They knew he wasn't telling the truth. They knew something about Operation Watchdog, and they knew he was involved, so he was their enemy now. There would be no consummation of the careful groundwork he'd laid, no development of trust for comrade Nicholai. It had all been a waste of his time... and to add insult to injury, he was now going to have to walk to the hospital.

Nicholai ground his teeth together, drowning, the impotent hatred like a diseased secret that was crushing him from the inside out. They had done this to him, stolen his sense of control as though they had a right to it.

My plans, my money, my decision. Mine, not theirs, mine—After a moment the mantra started to work, calming him slightly, the words soothing in their truth. *Mine, I decide, me.*

Nicholai took several deep breaths and fixated on the only thing that could bring him relief as he heard the trolley slowly rumble away.

He'd find a way to make them sorry. He'd make them beg for mercy, and laugh while they screamed.

FIFTEEN

Jill stood next to Carlos at the train's controls, looking out as the dark ruins of Raccoon slowly slipped past. They couldn't see much by the yellowed beam of the single headlight, but there were numerous small fires blazing unchecked and a partial moon shone its cold light down on it all—debris-packed streets, broken, boarded windows, living shadows that swayed and wandered aimlessly.

"Keep it slow," Jill said. "If the tracks are blocked and we're going too fast..."

Carlos shot her an irritated look. "Gee, I hadn't thought about that. *Gracias.*"

His sarcasm invited a reply, but Jill was too tired to banter, and her body felt like a single, massive bruise. "Yeah, okay. Sorry."

The tracks unrolled in front of them as Carlos carefully handled the controls, slowing to a virtual crawl with each curve. Jill wanted to sit, maybe go into the other car with Mikhail and lay down—it was a few miles to the clock tower and a jogger could easily keep up with them—but she knew that Carlos was tired, too; she could at least suffer aching feet along with him for another few minutes.

By some unspoken agreement, they hadn't discussed Nicholai yet, perhaps because speculation on where he was and what he was doing didn't serve any purpose; whatever he was up to, they were getting out of town. Assuming they survived, Jill was more committed than ever to seeing that Umbrella paid for their crimes, and it was Umbrella, not Nicholai, who held responsibility for the death of Raccoon.

Her intuition had been good on Nicholai, that he wasn't ignorant of Umbrella's evils, though she hadn't suspected the depth of his deception. From what she'd read in the journal Carlos had found, it appeared that the company had been prepared for Raccoon to be infected and had set up a secret team to make reports on the catastrophe. It was disgusting, but not surprising.

We're dealing with Umbrella, after all. If they can illegally design genetic viruses and breed killing machines to inject said viruses into, why not capitalize on mass murder? Take some notes, document a few fights—

Crash!

Jill stumbled against Carlos as the trolley rocked, the sound of shattering glass coming from the other car. A half second later, they heard Mikhail let out a fevered cry—of fear or pain, Jill couldn't tell.

"Here, take the controls," Carlos said, but she was already halfway across the car, the heavy revolver in hand.

"I got it, keep us going," she shouted back, not wanting to think about what it could be as she dashed toward the door. For the trolley to shake like that—

—*it has to be one of their monsters. And Mikhail probably can't even sit up on his own.*

She pushed the door open and stepped onto the connecting platform, the heavy clatter of the moving trolley seeming incredibly loud as she opened the second door, Mikhail's helplessness in the forefront of her mind.

Oh, shit.

The elements of the scene were simple, straightforward, and deadly: a broken window, glass everywhere; Mikhail, to her left, his back to the wall as he struggled to get to his feet, using his rifle as a crutch—and the S.T.A.R.S. killer standing in the middle of the car, misshapen head thrown back, its giant lipless mouth opening as it growl-screamed wordlessly. The remaining windows shook from the strength of its insane cry.

Jill opened fire, each shot a deafening explosion, the heavy rounds slamming into its upper torso as it continued to howl. The sheer force of the assault drove it back a few steps, but if there was any effect otherwise, she couldn't see it.

On the sixth round, Mikhail's rifle joined in, the smaller slugs peppering the Nemesis's gigantic legs as Jill went dry. Mikhail was still slumped against the wall and his aim was poor, but Jill would take any help she could get. She grabbed her Beretta—even with a speed loader the .357 would take too long—and opened up, going for head shots—

—*not working*—

—and the Nemesis stopped screaming and fixed its attention on her, its slitted white eyes like cataracts, its huge teeth shining and slick. Tentacles snaked around its hairless, lumpy head.

"Get out!" Mikhail shouted, and Jill spared him a glance, not even considering the idea as she fired again—until it registered an instant later that he was holding a grenade, one shaking finger hooked through its ring. She recognized the make without thinking about it—a Czech RG34, Barry had collected antipersonnel grenades—as she sent a round into the Nemesis's stitched brow to no effect. Impact grenade, once the ring was pulled it'd detonate on contact—

—*and Mikhail won't make it, it's suicide*—

"No, you go, get behind me," she screamed, and the S.T.A.R.S. killer took one massive step forward, almost halving the distance between them.

"*Get out!*" Mikhail ordered again and popped the ring, an expression of incredible concentration and purpose on his dead-white face. "*I'm dead already! Do it, now!*"

Her Beretta fired once more and was empty.

Jill spun and ran, leaving Mikhail to face the monster alone.

* * *

Carlos heard the yelling amidst the shots as he worked to bring the trolley to a stop, desperate to help Jill and Mikhail, but they were in the middle of a relatively tight curve and the poorly maintained controls fought his efforts. He was about a second from joining them anyway when the door behind him crashed open.

Carlos whipped around, one-arming his M16 as he instinctively kept his other hand on the throttle, and saw Jill. She practically flew into the car, her expression a mask of expectant terror, his name forming on her lips—

—and a tremendous shock of fire and sound bloomed up behind her, pushing her to dive, a clumsy shoulder roll that was punctuated by the echoing *boomcrash* from the second car. Tongues of flame burst through the back door's window as the floor tilted wildly. Carlos slammed against the driver's seat, the chair's arm whacking him mid-thigh hard enough to bring tears to his eyes.

Mikhail!

Carlos took one faltering step toward the back— and saw only burning pieces of the obliterated second car dragging behind them, falling away as the trolley picked up speed. There was no chance that Mikhail could have survived, and Carlos started having serious doubts about their own chances as Jill stumbled forward, her face haunted by whatever she'd seen.

The cable car hit another curve, and then it was out of control, tossing back and forth like a ship on stormy seas, except the thunder and lightning were caused by their car smashing mightily into buildings and autos alike, sending up great plumes of sparks. Instead of slowing them down, the trolley seemed to be picking up speed with each impact, hurtling through the dark in a series of fiery metal screams.

Carlos fought gravity to grab the throttle, aware that they'd jumped the tracks, that Mikhail was gone, that their only hope was the manual brake. If they were very lucky, the wheels would lock. He yanked back as hard as he could—

—and nothing happened, nothing at all. They were screwed.

Jill made it to the front, clutching at chair backs and support poles as the trolley continued to buck and screech. Carlos saw her staring at the useless throttle beneath his fingers, saw despair flash in her eyes, and he knew that they had to jump.

"*The brakes!*" Jill shouted.

"*No good! We have to bail!*"

He turned, grabbed his rifle by the barrel, and used the locked stock to break out a side window, a sudden shift of the floor sending the glass shards raining on his chest. He held on to the slick window frame with one hand, reached back to grab Jill—

—and saw her drive her elbow into a small glass panel set low into the console, a look of crazed hope on her face as she pulled a switch he couldn't see—

SKREEEEEEE—

emergency brake

—and incredibly, the trolley was slowing, tipping to the left a final time before settling back, sliding forward in a diminishing spray of bright sparks. Carlos closed his eyes and gripped the useless throttle, tensing, trying to prepare himself for the impact—and a few seconds later, a mild, anticlimactic *crunch* signified their journey's end; the car had come to rest against a pile of broken concrete pieces in the middle of a neatly trimmed lawn, a few shadowy statues and hedges nearby. A final tremor rattled through the car, and it was over.

Silence, except for the tick of cooling metal. He opened his eyes, hardly able to credit their nightmare ride through the city. Next to him, Jill took a shaky breath. It had all happened so fast, it was a miracle that he and Jill were still alive.

"Mikhail?" he asked softly.

Jill shook her head. "It was the Tyrant-thing, the S.T.A.R.S. Nemesis. Mikhail had a grenade, it kept coming at us and he—"

Her voice broke, and she reached into her pack and started to reload her weapons, concentrating on the simple movements. It seemed to calm her. When she spoke again, her voice was firm.

"Mikhail sacrificed himself when he saw that the Nemesis was coming after me."

She looked away, out into the dark as a chill wind drafted through the trolley's shattered windows. Her shoulders slumped. Carlos wasn't sure what to say. He stepped toward her, gently touching one abraded shoulder, and felt her body stiffen beneath his fingers. He quickly dropped his hand, afraid that he'd offended her somehow, and then realized that she was staring out at something, a look of pure amazement on her delicate features.

Carlos followed her gaze, looking out and up to see a giant, three- or four-story tower looming over them, silhouetted against a backdrop of clouded night sky. A glowing white clock face near the top read that it was almost midnight.

"Somebody loves us, Carlos," Jill said, and Carlos could only nod mutely.

They had reached the clock tower.

* * *

Nicholai walked along the moonlit tracks, not bothering to conceal himself as he plodded west. He'd be able to see anything coming and kill it long before it reached him; he was in a foul mood and almost welcomed the opportunity to blow the guts out of something, human or otherwise.

His anger had abated somewhat, giving way to a rather fatalistic state of mind. It no longer seemed feasible for him to track down the dying platoon leader and two young soldiers—basically, there just wasn't enough time. It would take at least an hour for him to make it to the clock tower; assuming they could figure out how to ring the bells, they'd be long gone by the time he got there.

Nicholai scowled, working to remind himself that his plans hadn't changed, that he still had an agenda to fulfill. Four people were unwittingly waiting for him. After Dr. Aquino, there were the soldiers—Chan and a Sergeant Ken Franklin—and the factory worker, Foster. When they were all out of the way, Nicholai still had to collate their data, arrange a meeting, and 'copter out. He had plenty to do... yet he couldn't help feeling cheated by the circumstances.

He stopped walking, cocking his head to one side. He heard a crash, an impact of some kind further west, perhaps even a small explosion muffled by distance. A second later he felt the slightest of vibrations coming from the trolley tracks. The tracks ran down the middle of a main street, anything solid could have given them a jolt—

—*but it's them, it's Mikhail and Carlos and Jill Valentine. They ran into something, or something went wrong with the engine, or...*

Or he didn't know what, but he was suddenly quite sure that they had encountered trouble. It reinforced for him the positive feeling he had that *he* was the one with skill; they were forced to rely on luck, and not all luck was good.

Perhaps we will meet again. Anything is possible, especially in a place like this.

Ahead of him and to the left, from in between an office building and a fenced lot, came a gurgling groan, then another. Three infected shambled out into the open, ten meters or so from where he stood. They were too far away to make out clearly in the waxy moonlight, but Nicholai could see that none of them were in good shape; two were missing arms and the third's legs had somehow been cut down, so that it seemed to be walking on its knees, each stumping footstep creating a noise like someone smacking their lips.

"Uhllg," the closest complained, and Nicholai shot it through its disintegrating brains. Two more shots and the other two joined the first, collapsing to the asphalt in wet *thumps*.

He felt much better. Whether or not he got an opportunity to see his duplicitous comrades again—and he found that he felt strongly that he would—he was the superior man, and he would triumph in the end.

The awareness filled him with a new energy. Nicholai broke into a trot, eager to meet whatever challenge came next.

SIXTEEN

The trolley's door was jammed, so Jill and Carlos had to climb out of a window, Carlos looking as drained as Jill felt. It was a frankly weird coincidence that the trolley had ended up exactly where they needed to go, but then the last several hours—hell, *weeks*—had been weird. Jill thought it would serve her well to stop letting things surprise her.

The clock tower yard seemed empty of life, nothing moving but a thin haze of oily smoke boiling up from the cable car's electrical system. They walked to the unused decorative fountain in front of the main doors, gazing up at the giant clock and the small belfry that topped the tower, Jill's thoughts heavy with images of Mikhail Victor. She'd never even been properly introduced to the man who'd saved her life, but she thought that they'd lost a valuable ally. The strength of character it took to die so that another might live... *heroic* was the only word that fit.

Maybe he even killed the Nemesis, it was practically on top of him when the grenade went off... Wishful thinking, probably, but she could hope.

"So, I guess we try to find the bell mechanism," Carlos said. "Do you think it's safe to split up, or should we—"

Caw!

The harsh cry of a crow cut him off, and Jill felt a fresh surge of adrenaline pump new life into her veins. She grabbed Carlos's hand as a fluttering sound filled the dark from above and around them, the sound of birds' wings pushing air.

The hall of portraits at the mansion, watched from above by dozens of shiny black eyes as they waited to attack. And Forest Speyer, from the Bravo team, Chris said he'd been ripped apart by dozens, perhaps hundreds of them.

"Come on!" She pulled at Carlos, remembering the relentless viciousness of the altered, oversized crows at the Spencer estate. Carlos seemed to know better than to ask questions as a dozen more hoarse cries pierced the air. They ran around the fountain to the front doors of the tower.

Locked.

"Cover me!" Jill shouted, reaching into her pack for her lockpick tools, the wheeling cries closing in on them—

—and Carlos threw himself at the doors, hitting the heavy old wood hard enough that splinters flew. He jogged back a few paces and ran at them again, *bam—*

—and they crashed inward, Carlos following through to trip and sprawl across the tastefully tiled floor, Jill quickly stepping in behind him. She grabbed the door handles and slammed the doors closed not a second too soon. There were two audible thumps from the other side, joined by a chorus of angry screeching and the brush of dark wings, and then they were retreating, the sounds fading away. Jill sagged against the doors, exhaling heavily.

God, is it ever going to stop? Do we have to face off with every demonic asshole in the city before we're allowed to leave?

"Zombie birds? Are you kidding me?" Carlos said, pushing himself to his feet as Jill manually bolted the doors. She didn't bother answering him, turning to take in the clock tower's grand lobby instead.

It reminded her of the Spencer mansion's foyer, the low lights and Gothic scrollwork giving it a kind of shabbily elegant atmosphere. A wide marble staircase dominated the large room, leading up to a second-floor landing with stained-glass windows. There were doors on either side of the room, a couple of polished wood tables in front of them, and to their left...

Jill sighed inwardly and felt something inside tighten a little. She hadn't *expected* the clock tower to be some kind of untouched sanctuary, even as far out of town as it was, but she realized that she had hoped—a hope lost at the sight of more death.

The scene told a story, a kind of mystery. Five male corpses, all of them dressed in somewhat military garb. Three of them lay next to the tables, apparently victims of a virus carrier; the carrier's bullet-riddled body was nearby. The victims' flesh had been gnawed, their skulls crushed and empty. The fifth corpse, a young man, had shot himself in the head, presumably after dispatching the zombie. Had he killed himself out of despair at the sight of his half-eaten friends? Had he been responsible somehow? Or had he known the virus carrier well, and taken his life after being forced to kill it?

No way we can ever know. It's just another handful of lives lost in some untold tragedy, one among this city's thousands.

Carlos moved closer to the bodies, frowning. From the grim look on his face, she got the impression that he knew who they were. He crouched down and pulled a blood-streaked duffel bag out from in between two of them, drawing a trail of red across the tile. Jill could hear metal touching metal inside, and it was obviously heavy, Carlos's bicep straining to lift the bag.

"Is that what I think it is?" Jill asked.

Carlos took the bag to one of the tables and eased the contents out. Jill felt a sudden, unexpected burst of glee at what was there; she hurried to the table, hardly able to believe their luck.

A half dozen hand grenades like the one Mikhail had used, RG34s; eight M16 thirty-round magazines, loaded as far as she could tell; and, more than she could have hoped for, a US M79 grenade launcher with a handful of fat 40mm cartridges.

"Weapons at the clock tower," Carlos said thoughtfully. Before Jill could ask what he meant, he picked up one of the rifle grenades and whistled softly.

"Buckshot loads," he said. "One of these would have blasted the living shit out of that Nemesis *espantajo*."

Jill raised her eyebrows. "'*Espantajo*'?"

"Literally, a scarecrow," Carlos said, "but it's used like weirdo, or freak."

Appropriate. Jill nodded toward the men who had carried the weapons. "Do you recognize these people?"

Carlos shrugged uncomfortably, handing her three of the hand grenades. "They're all U.B.C.S., I've seen them around, but I don't—I didn't know them. They were just dumb grunts, they probably had no idea what they were getting into when they joined Umbrella, or when we were sent here. Like me."

He seemed angry and a little sad, and he abruptly changed the topic, suddenly remembering how close they were to escaping Raccoon City. "Do you want to carry the grenade gun?"

"I thought you'd never ask," Jill said, smiling. She could use a weapon that would, as Carlos so colorfully put it, blast the living shit out of the Nemesis freak. "Now all we have to do is find a button somewhere, push it, and wait for our taxi to arrive."

Carlos smiled faintly in turn, tucking M16 mags into his vest pockets. "And try not to end up dead, like everyone else in this goddamn place."

Jill had no response to that. "Upstairs?"

Carlos nodded. Armed and ready, they started up.

* * *

The clock tower's second floor was really only a balcony that overlooked the front room. It ran along three sides of the building, and there was a single door where it ended, which had to lead to another set of stairs—to the belfry, if Carlos remembered the term correctly. Where the bells were.

Almost over, this is almost over, almost over... He let the repeating thought drive away almost everything else, too fatigued to consider his feelings of anger and sorrow and fear, aware that his breaking point wasn't all that far off. He could sort through his emotions once they left Raccoon behind.

The balcony itself was as richly adorned as the lobby, blue tiles that matched the blue of the stained-glass windows, an arched overhang supported by white columns. They could see almost all of the fine balcony from the top of the stairs, and it appeared to be clear, not a zombie or monster in sight. Carlos breathed easier and saw that Jill also seemed more at ease. She carried the Colt Python and wore the grenade gun on her back, using Carlos's belt as a sling.

How did Trent know there would be weapons here? Did he know I'd be taking them from dead men?

Carlos realized suddenly that he was overestimating

Trent's reach. There had to be another cache of weapons somewhere in the building, that was all, he and Jill had just happened across the duffel bag. The alternative—that Trent had somehow known about the dead soldiers—was too bizarre to consider.

They started down the first leg of the balcony side by side, Carlos wondering what Jill would say if he told her about Trent. She'd probably think he was kidding, the whole thing was so spy-novel mysterious—

Something moved. Ahead of them and around the first corner, something on the ceiling, a flash of dark movement. Carlos stepped to the railing and leaned out to look, but, whatever it was, it was either hidden behind one of the hanging arches or something that his exhausted brain had come up with to keep him awake.

"What?" Jill whispered at his shoulder, holding her revolver ready.

Carlos searched a few seconds longer and then shook his head, turning away. "Nothing, I guess, thought I saw something on the ceiling, but—"

"*Shit!*"

Carlos swung around as Jill jerked her weapon up, pointing at the ceiling just in front of them as a creature the size of a large dog skittered in their direction, a thing with a humped body and multiple legs, its thickly furred feet thumping stickily across the ceiling faster than seemed possible.

Jill unloaded three rounds into it before Carlos could blink, but not before he registered what he was looking at. It was a spider, big enough for Carlos to see his own reflection in its shining eyes as it crashed to the floor. Dark fluids spouted from its back as it thrashed its multicolored legs in the air, ichorous blood pooling beneath it. The wild, silent dance lasted only a second or two before it curled into itself, dead.

"I hate spiders," Jill said, a look of revulsion on her face as she started forward again, scanning the ceiling. "All those legs, that bloated stomach... *yuck.*"

"You've seen these before?" Carlos asked, unable to look away from the closed fist of its body.

"Yeah, at the Umbrella lab in the woods. Not alive, though, the ones I saw were dead."

Jill's apparent calm as they skirted the dead spider and continued on reminded Carlos how lucky he was to have hooked up with her. He'd come across a lot of tough men in his experiences, but he doubted very much that any one of them, put in her position, would be handling themselves as capably as Jill Valentine.

The rest of the balcony was clear, although Carlos uncomfortably noted a shitload of webbing on the ceiling, mounds of the thick white stuff accumulated in every corner; he didn't care much for spiders, either. When they reached the door and swept their way through, Jill going in low, Carlos was relieved to be outside again.

They'd come out on a wide ledge in front of the tower itself, a barren space surrounded by an ancient railing, a couple of defunct spotlights, and a few dead plants. There was a doorlike opening set a story higher up in the tower but no way to get to it. It seemed like a dead end, nowhere to go but back the way they'd come. Carlos sighed; at least the crows, if that's what they were, had migrated somewhere else.

"So what now?" Carlos asked, looking out over the dark courtyard, at the still smoking wrecked trolley car. When Jill didn't answer, Carlos turned and saw her standing by a copper plaque he hadn't noticed, set into the stone face of the tower. She reached into her bag and produced a wrapped set of lockpicks.

"You give up way too easy," Jill said, selecting a few pieces from the bundle. "Watch for crows, and I'll see what I can do about getting us a ladder."

Carlos covered her, vaguely wondering if there was anything she couldn't do, smelling rain on the cold wind that blew across the ledge. A moment later there was a series of clicks followed by a low hum of hidden machinery, and a narrow metal ladder descended from just beneath the opening above.

"How do you feel about standing guard for another few minutes?" Jill asked, smiling.

Carlos grinned, feeling her excitement; it really was almost over. "You got it."

Jill quickly scaled the ladder and disappeared through the open door above. She called down an all-clear a second later, and for the next several minutes, Carlos paced the ledge, thinking about what he was going to do after they were rescued. He wanted to talk to Trent again, about what needed to be done to stop Umbrella; whatever it took, he was there.

I bet he'd be interested in talking to Jill, too. When the 'copters come, we play stupid until they let us go, then plan out our next step—after a good meal and a shower and about twenty-four hours of sleep, of course...

He was so fixated on their deliverance from Raccoon that he didn't notice Jill's expression at first as she descended the ladder, didn't really think about the fact that there weren't any bells tolling. He smiled at her... and then felt his heart sink, understanding that their trial wasn't over yet.

"There's a gear missing from the bell mechanism," she said, "and we have to have it to make them ring. The good news is, I'm willing to bet that it's somewhere in the building."

Carlos arched an eyebrow. "How do you figure?"

"I found this next to one of the other gears," Jill said and handed him a tattered postcard.

The picture on the front was of three paintings hung in a row, each piece incorporating a clock. Carlos flipped the card over and saw "St. Michael Clock Tower, Raccoon City" in fine print on the upper left corner. Below that was a printed line of verse, which Jill said out loud.

"'Give your soul to the goddess. Put your hands together to pray before her.'"

Carlos stared at her. "Are you suggesting that we *pray* for the missing gear?"

"Ha ha. I'm suggesting that the gear is wherever these clocks are."

Carlos handed the card back. "You said that was the good news—what's the bad?"

Jill smiled sourly, an entirely humorless expression. "I doubt that the gear is going to be laying out in plain sight. It's some kind of puzzle, like the ones I ran across at the Spencer estate—and a few of those almost got me killed."

Carlos didn't ask. For the moment, at least, he didn't want to know.

SEVENTEEN

After tracking him for nearly half an hour, Nicholai found Dr. Richard Aquino on the fourth floor of Raccoon City's largest hospital. Seeing the Watchdog made Nicholai happy in a way he couldn't explain, not even to himself. A sense that all was right with the world, that things were unfolding as they should...

...with me on top, making the decisions. In a moment there will only be three left, three little doggies for me to hunt in the land of the walking dead, he thought dreamily. *Does it get any better than this?*

Aquino was just locking a door behind him, a look of sweaty fear on his pallid face as his gaze darted around nervously. He pocketed his keys and turned toward the hallway that led back to the elevator, pushing his smudged glasses to the bridge of his nose. Nicholai was amused to note that he wasn't even armed.

Nicholai stepped half out of the shadows, planning

to enjoy himself. After Nicholai had spent over an hour getting to the hospital, jogging most of the way, the mousy Dr. Aquino had had the nerve to try and hide from him—although looking at him now, Nicholai thought it was more likely that the scientist hadn't even known that he was being hunted and had eluded Nicholai by pure accident. Aquino looked like the kind of man who could get lost in his own backyard; even now, the "watchdog" didn't realize that he wasn't alone anymore, that Nicholai was only three meters away.

"*Doctor!*" Nicholai called loudly, and Aquino jumped around, gasping, involuntarily waving his hands in front of him; his surprise was absolute. Nicholai couldn't help a slight smile.

"Who, who are you?" Aquino stammered. He had watery blue eyes and a bad haircut.

Nicholai stepped closer, deliberately intimidating the scientist with his size. "I'm with Umbrella. I came to see how you were progressing with the vaccine... among other things."

"With Umbrella? I didn't—what vaccine, I don't know what you're talking about."

No weapon, no physical skills, and he can't tell a lie without blushing. He must be brilliant.

Nicholai lowered his voice conspiratorially. "Operation Watchdog sent me, Doctor. You haven't filed a details report lately. They've been worried about you."

Aquino seemed on the verge of collapsing with

relief. "Oh, if you know about—I thought you were—yes, the vaccine, I've been very busy; my, ah, contact wanted the initial synthesis broken down into stages, so there isn't an actual mixed sample cultivated—but I can assure you that it's only a matter of combining elements, everything's ready." The doctor practically babbled in his effort to submit.

Nicholai shook his head in mock wonder, playing his part. "And you've done this all yourself?"

Aquino smiled weakly. "With help from my assistant, Douglas, God rest his soul. I'm afraid that I've been running a bit ragged since his death, day before yesterday. That's why I've been remiss in my reports..."

He trailed off, then attempted another smile. "So... you're the one they sent to pick up the sample—Franklin, isn't it?"

Nicholai couldn't believe his own luck, or Aquino's naivete; the man was about to turn over the only TGViral antidote in existence, and all because Nicholai had said that Umbrella sent him. And now another one of his targets would be showing up—

"Yes, that's right," Nicholai said smoothly. "Ken Franklin. Where is the vaccine, Doctor?"

Aquino fumbled for his keys. "In here. I was just hiding it—the vaccine base, I mean, we've kept the medium separate—I hid it in here for safekeeping, until you arrived. I thought you were supposed to come in tomorrow night... no, the night after, you're much earlier than I expected."

He opened the door and gestured inside. "There's a refrigerated wall safe behind that rather tacky landscape—a recent addition by a wealthy patient, an eccentric as I understand it, not that that's important..."

Nicholai stepped past the driveling doctor, tuning him out, still feeling dumbfounded that Aquino had been selected as a Watchdog, when he suddenly realized that he'd allowed the scientist to get behind him.

It all came together in that instant, a complete scenario in Nicholai's mind—the stupid, gossiping science nerd, putting his enemies at ease, capitalizing on their underestimation of his abilities—

The awareness took only a fraction of a second, and then Nicholai was moving.

He dropped to his knees and swung his arms around, grabbing Aquino's calves and following through, literally sweeping him off his feet.

Aquino yelped and collapsed on top of Nicholai. A syringe clattered to the floor and Aquino lunged after it, but Nicholai still held his bony legs. The doctor had no muscle to speak of. In fact, Nicholai found it quite easy to hold the flailing doctor with one arm while reaching for the knife sheathed in his boot with his other.

Nicholai sat up, jerked Aquino closer, and stabbed him in the throat.

Aquino put his hands to his neck as Nicholai withdrew the blade, staring at his killer with wide, shocked eyes, blood pouring over his fingers as his heart continued its work.

Nicholai stared back at him, grinning and pitiless. Aquino had been slated to die, anyway, and that he'd attacked Nicholai only made his death a pleasure, in addition to its being a necessity.

The scientist finally fell over, still clutching his bubbling throat, and lost consciousness. He died quickly after that, a final spasm and he was gone.

"Better you than me," Nicholai said. He searched the cooling body and found several more syringes and a four-digit code on a slip of paper—undoubtedly the wall safe's combination. Aquino obviously hadn't expected Nicholai to be around to steal the vaccine.

Nicholai stood and walked to the safe, revising his plans as he always tried to do after any unexpected occurrence. Aquino had been expecting Ken Franklin to pick up the sample, which meant that Franklin would be putting in an appearance, unless the doctor had been lying. Nicholai didn't think so. Aquino had been so convincing *because* he had been telling the truth, an excellent technique to distract one's opponent...

...so I synthesize the vaccine, maybe enjoy some hunting while I wait for Sergeant Franklin to show up, get rid of him—and then destroy the hospital, Aquino's research along with it. If Umbrella's watching, they'll think everything is going according to plan. After that, there's only Chan and the factory worker, Terence Foster...

To hell with Mikhail and the other two, they weren't important anymore. As the soon-to-be only surviving Watchdog with information to sell, Nicholai would be worth millions. But with the TG vaccine in hand, there was no limit to what Umbrella might pay.

* * *

By the time they reached the building's back rooms, Jill was almost ready to admit defeat. They'd been everywhere, picking locks, slogging through each tastefully furnished room, stepping over corpses and creating a few new ones. A broken picture window outside the tower's chapel had allowed several carriers to get in, and they'd come across another viral spider in the hallway just past the library.

Along the way, she told Carlos a little about the mansion and grounds of the Spencer estate, history that she had dug up after the S.T.A.R.S.'s disastrous mission. Old man Spencer, one of Umbrella's founders, had been a fanatic for secret hiding places and hidden passages and had hired George Trevor, an architect renowned for his creativity, to design the mansion and to help renovate a few of the town's historical landmarks, tying parts of Raccoon to Spencer's spy fantasies.

"This was all thirty years ago," Jill said, "and the old man was completely crazy by then, so the story goes. As soon as everything was finished, he boarded up the mansion and moved Umbrella's headquarters to Europe."

"What happened to George Trevor?" Carlos asked. They stopped outside yet another door, what had to be one of the last rooms.

"Oh, that's the best part," Jill said. "He disappeared just before Spencer skipped town. No one ever saw him again."

Carlos shook his head slowly. "This is one nut job of a place to live, you know that?"

Jill nodded, pushing open the door and stepping back, revolver up. "Yeah, I've been thinking that myself."

Nothing was moving. Stacks of chairs to the right. Three statues, busts of women, straight in front of them. There were two corpses huddled together to the left of the door, a couple, holding each other, making Jill wince and look away—and there, hanging on the southern wall in heavy gold frames, were the three clock paintings.

They walked into the room, Jill nervously studying their surroundings. It *seemed* normal...

...*but so did that room in the mansion that turned out to be a giant trash compactor.* On impulse, Jill stepped back and used one of the chairs to prop the door open before going to take a closer look at the paintings.

Well, kind of paintings. She supposed technically they'd be called mixed media. The three pieces were of women, one on each canvas, but each also contained an octagonal clock—the first and last set at midnight, the one in the middle at five o'clock. A small, bowl-like tray protruded from the bottom of each frame. They were labeled as the goddesses of the past, present, and future, from left to right.

"On the postcard, it said something about putting your hands together," Carlos said. "That's like the clock hands, right?"

Jill nodded. "Yeah, makes sense. It's just obscure enough to be annoying."

She reached forward and lightly touched the tray on the middle frame, a dancing woman. There was a tiny click and the tray dipped like a scale, the weight of her hand pushing it down. At the same time, the hands of the clock started to spin.

Jill jerked her hand back, afraid that she'd set something off, and the clock hands quickly spun back to their previous settings. Nothing else happened.

"Hands together..." she murmured. "Do you think they mean that all of the clocks have to be set for the same time? Or do they mean literally, the hands aligned?"

Carlos shrugged and reached out to touch the tray of the future goddess, definitely the creepiest of the paintings. The past was a young girl sitting on a hill, the present a dancing woman... and the goddess of the future was the figure of a woman in a slinky cocktail dress, her body enticingly posed—but with the bald, grinning face of a skeleton.

Jill suppressed a shudder and didn't let any thoughts get started on the theme of imminent death, *like I don't have enough of that already.*

The tray Carlos touched dipped down, but again, it was the hands on the clock of the present goddess that moved. Apparently, the other two were fixed at midnight.

Jill stepped back from the wall, arms folded, thinking—and suddenly she had it, she knew how the puzzle worked, if not the exact solution. She turned around, hoping that the missing pieces were nearby, and she smiled when she saw the three statues—ah, the symmetry—and the shining objects they held in their slender stone fingers.

"It's a balancing puzzle," Jill said, walking to the statues. At closer inspection, she saw that each held a tray with a single, fist-sized stone. She picked them up, hefting each orb, noting the different weights.

"Three balls, three trays," she continued, walking back to the pictures, handing the black stone—made from obsidian or onyx, she wasn't sure—to Carlos. Another was clear crystal, the third a glowing amber.

"And the goal is to make the middle clock hit midnight," Carlos said, catching on.

Jill nodded. "I'm sure there's a motif to the solution, a color match, like black for death, maybe... or maybe it's mathematical. It doesn't matter, it won't take that long to try all of the combinations."

They set to work, trying each ball on one painting at a time, then using them all, Jill carefully studying the present clock's hand movements with each placement. It appeared that the different balls held different values, depending on which tray they were in. Jill was just starting to feel like she could figure it out—it was definitely mathematical—when they lucked across the solution.

With crystal in the past, obsidian in the present, and amber in the future, the clock in the middle struck midnight, chiming softly. The minute hand started to move backwards with a clattering sound—and then the face of the clock itself fell from the picture, pushed out by some machinery that Jill couldn't see. In the revealed hollow was the glittering gold cog that had been missing from the tower's bell mechanism.

Sneaky, you pricks, but not sneaky enough.

Carlos was frowning, his expression openly confused. "What the hell is all this, anyway? Who would hide the gear at all, and why in such a complicated way?"

Jill plucked the shining gear from its hiding place, remembering her own thoughts on that exact subject only six weeks before, standing in the dark halls of Spencer's mansion. Why, why such elaborate secrecy? The files Trent had given her just before the estate mission had been full of clues to the mansion's puzzles, lucky for her; without those, she might never have gotten out. Most of the bizarre little mechanisms had been much too intricate to be practical, time-wise or functionally. What was the point?

After giving it a lot of thought, Jill had finally concluded that Umbrella's *real* board of directors, the ones no one knew about, were paranoid fanatics. They were self-involved children, playing secret agent games and betting with other people's lives, because they could. Because no one had ever explained to them that hiding toys and making treasure maps was something people outgrew.

Because no one has stopped them. Yet.

Suddenly eager to wrap it all up, to place the gear and ring the bell and just *leave*, Jill phrased it much more simply to Carlos. "They're wacko, that's why. One-hundred-percent grade-A jacked-up *batshit*. You ready to get out of here, or what?"

Carlos nodded somberly, and after a final look around the room, they headed back out the way they'd come.

EIGHTEEN

Carlos watched Jill climb the ladder once more, trying not to get his hopes up again. If this didn't work, he was going to be deeply—no, *majestically* pissed.

Hell with it. If this doesn't work, we should just walk out, or see if we can get to that factory and steal ourselves a ride. She's right, these people are andar lurias, *lost in space; the sooner we get out of their territory, the better.*

He stared blankly out at the dark yard for a few moments, so bone-weary that he wondered how he would do one more thing, take one more step; it seemed impossible. All that kept him going was his desire to leave, to get away from this holocaust and try to recover.

When the first massive peal of sound rang out, its deep and hollow tone rolling out from the top of the tower, Carlos realized he couldn't keep a lid on his hope. He tried, telling himself that there was going to be a glitch in the program, telling himself that Umbrella would send assassins, that the pilot would be a zombie; nothing worked. A helicopter was coming for them, he knew it, he *believed* it; he just hoped the rescue team wouldn't have any trouble finding a place to land—

—*spotlights!* There were four of them on the ledge and a crusty-looking control box near the door that led back inside; the light would guide the transport in faster. Carlos hurried toward it, glancing up to see if Jill had started down yet. She hadn't—

—and when he looked ahead again, he saw that he wasn't alone. As if by magic, the giant, mutilated freak that had been chasing Jill was simply *there*, close enough for Carlos to smell a burnt meat smell, snarling, its piggy, distorted gaze turned to the top of the ladder.

"*Carlos, look out!*" Jill screamed down, but the Nemesis-monster ignored him completely, taking a mammoth step toward the ladder, the eyeless snakes that were its tentacles whipping around its colossal head. One more step and it would be at the base of the ladder—and Jill would be trapped.

—*she said bullets don't hurt it*—

Desperate to do something, Carlos saw the large green power switch on the spotlights' control panel and lunged for it, not sure what he expected. To distract it, if they were lucky—

—and all four lights snapped on at once, blinding, instantly heating the air around them and illuminating the tower, probably for miles to see. One of the beams was full-on blocked by the freak's hideous face. The light actually forced the thing to stumble backwards, giant hands covering its mutant eyes, and Carlos acted.

He ran at the blinded Nemesis, M16 held high, and slammed the rifle against its chest, pushing as hard as he could. Off balance, it stumbled backwards, its legs slapping the ancient railing—

—and with a brittle snap, a wide section of the railing gave way, falling into the darkness, the Nemesis plummeting after it. Carlos heard a sickly *thump* from the ground below at the same instant that the overheated spotlights shut down, making glowing dark shapes float in Carlos's eyes for a moment.

The huge, mellow sound of the bells continued to fill the air as Jill scrambled down the ladder and un-slung the grenade launcher, joining Carlos at the broken railing.

"I... thanks," Jill said, looking into his eyes, her own gaze sincere and unwavering. "If you hadn't hit the lights, I would have been dead. Thank you."

Carlos was impressed and a little flustered by her candor. "*De nada*," he said, suddenly very aware of how attractive she was—not just physically—and how little experience he actually had with women. He was a self-educated twenty-one-year-old merc, and he hadn't exactly had a whole lot of time or opportunity to date.

She can't be much older, twenty-five at the outside, and maybe she—

Jill snapped her fingers in front of him, bringing him back to reality and reminding him of how tired he really was. He'd totally spaced out.

"You still with me?"

Carlos nodded, clearing his throat. "Yeah, sorry. Did you say something?"

"I said we need to move. If it's still that feisty after a grenade in the face, I doubt a two-story drop will kill it."

"Right," Carlos said. "We should circle around front, anyway. They'll probably drop a harness if they can't set down."

Jill nodded. "Let's do it."

Ushered inside by the deep voice of hollowed metal, Carlos suddenly wondered if Nicholai was still alive—and if he was, what he would do when he heard the tolling bells.

* * *

Nicholai heard the bells on his walk back into town and scoffed irritably, refusing to be baited. He hadn't expected the barely skilled trio to make it, but so what if they had? Davis Chan had filed another report, from a woman's boutique of all places, and Nicholai meant to track him down.

And why should I care if they limp away with their miserable lives, with what I've got?

Nicholai pulled the slender metal case out of his pocket for the third time since leaving the hospital, unable to resist. Inside was a glass vial of purplish fluid that he'd synthesized himself, with a little help from an instruction sheet that Aquino's assistant had thoughtfully left behind.

Nicholai knew it would be safest to store the sample someplace, but the small container represented his authority over the other Watchdogs and a newly elevated status with Umbrella; he was a leader, a supervisor of lesser men, and he found that carrying the vaccine with him and occasionally holding it made him feel powerful. Grounded, in a way.

Smiling, Nicholai slipped the container back into his pocket, within easy reach, and started walking again, deliberately ignoring the bells. Things were going very well—he had the vaccine; he knew where Chan was and where Franklin was going to be in just under forty-eight hours; he'd already rigged the hospital to blow; and he would push the button as soon as his meeting with Franklin was over. Nicholai thought he might duck over to the factory and get rid of Terence Foster while he waited on Franklin, there was plenty of time—

—*just like there was plenty of time to track Mikhail, to play at being a noble team member, to decide who would die first among them...*

The clamorous bells pounded at him, seeking to remind him of his failure, but he refused to be distracted by the escape of three incompetents. He was getting closer to town, he could see the combined glow of hundreds of small and not so small fires encasing the dark city; even if he wanted to, he wouldn't make it back to the clock tower before the first helicopter came. And he *didn't* want to, he'd had the opportunity after killing Aquino and had decided that it wasn't worth his time. It was the right decision... and the strange doubts that curled up inside of him at the sound of the bells were to be disregarded; it meant nothing, that they had survived, it didn't mean that they were as good as him.

Besides, he still had a few dogs to put down to ensure his monopoly on information. He thought that Chan might choose to bunk down at the store he'd reported from, as late as it was. Nicholai would kill him, take his data, and retire for the evening somewhere in the city. At the Watchdog briefing he'd heard that food was scarce, but he was certain that he could manage—raid a few pantries for canned goods, perhaps. In the morning he would file his own report, to keep up his cover, and spend the day hunting up information of his own before heading west again.

Everything was fine, and as he gradually crossed over from the suburbs into the city, the sound of the approaching helicopter didn't bother him a bit. Let those spineless, shit-eating bastards run, he felt great, in control, *better* than great. He only had a headache because of those damned bells.

* * *

They retraced much of their winding path through the clock tower, Jill wanting to make sure the Nemesis either got confused or had plenty of time to wander away before they went out to meet the 'copter. As they walked, they hammered out a story to tell whoever was running the evac—Jill was Kimberly Sampsel (the name of Jill's best friend from fifth grade), she'd worked at a local art gallery, no family, and she'd only moved to Raccoon recently. Carlos had found her just after his platoon leader, the only other U.B.C.S. member to have survived, had been killed by zombies. Together, they'd made it to the clock tower, end of story.

They decided not to mention Nicholai, the Nemesis, or any unidentifiable creatures they'd seen running around; the idea was to appear as ignorant of the facts as possible. Neither of them wanted to take any chances on the allegiance of the rescue team, and Jill had no doubt that there would be someone on the transport waiting to debrief them, so the simpler the story, the better. They'd just have to pray that no one had her pic on hand. They could worry about how to slip away once they got out of the city.

At the front doors of the clock tower they paused for a moment, readying themselves, Jill feeling a strange mixture of happiness and anxiety. Rescue was coming, but they were so close to getting out now that she was afraid something would go wrong.

Maybe that's just because Umbrella is doing the rescuing, God knows they don't have a very good track record for keeping their shit together...

"Jill? Before we leave, I want to tell you something," Carlos said, and for a few seconds, Jill thought her anxiety was about to be confirmed, that he was going to tell her some terrible secret he'd been holding back—but then she saw his careful, thoughtful expression and thought different.

"Okay, shoot," she said neutrally, thinking about the way he'd looked at her out on the balcony. She'd seen that look before, from other men—and she wasn't sure how she felt about it from Carlos. Before he'd left for Europe, Chris Redfield and she had been getting pretty close...

"Before I came here, I was approached by this guy about Raccoon, about what was going on here," Carlos started, and Jill had just enough time to feel stupid about her assumption before his words sank in.

Trent!

"He told me that we were in for a rough time, and offered to help me out. I thought he was crazy at first—"

"—but then you got here and found out he wasn't."

Carlos stared at her. "You know him or something?"

"Probably as well as you do. It was the same with me, just before the estate mission, he gave me information about the mansion—and told me to be careful who I trusted. Trent, right?"

Carlos nodded, and although they both opened their mouths to speak, neither of them said a word. It was the sound of the approaching helicopter that cut them off, that made both of them grin and exchange looks of joy and relief.

"Let's talk about him later," Carlos said, pushing open the front doors, the chop of the 'copter's blades filling the tower's lobby as they both stepped out into the yard.

Jill only saw one transport helicopter but didn't care, there obviously wasn't anyone else to evacuate, and as it swung over the crashed trolley, she and Carlos both started to wave their arms and shout.

"*Over here! We're over here!*" Jill screamed, and she actually saw the clean-shaven face of the pilot, his smile glowing by the lights in the cockpit as he flew closer—

—close enough that she could see the smile disappear in the same instant that she heard the weapon discharge to their right, a look of horror dawning on that youthful face.

Shhhh—

A line of colored smoke, streaking toward the hovering ship from someone on the roof of the tower's adjunct buildings, *surface to air, bazooka or rocket launcher—*

—*BOOM!*

"No," Jill whispered, but the sound was lost as the missile slammed into the 'copter and exploded, Jill numbly thinking that it had to be a HEAT rocket to do the damage it was doing as the airship spun toward them, listing badly to one side, fire spouting from the shattered cockpit.

Carlos grabbed her arm and yanked, almost jerking her off her feet, pulling her out into the yard as a high, climbing, whining noise blew over them, the burning helicopter stuttering forward as they huddled behind the fountain—

—and then it crashed into the clock tower. Flaming chunks of metal and stone and wood showered down upon them as the transport plunged through the roof of the lobby, and like the voice of destruction, Jill heard the Nemesis's triumphant scream rising above it all.

NINETEEN

Carlos heard the monster's screaming howl and started to get up, still holding Jill's arm. They had to get away before it saw her—

—and the front of the building cracked open as though it were made of balsa wood, wreckage from the helicopter spewing out in a burst of smoking debris.

Before Carlos could get down, a large piece of blackened rock from the building's outer wall smacked into his left side. He heard and felt a rib give way as he fell, the pain instant and intense.

"Carlos!"

Jill leaned over him, her gaze darting back and forth between him and part of the tower he couldn't see, the grenade launcher still clutched in her hands. The Nemesis had stopped roaring; between that and the sudden, brutal silencing of the bells, Carlos could hear something thumping heavily to the ground, followed by the crumble of powdering rock in a slow, even rhythm. *Crunch. Crunch.*

It's coming, it jumped off the roof and it's coming—

"*Run,*" Carlos said, and he saw that she understood, a second before she took off, that she had no other choice. Boots kicking the ground away, she left him alone as fast as she could.

Carlos turned his head as he sat up, willing himself not to feel pain, and saw the creature standing in a pile of broken concrete and burning wood, unaware that the hem of its leathery coat was on fire as its aberrant gaze tracked Jill. As before, it didn't seem to see him.

As long as I don't get in its way, Carlos thought, propping himself against the cool stone of the fountain, lifting his rifle. *It doesn't hurt, it doesn't, doesn't.*

In a single, powerful motion the Nemesis lifted a rocket launcher to its giant shoulder and took aim, as Carlos started firing.

Each chattering round from the M16 sent a fresh pulse of muffled agony through his bones, but his aim was good in spite of the pain. Tiny black holes appeared on the creature's face, and Carlos could hear the *ping* of ricochet off the battered launcher. The fleshy tentacles that rose up from beneath the monster's long jacket whipped around its upper body as if outraged, coiling and uncoiling with incredible speed.

Carlos saw that it was swinging the bazooka toward him, but he kept firing, knowing that he couldn't get up in time to run. *Get away, Jill, go!*

It sighted Carlos and fired, and Carlos saw a burst of light and motion coming at him, felt the heat of the high-explosive anti-tank missile radiating against his skin—

—and somehow, he wasn't dead, but something not far behind him blew up. The force of the blast lifted and threw him roughly against the side of the fountain; the pain was spectacular but he raggedly held on to consciousness, determined to buy Jill a few more seconds.

Half laying across the lip of the fountain, Carlos started firing again, shooting for its face, rounds going everywhere as he struggled to control the weapon.

Die, just die already... But it wasn't dying, it wasn't even flinching, and Carlos knew he only had a half second left before he was blown into a greasy stain on the lawn.

The rocket launcher was pointed directly at Carlos's face when it happened, a one in a million shot—

¡Carajo!

—as one of the metallic *pings* turned into an explosion, a sudden white-hot light show. The monster pitched backwards as its weapon disintegrated, dropping out of sight.

Carlos's rifle went dry. He reached for a new magazine, and there was new pain. He lost track of the light, darkness pulling him down.

* * *

Jill saw Carlos collapse and made herself stay where she was, standing between the trolley and a hedge row. She'd seen the Nemesis go down, thrown into the burning rubble by the misfire that had obliterated its bazooka, but its confirmed ability to avoid death kept her from going to Carlos. If it was still coming, she wanted to keep it focused on her alone.

The grenade launcher felt light in her hands, high adrenaline giving her a second wind with a vengeance—and when the Nemesis rose up, one shoulder burning, blistering black and red flesh visible beneath its ruined clothing, Jill fired.

The buckshot-loaded "grenade," like a super shotgun shell, sent a concentrated blast of thousands of pellets across the yard—but she missed the howling Nemesis entirely, the shot tearing new holes in what was left of the tower's front wall.

The Nemesis stopped screaming even though its chest was still burning, the skin crackling and black now. It squared its body toward Jill as she broke open the grenade launcher and snatched another load out of her bag, praying that it was more seriously injured by Carlos's lucky shot than it appeared.

It lowered its head and ran at her, its gigantic stride carrying it toward her incredibly quickly. In a second it was across the yard, its snaking appendages spread out as if to grab her up.

Jill leaped to her left and took off at a dead run, still holding the grenade, in between the row of hedges and the undamaged west wall of the tower. She could hear it enter the row behind her as she reached the end; it still almost had her, its speed extraordinary, putting it an arm's length away as she rounded the end of the row—

—and something struck her right shoulder as she tore around the hedge, something solid and slick, burrowing into her flesh like a giant, boneless finger. It stung, a thousand hornets at once flooding her system with poison, and she understood that one of the searching tentacles had pierced her.

Oshitoshitoshit, she couldn't think about it, there wasn't time, but the Nemesis stopped suddenly, threw its head back and bellowed its victory to the cold stars above, and Jill stumbled to a halt, shoved the load into the gun and snapped the breech closed—

—and fired as it lunged toward her again. The shot clipped the howling Nemesis just below its right hip and tore into the meat of its upper thigh, bits of skin and muscle flying out behind it—

—and it crashed, a few more momentum strides and it went down in a spray of ravaged tissue, monstrous and silent and suddenly still.

In a fever to reload, Jill dropped the second to last buckshot grenade, and it rolled away. She managed to get a firm grip on the fifth and was just snapping the gun closed when the Nemesis sat up, facing away from her.

Jill aimed for its lower back and fired, the thunder of the weapon just another dull sound beneath the ringing in her ears. The Nemesis was moving, standing up when it was hit, and the pellets hit low and left, what would be a lethal kidney shot for a human. Apparently not for the S.T.A.R.S. killer. It stumbled, then stood up and started to limp away, one giant hand clapped over its new wound.

Leaving, it's leaving—

Her thoughts were slow and heavy. It took her a moment to understand that its departure wasn't good news. She couldn't let it get away, let it repair itself and come back—she had to try and kill it while it was weak.

Jill drew the Python and tried to take aim, but her vision doubled suddenly and she couldn't focus on the receding figure as it dragged itself through the fiery wreckage. She felt light-headed and flushed and thought it very likely that she'd been infected by the T-virus.

She didn't have to see the shoulder wound to know it was bad, she could feel hot blood coursing down her side, soaking into the waistband of her skirt. She wished she could believe that the virus was being washed out of her system, but she couldn't kid herself, even so direly injured.

For a few seconds she considered the loaded .357 she still held—and then thought of Carlos and knew she had to wait. She had to help him if she could, she owed him that much.

Summoning the last of her rapidly draining strength, Jill started toward Carlos. He lay by the fountain, groaning and half conscious, hurt, but at least she couldn't see any blood, *maybe he's okay...*

It was her last thought before she felt her body betray her by giving up, dropping her to the ground and putting her into a very deep sleep.

Dark, elsewhere ringing and escape, fire and dark and bullets, can't hear, Jill running from the fire and the thing firing, high-explosive missile aimed—

aimed at my—

face.

Carlos came to in a rush, confused and hurting and looking for the fight, for the Nemesis and Jill. She was in trouble if that thing got hold of her...

It was a quiet, still night, and low fires burned all around, providing a dancing orange light and enough heat to make him sweat. Carlos forced himself to move, crawling to his feet and holding his ribs tightly, jaw clenched from the pain. Fractured or broken, maybe two of them, but he had to think about Jill now, had to shake off the effects of the multiple blasts and—

"Oh, no," he said, forgetting about his aching exhaustion as he hurried toward her. Jill was lying on a patch of burnt grass, perfectly still except for the steady ooze of blood from her right shoulder. Still alive, but maybe not for much longer.

Carlos swallowed his pain and picked her up, the dead weight of her body making him want to scream in anger, at the insanity that had unfolded and grown in Raccoon, that had imposed its merciless grasp on Jill and on himself. Umbrella, monsters, spies, even

Trent—all of it was crazy, it was a nightmare fairy tale... but the blood was real enough.

He held her close, turning, searching. He had to get her inside, safe, somewhere he could dress her wounds, where they could both rest for a little while. There was the chapel in the mostly undamaged west wing; there were no windows and good locks on the door.

"Don't die, Jill," he said, and hoped she was listening as he carried her across the burning yard.

TWENTY

Time passing. Dark and dark, and fragments of a thousand dreams, spinning into focus for a brief glimpse before spinning away. She was a child at the beach with her father, the taste of salt on the wind. She was a gawky teenager, in love for the first time; a thief, stealing from wealthy strangers as her father had taught her to do; a student, training for the S.T.A.R.S., learning to apply her skills to help people.

Darker. The day her father went to prison for grand larceny. Lovers she had betrayed, or who had betrayed her. Feelings of loneliness. And her life in Raccoon City, the very death of light.

Becky and Priscilla McGee, ages seven and nine, the first victims. Eviscerated, parts of them eaten. Finding the crashed Bravo team helicopter outside of the mansion; the smell inside, of dust and rot. Learning about Umbrella's conspiracy and the corruption and collaboration of at least a few

S.T.A.R.S. members. The death of the traitorous team leader, Albert Wesker, and the Nemesis's final attack.

Several times, half awake, she swallowed cool water and then slept again, more recent memories taking over. The lost survivors, the people she'd tried to save, the faces of the children, mostly. All of them, gone. Brad Vickers's brutal death. Carlos. Nicholai's flat, emotionless gaze, and Mikhail's sacrifice. And reigning over it all like the demonic epitome of evil, the beyond-Tyrant monster, the Nemesis, its terrible voice calling for her, its terrible eyes seeking her wherever she went, whatever she did.

The most troubling thing, though, was that there was something happening to her—a distant feeling, because it was happening to her body and she was very much asleep, but no less unpleasant for that. It felt like her veins were heating up and expanding. Like her every cell was becoming thick and heavy with strange spices, sticking to the cells around it, all of them boiling gently. Like her whole body was a vessel filled with moving wet heat.

Finally, the gentle sound of falling rain lapped at the edges of her awareness and she yearned to see it, feel its coolness on her skin, but it was a long, tiring struggle to leave the dark behind. Her body didn't want to, protesting louder the closer she got to the surface of gray, the twilight between the dreams and the rain—but determined, she won out.

After deciding that she was alive, Jill opened her eyes.

TWENTY-ONE

Carlos was sitting with his back to the door eating fruit cocktail out of a can when he heard Jill stir, the regular, consistent sound of her deep breathing becoming lighter. She turned her head from side to side, still asleep, but the movement was the most deliberate action he'd seen in forty-eight hours. He stood as quickly as he could, forced to be careful by the pinch of his tightly taped ribs, and hurried to the raised altar where she lay.

He picked up the bottle of water at the base of the dais, and when he stood up again, she opened her eyes.

"Jill? I'm going to give you some water now. Try and help me out, okay?"

She nodded, and Carlos felt sappy with relief, holding her head up while she drank a few swallows from the bottle. It was the first time she had responded clearly to anything, and her color looked good. For two days she had drunk when he'd pushed it on her, swallowing at least but white as a ghost and completely out of it otherwise.

"Where... are we?" Jill asked weakly, closing her eyes as she lay her head back down on the makeshift pillow, a piece of rolled-up carpet. Her blanket was made from unburned drapes he'd salvaged from the foyer.

"The chapel of the clock tower," he said softly, still smiling. "We've been here since—since the helicopter crashed."

Jill opened her eyes again, obviously aware and reasonably focused. She *wasn't* infected, he'd been so afraid for a while, but she was okay, she had to be.

"How long?"

Talking seemed to be tiring for her, so Carlos tried to summarize everything that had happened, to save her the questions. "The Nemesis shot down the helicopter, and you and I were both wounded. Your shoulder was... injured, but I've been changing the dressings and it doesn't seem to be infected. We've been here two days, recuperating, you've been sleeping mostly. It's October first, I think, the sun set an hour ago and it's been raining off and on since last night..."

He trailed off, not sure what else he could tell her but not wanting her to fall asleep again, not right away. He'd been stuck with his own thoughts for long enough.

"Oh, I found a case of fruit cocktail, of all things, in the trunk in that one sitting room—the one with the chessboard, remember? Water, too, someone was hoarding, I guess, lucky for us. I didn't want to leave you alone, I've been, ah, taking care of you." He didn't add that he'd been cleaning her up, changing the drapes she lay upon when it was necessary; he didn't want her to feel embarrassed.

"You're hurt?" she asked, frowning, blinking slowly.

"Couple of fractured ribs, no big deal. Well, maybe when I have to pull the tape off, *that's* gonna hurt like a son of a bitch. All I could find was duct tape."

She smiled faintly, and Carlos softened his tone, almost afraid to ask. "How are you doin'?"

"Two days? No more helicopters?" she asked, looking away, and he felt himself tense slightly. She hadn't answered his question.

"No more helicopters," he said and noticed for the first time that the color in her cheeks was overly red. He touched the side of her neck, and his tension grew; fever, not too bad, but she hadn't had it the last time he'd checked, an hour before. "Jill, how do you feel?"

"Not bad. Not bad at all, hardly any pain." Her voice was flat, inflectionless.

Carlos smiled crookedly. "*Bien, si*? That's good news, that means we can pack up and get out of here soon..."

"I'm infected with the virus," she said, and Carlos froze, his smile fading.

No. No, she's wrong, it's not possible.

"It's been two days, you can't be," he said firmly, telling her what he'd been telling himself since he first woke up. "I saw one of the other soldiers turn into a zombie, couldn't have been more than two *hours* from the time Randy was bit until he changed. If you have it, something would have happened by now."

Jill carefully rolled onto her side, wincing a little, closing her eyes again. She sounded incredibly tired. "I'm not going to argue with you, Carlos. Maybe it's a different mutation because it came from the Nemesis, or maybe I picked up some kind of immunity, from being at the Spencer estate. I don't know, but I have it." Her voice shook. "I can *feel* it, I can feel myself getting worse!"

"Okay, okay, shhh," Carlos said, deciding that he would leave immediately. He'd take Jill's revolver in addition to the assault rifle, and definitely a couple of hand grenades.

The hospital was close, and there was at least one vaccine sample there, that's what Trent had said. Carlos had wanted to find the hospital earlier, for supplies, but he'd been too exhausted and hurt to go looking, at first—and then he hadn't wanted to risk leaving Jill alone and unconscious, dangerous for several reasons.

I'll go out front and head west, see if I can find a sign or something... Trent had also said something about the hospital not being there for much longer; Carlos hoped he wasn't too late.

"Try and get back to sleep," Carlos said. "I'm going to take off for a while, to try and find something that might help you. I won't be gone long."

Jill already seemed to be half asleep, but she raised her head and made an effort to be clear, enunciating carefully. "If you come back and I'm—sicker, I want you to help me. I'm asking you now, I may not be able to ask you later. Do you understand?"

Carlos wanted to protest but knew that he'd want the same thing if he had the disease. Being dead sucked, but Raccoon was proof that there were worse things.

Like having to shoot someone you care about.

"I understand," he said. "You rest now. I'll be back soon."

Jill slept, and Carlos started to load up. Just before he left, he gazed into her sleeping face for a long moment, silently praying that she'd still be Jill when he got back.

The hospital turned out to be much closer than he thought, less than two blocks away.

* * *

Nicholai waited for Ken Franklin eagerly, knowing that the Watchdog's death would mark the beginning of the end game. Nicholai's growing frustration was about to come to an end.

If the bastard ever shows up... But no, he was coming, and then Nicholai would be on track again. He checked the corner window of the office he'd chosen, overlooking the dark, empty street—also his escape route, if the sergeant turned out to be troublesome—

for the tenth time in half as many minutes, willing the errant Watchdog to hurry.

Nothing had gone as he'd planned, and although he'd made the best of it, Nicholai was losing his patience. The search for Davis Chan had been spectacularly unsuccessful; Nicholai hadn't even caught a glimpse of him during the two days he'd stayed in the city—and twice more the elusive soldier had managed to avoid a confrontation after filing his reports, sending Nicholai running all over town.

Nicholai had also been planning to head to Umbrella's "water treatment" facility to get rid of Terence Foster earlier in the day, but he'd been further side-tracked in a wild-goose chase—he'd seen an uninfected woman near the RPD building, a tall, Asian-American woman wearing a tight, sleeveless red dress and holding a gun like she knew what to do with it. She'd slipped into the building and was gone. Nicholai had searched for nearly four hours but hadn't seen the mystery woman again.

So, all three of his targets, still alive. He'd been able to collect some Watchdog information, at least, uncovering a couple of private lab reports on the strength of the average zombie—but he'd had enough, enough eating cold beans out of cans, enough sleeping with one eye open, enough playing big game hunter. By his count, he'd killed four Beta Hunters, three giant spiders, and three brain suckers. And dozens of zombies, of course, although he didn't really count those as worthy of note, not anymore. They just kept getting slower and stickier; Raccoon already smelled like a giant cesspool, and it was only going to get worse as the virus carriers continued to decay, turning into great sludgy piles of malodorous stew.

I'll be gone by then. After all, Franklin will be here any minute.

After two days of unmet objectives, Nicholai had come to see Franklin's appointment at the hospital as something solid, something he could hold on to—a sure kill. And as he'd passed long, solitary hours immersed in the growing chaos of uncertainty, the death of Ken Franklin had become extremely important. Once he was dead, Nicholai could blow up the hospital; once the hospital was destroyed, Nicholai could hunt down Chan and Foster, and then he could leave. Everything would fall into place as soon as he killed Franklin.

Even as Nicholai embraced that thought, he heard footsteps out in the hall. Heart swelling with pleasure, Nicholai took his position by the window and waited for Franklin to find him. The cluttered office/supply room was on the fourth floor, not far from where he'd killed and hidden Dr. Aquino.

Come along, Sergeant...

When the Watchdog opened the door, Nicholai was leaning casually in the corner, arms folded. Franklin was carrying top of the line, a 9mm VP70, and he had it trained on Nicholai's face in the blink of an eye. Nicholai didn't move.

"You're not supposed to be here," Franklin said coolly, his voice deep and deadly. He stepped further into the room, not taking his gaze—or the semiautomatic—off of Nicholai.

Time for him to find out who's smarter. Anyone could stage an ambush, but it took a certain amount of intelligence and skill to make one's opponent willingly walk into one. Nicholai feigned a mildly surly nervousness.

"You're right, I'm not. Aquino should be here—but he stopped filing reports yesterday. They thought he was too busy, working on the antiviral, but I've been looking since last night and can't find him." Nicholai had actually filed several status reports with Dr. Aquino's name on them since killing him, to keep up appearances.

"Who are you?" Franklin asked. He was tall and well muscled, with very dark skin and rather delicate-looking wire rimmed glasses. There was nothing delicate in the way he looked at Nicholai, however.

Nicholai uncrossed his arms and lowered them very slowly. "Nicholai Ginovaef, U.B.C.S.... and Watchdog. I was tapped to check things out when the doctor went AWOL. You're Franklin, right? Have you had any contact with Aquino since your arrival? Did he talk to you about where he was going to secure the sample, or give you a combination, or a key?"

Franklin didn't lower his weapon, but he was obviously confused. "Nobody told me about any change in plans. Who did you say sent you?"

This part was a risk. Nicholai knew the names of four men important enough to have made changes to

Umbrella's agenda, and chances were good that one of them was Franklin's contact and would already have informed Franklin.

"I didn't say," Nicholai said. "But I guess it's okay to tell you... Trent called me in on this."

He'd chosen the man he knew least about, even after all of his careful research, in the hope that Franklin wouldn't know anything about him, either. Trent was an enigma, skulking around the other top brass like some cryptic shadow. Nicholai didn't even know his first name.

It worked for the sergeant. Franklin lowered his weapon, still wary but obviously willing to believe. "So, you couldn't find Aquino? What about the vaccine?"

Nicholai sighed, shaking his head and then deliberately looking to his left, a space hidden from Franklin's view by an overstuffed shelf. "No sign of the doc... but this was his office, and there's a wall safe back here. Do you know anything about getting one of these things open?"

Nicholai knew that Franklin did—on his personnel file, safecracking was listed among his skills. Nicholai didn't give a shit whether or not Franklin could open the safe; what mattered was that to get to the safe, the sergeant would have to turn his back on Nicholai.

I'm better, better at this than Aquino or Chan or this fool, and this will prove it. I'd never turn my back on anyone, ever. Yes, that would be unworthy of him...

Franklin nodded, holstering the VP70 and walking toward the corner where Nicholai stood. "Yeah, I know a little. I can take a look at it, anyway."

Nicholai nodded briskly. "Good. I was starting to think that I was going to be stuck here for a while."

"Maybe that's for the best," Franklin said, stepping past Nicholai to a small safe inset behind the shelf. "With the way things are going out there, I've been thinking about holing up someplace for a while, waiting until things die down a little."

Nicholai took a silent step closer to Franklin, eyeing the VP70's unsnapped holster. "Not a bad idea."

Franklin nodded, frowning at the keypad. "Chan is doing it, he says the info will still be there tomorrow so why not, right?"

Davis Chan!

Nicholai held very still, deciding—and then he darted forward and snatched up the 9mm, not willing to dance for what he wanted. He shoved Franklin at the same time, pushing him off balance, using the split second of his recovery time to sight the heavy handgun.

"Chan—tell me where he is, and you live," Nicholai barked. With his free hand, he reached into his pocket and touched the vaccine case, for luck. It had become something of a talisman for him, a reminder of how good he was—and it *was* lucky, he knew it.

Franklin and now Chan, the only two Watchdogs with no assigned filing locale. Incredible.

Franklin backed up a step, hands up. "Hey, take it easy—"

"*Where is he?*"

Franklin was sweating. "At the radio setup, okay? At the cemetery. Look, I don't know you, and I don't care what you're doing—"

"Terrific," Nicholai said, and shot Franklin in the abdomen, twice.

"*Uuh!*" Franklin grunted heavily as blood splattered the wall behind him. The sergeant fell backwards and landed on his butt, arms still outspread, an expression of surprise on his dark features. Nicholai was a little surprised himself; he'd expected better from one of the soldier dogs.

Nicholai raised the weapon, aiming it at Franklin's forehead—

—when he heard the door open, boot steps jogging into the room. Handgun still pointed at the dying Franklin, Nicholai ducked down and peered through an opening in the shelf—

—and saw Carlos Oliveira standing there, staring around wildly and hefting a .357 revolver, obviously trying to figure out where the shots had come from.

It was a gift from the fates. Nicholai stepped into view, Carlos's stupid face targeted before the soldier even realized that there was somebody else in the room.

"Gotcha," Nicholai whispered.

TWENTY-TWO

Nicholai had him, dead to rights. Carlos dropped the revolver and raised his hands. He had to buy some time.

Talk to him, get his attention. Jill needs you to come back, with or without the vaccine.

"*Hola*, dickhead," Carlos said lightly. "I wondered if I was going to see you again, after our ride out of town got blown to shit. A monster did it, believe it or not. So, what's your story? Kill anything interesting lately?"

From behind the tall shelf unit jutting out from one wall, somebody groaned in pain. Nicholai didn't look away, and Carlos could see that he'd taken the right tact. Nicholai was smug, irritated... and intrigued.

"I'm about to kill you—so no, nothing interesting. Tell me, has Mikhail died yet? And how is your bitch friend, Ms. Valentine?"

Carlos glared at him. "Both dead. Mikhail died on the trolley, and Jill contracted the virus. I... I had to put her down just a few hours ago." He probably wasn't going to walk away from this, and he didn't want Nicholai going after Jill; he quickly changed the subject. "You shot Mikhail, didn't you?"

"I did." Nicholai's eyes sparkled. He reached into his front pocket as he spoke, pulling out what looked like a metal cigar holder. "And as luck would have it, this is the cure to what killed your other friend. If only you'd come sooner... in a way, I suppose you could say I'm at least partly responsible in both deaths, couldn't you?"

The sample. The only thing that could save Jill now, and Carlos was being held at gunpoint by the madman who had it.

Think! Think of something!

There was another gruff wail of pain from behind the shelf. Carlos tilted his head and could see a man slumped in the back corner of the room, just visible between two stacks of files. Carlos couldn't see his face, but the man's lower half was drenched with blood.

"And that guy makes three," Carlos said, desperately trying to keep the conversation going, trying not to stare at the silver case that Nicholai held up. "Aren't you a go-getter? Tell me, is this a means to an end, or do you *like* killing people?"

"I enjoy killing people who are as useless as you," Nicholai said, slipping the vaccine into an open pocket. "Can you think of one reason you deserve to live?"

Another moan came from the dying man behind the shelf. Carlos glanced between the stacks again and saw an impact grenade clenched in shaking hands, the ring already pulled; Carlos realized that the man must have groaned to cover the sound, and some part of him admired the clear thinking, all in the instant before he started to back up, hands still raised. The grenade was an RG34, the same kind that Carlos had tucked in his vest, and he wanted as much distance as he could get.

Make it look good...

"I'm an excellent shot, I have a generous nature, and I floss every day," Carlos said, backing up another step, trying to appear that he was deeply afraid and covering it up with bravado.

"Such a waste this will be," Nicholai said, smiling, extending his arm.

Throw the goddamn thing!

"Why?" Carlos asked quickly. "Why are you doing this?"

Nicholai's smile stretched into a grin, the same predatorial grin that Carlos had seen him wearing on the transport, what felt like a million years before.

"I possess leadership qualities," Nicholai said, and for the first time, Carlos could see the insanity in his murky eyes. "That's all you need to know—"

"*Die!*" the bleeding man screamed. Carlos caught a flicker of motion behind the shelf, and then Carlos was diving sideways, trying to get behind a table as a window broke and—

—*BOOM*, folders and books were airborne and exploded materials rained down, wood and paper and chips of metal, the heavy shelf tipping over with a thundering creak. It slammed to the floor with a tremendous crash, and then everything was quiet, and shit was everywhere.

Carlos sat up, one arm wrapped around his throbbing rib cage, tears of pain in his eyes. He blinked them away and got to his feet, grabbing the revolver he'd dropped as he stood up.

Nicholai was gone. Carlos kicked his way through the debris to the corner, remembering that a window had shattered *before* the grenade exploded. Although it was dark and rainy outside, Carlos could see the roof of an adjacent building one floor below.

Bam! Bam!

Carlos jumped back as two rounds hit the outer wall, hardly a hand's width from his face. He silently berated himself for sticking his head out the window, like some half-witted *baboso*. He backed away from the window and turned, only to find himself staring at the burnt, bloody remains of the grenade thrower.

"*Gracias*," Carlos said quietly. He wished he could think of something else to say, but then he decided it would only be useless symbolism; the guy was dead, he wasn't hearing shit.

Carlos walked back across the room, thinking, wondering how he was going to catch up with Nicholai. It wasn't going to be easy, but there was no other choice—

—and he saw the glint of metal from the corner of his eye, and stopped. He blinked, feeling a kind of awe as he realized what he was looking at—and then scooped it up, a giant weight lifting from his shoulders and from around his heart.

He was going to be able to save Jill. The crazy *pendejo* had dropped the vaccine.

* * *

Nicholai moved quickly through the rain toward the front of the hospital. *Everything is fine, he's dead at the push of a button and I control it, I can shut down the power and trap him—*

He laughed out loud suddenly, thinking about the containment tubes in the basement where the Hunter Gammas were stored, each floating in its own see-through womb. Shut down the power and there was automatic drainage so they wouldn't drown in the unaerated fluid.

Die, or fight and die, Carlos. Nicholai had been smart, he'd thought ahead and now all he had to do was hit a few switches and Carlos would be in the dark and the amphibious Hunters would be squelching toward him, and maybe Carlos would actually be dead before the hospital was blown apart, but he was dead no matter what.

* * *

Jill was sleeping again, and she was sick. Hot and achy, and her dreams were gone, pulsing, squirming shadows in their place. Shadows with textures, rough and wet. Nausea warred with an unfulfilled emptiness, with a dying thirst and a growing heat.

She rolled to one side and then the other, trying to find relief from the crawling itch that had embedded itself in every part of her, that made the ugly shadows get bigger as she slept on.

* * *

Carlos found needles, syringes, and a half bottle of Betadine in a doctor's office on the third floor. He also found a cabinet full of drug company samples and was trying to decipher the labels, looking for a mild painkiller, when the lights when out.

"Shit." He put down the sample, trying to get his bearings in the sudden dark. It took him about a second and a half to decide it was Nicholai, and a second longer to decide he needed to get out, and get out fast. Nicholai probably hadn't shut down the power just to make him stub his toe in the dark. Whatever Nicholai was planning, Carlos thought he'd take a rain check.

He edged out of the room and into the hall, moving slowly, his hands out in front of him. Just as he reached the stairwell, the hospital's emergency backup lights hummed into soft red life. The effect was otherworldly, the light just bright enough to see by, casting everything in murky shadow.

Carlos started down the stairs, taking them two

at a time, thumb on the hammer of the Python. He ignored his aching side, deciding that he'd collapse later, when he wasn't in such a hurry. He only knew of two options for getting out of the hospital—the window Nicholai had jumped from and the front door. There were certainly more, but he didn't want to waste time trying to find them; in his experience, most hospitals were mazes.

The front door was his best bet. Nicholai probably didn't think Carlos had the nerve to charge straight out of the most obvious exit, or so Carlos hoped.

He'd reached the landing between the first and second floors when he heard a door crash open somewhere far below, echoing up the stairwell, making him freeze. The sound that followed—the furious, piglike battle cry of some distinctly mutant creature— got him moving again. His feet hardly touched the steps, but he still wasn't fast enough; just as he was bounding down the last flight, a monstrous figure leaped in front of the exit to the ground floor.

It was giant, humanoid, tall and wide and dripping slime. Its body was a dark blue-green, almost black in the dim red light. With its webbed oversized hands and feet and its huge rounded head and mouth, it resembled nothing so much as a mammoth, hideously squashed frog.

Its powerful lower jaw dropped open, and another piercing, squealing screech filled the stairwell, rebounding throughout. Carlos heard at least three more answer the first, a fierce and freakish chorus erupting from somewhere down below.

Carlos opened fire, the first round hitting the metal door and creating a deafening tornado of sound. Before he could squeeze the trigger again, the amphibious creature was springing, squealing as it leaped toward Carlos, stretching its muscular arms wide.

Carlos reflexively dropped, firing as he slid down several steps, rolling to his uninjured side so he could follow the creature's descent. Three, four rounds plugged into the shrieking frog-thing's slimy body as it flew overhead—

—and it was dead by the time it landed, dark gouts of watery, brackish fluid spuming from its spasming body.

Carlos was on his feet running and halfway through the door even as the creature's siblings began their feral, earsplitting lament. Not too hard to kill, maybe, but he didn't want to consider his chances if there were three or more of them all leaping at once.

Into the lobby and he slammed the door, saw that it required a key to lock, and he turned to look for something he could use to block it—

—and instead he saw a tiny, blinking white light from across the room, its brightness drawing his gaze from the midst of a shady red ocean of trashed furniture and dead bodies.

A blinking white light on a small box, the box affixed to a pillar. A timer light for a detonating compound.

Carlos tried to think of something else it might be and came up blank, knowing only that it hadn't been there when he'd arrived; it was a bomb, Nicholai had put it there, and suddenly the frog monsters were a much smaller deal.

His mind was curiously blank as he pounded through the lobby, a thoughtless, wordless panic overtaking him, pushing him to run fast and far, to not waste time thinking. He tripped over a shredded couch and didn't notice whether or not he fell or felt pain, he was moving too fast, the glass doors at the front of the building all he could see.

Bam, through the doors, shining black asphalt splashing under his feet, rain misting on his sweaty face. Rows of smashed and abandoned cars, shining like wet jewels beneath a streetlight. The drum of his shuddering heart—

—and the explosion was so massive that his hearing couldn't encompass it all, a kind of *ka-WHAMM* that was as much motion as it was sound. His body was thrown, a leaf in a hot and violent hurricane, the ground and sky becoming connected, interchangeable.

He was skidding across wet pavement, tumbling to a gritty stop against a fire hydrant, feeling the enormity of pain in his side and tasting salt from a nose-bleed.

Barely a block away, the hospital had been reduced to a smoking ruin, smaller pieces of it still coming down, cracking against the ground like deadly hail. Parts were on fire, but a lot of it had just disintegrated, matter blown to dust, the dust settling and turning to mud as the skies continued to dump water on everything.

Jill.

Carlos pulled himself up and started to limp back to the clock tower.

* * *

Nicholai realized he'd lost the vaccine sample as he was running away from the hospital, when there was one minute left before all of it went sky high. When it was already too late.

There was no choice but to keep running, and he did, and when the hospital exploded, Nicholai paced back and forth in the street three blocks away, lost in anger. So lost that he didn't realize that the agonized moaning, whining noise he heard was coming from him, or that he'd clenched his jaw hard enough to crack two teeth.

After a long time, he remembered that he still had to kill two more people, and he started to calm down. Being able to express his anger would be constructive; it wasn't healthy to keep feelings bottled up.

The Watchdog operation was his interest. The vaccine had been an extra, a gift—so in a way, he hadn't really *lost* anything.

Nicholai told himself that several times on his way to get Davis Chan; it made him feel better, though not as good as when he remembered that he'd had his hunting knife sharpened just before he'd come to Raccoon. He was sure Chan would appreciate it.

TWENTY-THREE

When Jill woke up, it was still raining outside, and she felt like herself again. Weak, thirsty, and hungry, definitely in pain from her shoulder wound and about a thousand lesser aches—but herself. The sickness was gone.

Disoriented and a little confused, she sat up slowly and looked around, trying to piece together what had happened. She was still in the clock tower chapel, and Carlos was crashed out on one of the front pews. She remembered telling him that she had the virus, and him saying that he was going to get something...

...but I was sick, I had the disease... and I don't just feel better now, I absolutely don't have it anymore. How could—

"Oh my God," she whispered, seeing the syringe and empty vial on the organ bench next to the altar, suddenly understanding what had happened, if not how. Carlos had found an antidote.

Jill sat for a moment, slightly overwhelmed by the mix of emotions that hit her—shock, gratitude, a reluctance to believe she was actually okay. Her happiness at being alive and reasonably well was tempered by guilt, that she should have been cured when so many others had died. She wondered whether or not there was more of the antidote but found she couldn't consider that too carefully; the thought that there might be gallons of it lying around somewhere when tens of thousands had died was simply obscene.

Finally, she eased herself off her sickbed and stood, carefully stretching, checking herself over. Considering all that had happened, she was surprised at how well-off she was. Except for her right shoulder, she had no serious injuries, and after drinking some water, she actually felt awake and able to move around without any trouble.

Over the next couple of hours, Jill ate three cans of fruit cocktail, drank a half gallon of water, and reloaded and wiped down all of the weapons. She also cleaned herself up, as much as she could, with bottled water and a dirty sweatshirt. Carlos didn't stir once, deeply asleep—and from the way he was curled up and holding his left side, she thought that his trip to the hospital had probably been rough.

Jill also gave a great deal of thought to what they would do next. They couldn't stay. They didn't have the supplies or ammo to keep themselves alive indefinitely, and they had no way of knowing when— or even if, she didn't want to take it for granted anymore—rescue was coming. As hard as it was to believe, it seemed that Umbrella had managed to keep a lid on what had happened, and if they could do it for this long, it might be several more days before the story broke. To add to the pressure, she also couldn't convince herself that the Nemesis was dead; once it had recuperated, it would be coming back. They were incredibly lucky that it hadn't attacked already.

Before she'd hooked up with Carlos, she had tentatively planned to head for the abandoned Umbrella-owned plant north of the city. She'd come to believe that there was no such thing as a deserted Umbrella facility—they loved their secret operations too much—and thought that they might have kept the roads clear around the plant so their employees could get out. It was still worth a shot, and it was also the best she could come up with. Besides, the fastest way out of town from their current position was straight past the facility.

Carlos continued to sleep, perfectly still except for the rise and fall of his chest, his face slack from exhaustion... and once Jill had decided on a course of action, she watched him for a little while and realized that she had to leave him behind. It was a much harder decision to make, but only because she didn't want to be alone, a selfish reason at best. The truth of it was, he was hurting because he'd gotten in between her and the Nemesis, and she couldn't put him in that position again.

I'll go check out the plant, maybe find a radio and

call for help. If things look good, safe, I can come back for him. If they look shitty... well, I guess I'll just come back if I can. The facility was barely a mile away if she remembered right, she could get there by cutting through Memorial Park, just behind the clock tower, a very short trip. It was just after two in the morning, she'd be able to get there and back well before dawn. With any luck, Carlos would still be asleep when she returned, perhaps bearing good news.

She decided to leave him a note in case something happened to her so he'd know the route, at least. She couldn't find a pen or pencil, but she uncovered an ancient manual typewriter, of all things, beneath a stack of hymnbooks. She used the back of a fruit cocktail label for paper. The soft clack of keys was as soothing to her as the rain that continued to patter down on the roof, sounds that made her very glad to be alive.

She took the grenade gun even though there was only one round left—Carlos must have found the one she'd dropped in the yard—remembering the damage it had inflicted on the S.T.A.R.S. killer. She also took the Beretta, but she left the revolver for Carlos so that he'd have something a little heavier than the assault rifle. Just in case.

Jill left the note on the altar, where Carlos would see it as soon as he woke up, and she crouched next to him, reaching out to touch his cool brow. He was definitely out, not even a twitch as she brushed his dirty hair off his forehead, wondering how she could ever thank him for all he'd done.

"Sleep well," she whispered, and before she could change her mind, she stood up and turned away, hurrying to the door and not looking back.

* * *

There was a cabin behind the small cemetery in Memorial Park, ostensibly used for tool storage. It had been taken over as one of several Umbrella receiver stations for the duration of the Raccoon outbreak— kind of a rest stop for operatives, each in a private place where they could organize files without being seen and get general updates from Umbrella, if they didn't have immediate access to a computer.

Nicholai had not planned to stop by any of the receiver stations; he thought they were an unnecessary risk on Umbrella's part, even as well hidden as they were—the setup at the cemetery cabin was behind a false wall. Umbrella didn't want anyone tracking signals coming out of the city, so the stations were set to receive only, another precaution, but Nicholai still thought they were dangerous. If he wanted to trap an agent, he'd stake out one of the receiver stations.

Or if I wanted to kill one. Although in this case, I only have to walk in… or wait for a little while.

He stood in the shadows of a large monument a few meters from the false room, thinking of how fine it was going to be to kill Captain Chan. Nicholai had considered just barging through the concealed door and shooting him, but he needed to relax, to get into a better frame of mind. Chan would come out for a bathroom break or a smoke sooner or later, and by allowing his anticipation to build, Nicholai was able to let go of some of his more unpleasant emotions. He didn't do it often; he wasn't crazy or anything, and he generally preferred to keep things moving along—but sometimes, savoring the suspense before an intimate killing was just the thing to lift him out of a depression.

Nicholai watched the door—actually a hinged corner of the building—enjoying the cool rain in spite of how miserable he knew he'd be later, running around in wet clothes. He was going to take someone's life. Things had been a little out of control for a few moments, when he'd realized he'd lost the vaccine, but who was in control now? Davis Chan was about to die and Nicholai was the only one who knew it, because he had decided Chan's fate.

And Carlos is dead, I caused that. And Mikhail, and three Watchdogs so far. He couldn't really make a claim on Jill Valentine, but Nicholai *had* enjoyed the stricken look on Carlos's face when he'd suggested it. What counted, though, the only thing that had ever really mattered, was that his enemies were dead and he was still walking.

When Davis Chan stepped out into the rain a few moments later, Nicholai had released most of his negative feelings of self-pity and undirected frustration. And by the time his knife had finished with Chan, fifteen minutes later, he was his old self again. Chan, of course, no longer resembled anything human, but Nicholai sincerely thanked the remains for getting him back on track.

0250 HOURS OCTOBER 2

Carlos:

I've gone to the water treatment facility directly northeast from the clock tower, a mile give or take. Umbrella owns it, there may be resources there that we can use. I'll be back as soon as I take a look around. Wait here for me, for at least a few hours. If I'm not back by morning, you should probably try to get out on your own.

I'm grateful to you, for a lot of things. Stay here and get some rest, please. I shouldn't be long.

Jill

Carlos read the curled paper twice more, then grabbed his vest and stood up, checking his watch. She'd been gone less than a half hour. He could still catch up with her.

Staying wasn't an option. She'd left him behind either because he was injured or because she didn't want to put him in further danger... neither of which was acceptable to him. And he'd never had a chance to tell her what Trent had said, about there being helicopters at an Umbrella facility northwest of town, but northeast from where they were now, after the trolley ride. Obviously the same place.

"You may kick ass all over Umbrella's monsters, but can you pilot a helicopter?" Carlos mumbled, locking a new mag to the M16. If only she'd waked him up...

He headed for the door, as ready as he was going to be, trying not to breathe too deeply. It hurt, but he'd manage. He'd been in worse pain and still gotten things done; once, he'd walked six klicks on a fractured ankle, and it didn't get a whole lot worse than that.

Carlos didn't waste time trying to convince himself that wanting to share Trent's info was why he was going after her. He couldn't stand by and do nothing, that was all. She was trying to protect him, he could appreciate the sentiment, but he just couldn't stay there and—

Nicholai. He's out there and she doesn't know.

He suddenly felt sick thinking of that mad glimmer in Nicholai's eyes. Carlos hurried out of the chapel and into the moonlit rain. He had to find her.

TWENTY-FOUR

The rain had turned into a drizzle, but Nicholai didn't notice, walking beneath the thick canopy of autumn leaves back through the cemetery. Another fifty or sixty meters and he could cut east, parallel the trail that ran straight to the water treatment facility's back entrance. He never used paths in public places when he could avoid them, not liking the sense of exposure.

On last check, Terence Foster was still alive and well and filing environmental status reports from the treatment plant, perfectly unaware that, as the last surviving Watchdog, his hours were numbered. Nicholai had already decided to just kill the man outright, to hell with talking. He'd found Chan's Watchdog data easily enough, sitting on the small table in the receiver station; he'd find Foster's, too. A quick encryption on the combined files—a little health insurance—then he'd radio for pickup and go take a meeting with the decision makers.

Nicholai had just reached the copse of pines behind the fence of one of the park's reflecting pools when he saw Jill Valentine, walking casually past the water's edge beneath a row of wrought-iron lamps and headed in the direction he wanted to go. The low lights reflected off the water at her, giving her a ghostly appearance, but she was definitely alive.

He supposed he shouldn't be surprised, but he was. The look of pain on Carlos's face when he'd talked about her... Nicholai had been sure it was real, he hadn't doubted for a second that she was dead.

Ah, well, it was the last lie he ever told. Very noble of him, to try and protect the girl from who he believes to be the dastardly villain... as if I would waste my time.

No time wasted if he killed her now. Nicholai raised the assault rifle, carefully took aim at the back of her head—and hesitated, curious in spite of his resolve to finish his business in Raccoon. How had she managed to evade the S.T.A.R.S. seeker all this time? Where had she been when her Latin lover had so idiotically wandered into Nicholai's path at the hospital? And where, exactly, did she think she was going?

He decided to follow her, at least until an easy opportunity presented itself for him to get the answers to his questions. As it was, with her on the main trail through the park and him behind a waist-high railing, he couldn't maneuver very well; telling her to freeze, drop her weapons, and then hold still while he climbed the fence wasn't the most desirable option.

Nicholai sank back into the shadows and counted

slowly to twenty, letting her get far enough ahead that she shouldn't be able to hear him moving through the trees. He would trail her until the main path became the bridge over the park's large duck pond, confronting her once she was halfway across, out in the open with nowhere to run.

Satisfied with his plan, Nicholai started walking, moving as quietly as he could. He'd lost sight of her on his count, but unless she was jogging, he'd catch up with her just before—

"Freeze." Her voice was calm and clear, the semiautomatic's muzzle hard against the side of his head. "Oh, but drop the rifle first, if you would."

Nicholai did as he was told, shocked into it, unslinging his rifle and letting it fall. How had she spotted him? How had she managed to circle back so quietly, without his notice?

And how much does she really know about me?

"Please don't shoot," he said, his voice cracking. "Jill, it's me, Nicholai."

The gun stayed where it was. "I know who you are. And I know you're working for Umbrella, not just as a soldier. What's Operation Watchdog, Nicholai?"

She already knew something about it. If he lied, he lost any credibility he might still have with her.

Say and do whatever it takes. "Umbrella sent me and several others in to gather information about the virus carriers," he said. "But I didn't know it was going to be like this, I swear, I never would have agreed to it if I had known. I just want to get out with my life, that's all I care about anymore."

Still the muzzle stayed pressed to his temple. She was careful, he had to give her that much.

"What do you know about the water treatment plant near here?" she asked.

"Nothing. I mean, I know Umbrella owns it, but that's it. Please, you must believe me, I just want to—"

"What about the vaccine for the virus, what do you know about that?"

Nicholai's gut knotted at the very mention, but he stayed in character. "Vaccine? There's no vaccine."

"Bullshit, or I'd be dead. Prove to me that you want to cooperate here, and maybe we can work something out. What have you heard about a T-virus vaccine?"

Carlos. The look on his face when he talked about her... and when he saw the sample case.

Nicholai didn't trust himself to speak, the depth of his sudden and complete inner turmoil like a physical force, pushing him to act—but he couldn't, and he had to convince her that he was just another Umbrella pawn or she was going to shoot him. He opened his mouth, not sure what was going to come out—

—and he was saved by the very ground beneath them. There was a deep rumble and the earth shook, pitching both of them into a drunken stumble, leaves and sticks jumping around their feet. The gun swung away from his head as Jill struggled for balance.

Even as disorienting as it was to try and stay upright, Nicholai didn't think it was a real earthquake. It was localized around them; for one thing, he could see that the water in the pool was barely moving. The tremor went on and on, seeming to increase in magnitude, and Nicholai knew he wasn't going to get a better opportunity to get away.

Feigning panic, Nicholai threw up his arms and shouted, carefully noting where his rifle lay on the shaking ground. "It's one of the mutants! Run!"

It was as likely to be some viral monster as it was anything else, and telling her to run would work for him—she'd think twice about shooting someone trying to help her.

The quake was intensifying as Nicholai ran away from Jill, one arm still waving frantically. He yelled again for her to run as he snatched up the rifle and sprinted away, not looking back, hoping she'd bought his performance. If not, he'd feel the bullet soon enough—

—and within twenty meters, the ground that *he* was on was practically still, although he could still feel and hear the rumbling earth behind him.

Far enough, find cover and shoot her—

There was a big oak tree straight ahead. Still running, Nicholai reached out with his right arm and veered left, grabbing the tree and letting his own weight swing him around. As soon as he was safely behind the gnarled trunk, he darted a look back, readying the M16 as he spotted her, weaving slowly away from the quake in the opposite direction.

Now you die, you billion dollar bitch—

—and the rumbling was suddenly a roar, and a

huge fountain of muddy white spewed up from the ground, blocking his shot, trees crashing all around. A strange and horrible bellowing erupted from the fountain, a hissing bass note, and as the pale column twisted five meters into the air and then curved down suddenly, Nicholai realized it was an animal, one that had surely never existed before—the gnashing circle of pointed tusks and teeth that tipped the massive white worm-body were proof enough.

It bellowed again, arching, a titan hybrid of maggot and lamprey eel, of waxworm and snake, as big around as a man was tall—and it dove away from Nicholai.

Toward Jill Valentine.

Nicholai turned and ran away, giggling, cursing Jill and Carlos as he dodged trees in the dark, heading for the plant, laughing as he damned them to everlasting hell.

* * *

Jill was running, skirting the water's edge, and didn't know it was coming until it crashed to the ground only a few meters behind her. A wash of foul air blew over her, a smell of dirt and wet meat coming from the mouth of the carnivorous worm.

Holy crap!

She ran faster, wanting to get some distance before she dared to look back, *one grenade load's not enough, have to run for it—*

Ahead, the rounded reflecting pool curved, a few benches at the corner, a stand of trees behind them. The ground was rumbling again, but Jill was almost there; if she could get around the corner she should be clear—the man-made pool was lined with cement, the thing would knock itself out if she was lucky—

—and the benches and trees in front of her suddenly blew up into the air, raised up on a wave of dirt, the blind, probing worm vomiting soil from its toothed maw as it swept its head toward her.

Jesus, it's fast! Jill raised the Beretta she still held tightly and buried two rounds in its bloated underbelly, the worm screaming again, deep and hissing like the roar of an attacking crocodile.

Jill spun and took off, heart pounding, already hearing and feeling the start of another quake as she grabbed her Beretta. It would get in front of her again, she knew it, she'd never make it around either end of the long pool. Going across would slow her down too much. *Think, if you can't run what can you use to stop it, dirt, water, trees, lamps—*

Lamps. Several were leaning wildly from the underground movements of the mammoth grub, like uprooted saplings about to fall. Into the pool.

No time to plan, she had to get it into the water, she'd have to bait it out. She took a last running step and paused long enough to pivot ninety degrees right, dashing toward the pool. It was damaged, rivulets of scummy water draining from the concrete lip.

It rises up then crashes down, takes it a second or

two to raise itself again—A second or two, that's how long she'd have to get out of the water. Assuming she could knock a lamp over with bullets first, and that the monstrous worm would obligingly dive into the pool.

Calculating the odds meant she'd have to think, and the ground was already trembling, shaking hard enough to send her to her knees. She fell and slid through a thick layer of grass and mud, and then she was trying to get to her feet and keep the gun dry—

—and it was bursting up through the edge of the pool not ten feet to her right, blotting out the cloudy sky in a blast of mud and stone, concrete and water. There was a single lamp between her and the monster, already almost touching the water.

Move!

Jill scrambled backwards, moving faster than she would have thought possible, stopping as she saw that the creature had peaked and was starting to bend over, sheets of water pouring from its swollen form.

She opened fire as she rolled up onto her feet, the first shots wild, the third and fourth clanging off the metal post. The worm was coming down, creating a tidal wave of mud as the fifth shot blew out the light. It was going to crush her if she didn't move, *close, gonna be close*—

Bam! Bam!

It was the seventh shot that did it, and the results were spectacular. There was a giant, buzzing *pop* as Jill threw herself backwards and to the side, the lamp immersed in the rapidly draining pool. The semi-gelatinous flesh of the screaming worm shivered and shook as it raised itself up, twisting in agony. Its pallid skin began to blacken and crisp as an oily, noxious smoke poured out of its throat, the hidden length of its body thrashing up giant sprays of dirt and rock. It bellowed once more, the unearthly sound becoming choked, gurgling—

—and then it collapsed, dead before it hit the ground, before its outer layer of skin began to curl away, revealing the cooking meat of its innards.

Jill staggered to her feet, left hand pressed to her throbbing shoulder as she backed away from the frying worm, the smell of it making her gag repeatedly. She'd actually done it, she'd killed the goddamn thing! A warm swell of triumphant victory surged through her as she breathed in another wave of roasting worm smell, *I did it*, and then she bent over and vomited her guts out.

When there was nothing left to purge, Jill shakily stood up and started walking east again, thinking about her confrontation with Nicholai. He wasn't as good a liar as he thought, and if she'd had only suspicions before, she was now certain that he was extremely bad news.

Her plans hadn't changed, but she was going to have to be very careful when she got to the water treatment plant. Nicholai was going to be there, she had no doubt... and if he saw her first, she'd be dead before she knew what hit her.

* * *

The roadblock was a massive pileup of cars that had actually been stacked three and four high, stretched between several buildings at the end of a block in a rough semicircle. Carlos could still see the crisscross of greasy treadmarks from whatever piece of heavy machinery had managed the feat, just as he'd spotted them on the last three streets he'd tried. Umbrella and the RPD hadn't been screwing around when they'd sealed the city.

He stood in front of the stacked, partly crushed metal wall, experiencing an almost desperate indecision. Go back, try heading north first, then east—or try climbing over one of the precarious barricades, which seemed to have been specifically set up to deter him from finding Jill.

That's what it feels like, anyway. All that was north of the clock tower was a big park, but maybe that *was* the only way to get to the Umbrella facility; he couldn't imagine Jill scaling a wall of cars with a bad shoulder, and crawling through them was too dangerous...

...but you're assuming she even made it this far, a nagging little voice whispered. *Maybe she's already dead, maybe the Nemesis came for her, or Nicholai, or—*

Carlos cocked his head to one side, frowning, his thoughts disturbed by a distant sound. Shots? Possibly, but the light mist that was falling was having a dampening effect, distorting and muffling noises. He couldn't even be sure from which direction the sound had come... but he was suddenly even more frantic to find Jill than before.

"After all I went through to get that vaccine, you better not get yourself killed," he murmured lightly, but it was too close to the truth to be funny. He had to do something, now.

Carlos stared at the wall of cars for another moment, picking what appeared to be the most stable route, over a minivan and two compact cars. He took as deep a breath as he was able to manage, mentally crossed his fingers, and started to climb.

TWENTY-FIVE

"No, listen, you gotta listen—I don't know anything, you don't want to do this. They've had me doing reports on water and soil samples, that's it, I'm no threat to you! I swear!"

Foster was working himself into a froth, and Nicholai decided that making a man wait for his death, particularly such a sad little man, was cruel. The researcher was already cowering in the corner, pressed against the door in the northeast corner of his office, his pinched, ratty features flushed and sweaty. It had taken Nicholai less than five minutes to find him once he'd reached the facility.

"... and I'll just leave, okay?" Foster was still babbling. "I'll be gone and you'll never hear from me again, swear to God, why do you want to kill *me*, I'm nobody. Tell me what you want and I'll do it, whatever it is, talk to me, man, okay? Let's just talk, okay?"

Nicholai suddenly realized that he was just staring

at Foster, as if he'd been lulled into a trance by the rise and fall of the man's hysteria. It had been an endless day in a series of them... but as much as he wanted to get out, to be done with the entire operation, Nicholai felt oddly compelled to say something.

"There's nothing personal in this, I'm sure you understand," Nicholai said. "It's about money... or it was at the beginning, but things are different now."

Foster nodded quickly, eyes wide. "Yeah, sure they are, different."

Now that he'd started, Nicholai found he couldn't stop. It suddenly seemed important for someone else to understand what he'd gone through, what he was still up against—even if it was only someone like Foster.

"The money is still most of it, of course. But after I got here, after Wersbowski, I started to feel like I had come to a very special place. I felt... I felt that things were finally becoming the way they were supposed to be. The way my life should have been all along. Extreme circumstances, you see?"

Foster bobbed his head again but wisely said nothing.

"But then Carlos tricked me; he couldn't have died in the explosion, because Jill received the antidote. And I'm starting to think that *she's* the cause, that things changed because of her." As he spoke, he sensed the truth of it, as though a light was dawning in his mind's eye. It was true, talking helped.

"Even at the beginning, she ruined the setup I had with Carlos and Mikhail. Manipulative, controlling woman, there are a lot of them like that. She probably slept with both of them, too. Seduced them."

"Bitches, all of 'em," Foster sincerely agreed.

"Then she got sick and sent Carlos to steal the vaccine. I'm not excusing his part in all of this, not at all, but there's something about her... it's like her presence alters things, makes everything wrong somehow. I don't even think she's dead now. If a seeker can't kill her, a mutant certainly can't."

Nicholai stood silently, lost in thought for a moment. He'd never been a superstitious man, but things really were different. Jill Valentine was—

—*a woman, she's just a woman and you're not thinking clearly, haven't been for days*—

Nicholai blinked, and the thought was gone, and Foster was still in the corner, watching him with an expression of cautious terror. As though he thought Nicholai was crazy. Nicholai felt a rush of hatred for the little man, for trying to trick him, telling him to talk and then judging him for it. He deserved to die, as much as any of them.

"I'm not crazy," Nicholai shouted angrily, "and I'm done talking about this! You're the last one, after you it's over and that's just the way things are, so *be a man and accept it!*"

Three rounds, a burst of *tat tat tat* through one of Terence Foster's pleading green eyes, and the researcher's head snapped back, blood splashing the door he leaned against, his body collapsing lifeless to the cold floor.

Nicholai felt nothing. The last Watchdog, dead, and there was no sense of accomplishment, no feeling of conquest. Just another corpse on the floor in front of him and a deeply felt desire to get out of Raccoon, where things had gone so sour.

Nicholai shook his head, his heart heavy, and started to search the office for Foster's data.

* * *

Jill stood in front of the narrow bridge that connected Memorial Park's back gate to the second floor of the Umbrella facility, suspended over what had to be a marsh or swamp, from the gassy-mud smell. It was too dark to tell by looking, but the odor was unmistakable—and so were the fresh bootprints that led from where she stood to the door on the opposite side. As she'd expected, Nicholai was here.

Wonderful. What a treat.

Nicholai aside, she was glad to have found the bridge; she'd been concerned that the park would turn out to be a dead end and that she'd have to backtrack. The bridge also conveniently led to the second floor; it made sense that the offices and control rooms—hopefully at least one of them would have a transmitter system—would be on the second floor of the two-story building, the first floor being where the water treatment took place. Assuming Umbrella had bothered with a sensible layout, she should be able to get in and out easily enough. If there was no radio, she'd circle around to the front of the building's first floor and see about the roads.

She carefully edged out onto the wood-and-metal span, breathing deeply, focusing herself as she reached for the low wood railing to steady herself. Dealing with Umbrella's creatures, bred or created, took skill and concentration, but facing a human adversary took more than that; people were much less predictable than animals, and if she meant to keep away from Nicholai, she had to be as fully alert as possible, her intuition and awareness jacked up to feel an oncoming attack—

—like now—

Jill froze halfway across the bridge, feeling for the Beretta's safety with her thumb, something was very wrong but she couldn't tell—

Ka thud! Behind her.

Jill spun, heart racing, and saw the Nemesis standing twenty feet away, its freakish body hideously transformed by fire and buckshot. Its chest and arms were bare, giving her a clear look at how the waving tentacles were attached, sprouting from its upper back and shoulders. Much of its skin had burned off, revealing fibrous red muscle tissue in patches of ashy black.

"Starsss," it rumbled, limping forward a step, and she saw that much of its lower right side was mangled from where she'd hit it with the grenade gun. The flesh from the bottom of its rib cage to about midthigh looked like burned spaghetti, smashed and shredded—but she doubted very much that it felt pain, and she had few illusions about its strength being overly affected.

In an instant, her adrenaline-pumped mind flashed through a hundred options and latched on to her best bet. The ledge at the clock tower. Carlos had pushed it right off, but it had been blinded, distracted—

—*distract this, freak!*

She opened fire, aiming at the most obvious part of its deformed face, its improbably white teeth—and saw at least two shots shatter through the eerie grin, pale splinters exploding out in a spray.

The S.T.A.R.S. killer howled, its flesh tentacles spreading like a cape behind it, framing the beast in a coiling, quivering sunburst.

—*not in pain, maybe, but it feels something—*

—*GO NOW!*

Jill continued to fire as she ran for it, her instincts screaming at her to run the other way, her logic reminding her that she couldn't possibly run fast enough.

The Nemesis was still howling when Jill smashed into it, pushing up and out to smack into its chest the way Carlos had, inwardly cringing at the feel of its skin against her palms, wet, gritty, cold—

—and it staggered backwards, landing heavily at the very edge of the bridge, inches from empty space. Its weight and mass worked for Jill as she'd prayed it would, she could hear the explosive crack of the weathered board beneath its heels, the side rail crunching as the giant fell against the slats—

—but two, three of the twisting tentacles were grabbing at the undamaged railing on the other side, the reeling Nemesis putting its hands out, struggling to regain its balance.

Jill jumped, twisting, knowing that she couldn't let it stand up again, and landed both feet against its ravaged abdomen, kicking off from the monster's body with all of her strength.

She fell solidly to the wood planking, involuntarily crying out in pain as her wounded shoulder absorbed much of the impact—but the sight of those fleshy ropes, flailing at air as the Nemesis lost its grip and plunged over the side, did her a world of good... as did the murky, thunderous splash she heard a beat later.

She stumbled to her feet and across the rest of the bridge, silently cheering as the door that led into the facility swung open, unlocked. Inside, a short hall turned left fifteen feet ahead, all utilitarian metal grate floors and concrete walls. She quickly deadbolted the door behind her and sagged against it, pointing her weapon at the blind corner while she caught her breath.

No footsteps outside or in, nothing but a faint mechanical hum coming from somewhere deeper in the facility. When she could breathe almost normally again, she moved forward, anxious to get out before the Nemesis returned. She had to get out a call for help, or just get out; the Nemesis wasn't going to give up, and she couldn't hope to elude it forever.

She edged further down the hall and saw that a metal shutter stood at the right end, facing the corridor she couldn't see. Another step forward, and she darted a look around the corner. Clear, another short hall that turned right. She stepped back and took a closer look at the metal shutter, the kind that opened with a key card.

The room's name was just above the door, in black stencil: COMMUNICATIONS. Jill felt a rush of hope, then saw that there was no manual lock. The key card reader to the right of the shutter was the only way in.

Frustrated, Jill turned away. Running into the Nemesis had changed things. She could leave, get far away from it and Nicholai and try to come up with something new, or she could continue on, search for the card and keep looking for other possibilities.

Jill smiled wearily. Both options sounded terrible, actually, but the latter seemed to suck a little less. At least her clothes would have a chance to dry.

Shivering, Jill started down the adjoining corridor, feeling vaguely envious of Carlos, warm and sleeping back at the chapel.

* * *

The Umbrella facility was a series of small single-level buildings and one large two-story one, set among several open areas that had been stacked high with crap—piles of lumber, old cars, and scrap metal being the main competitors for space. If there were helicopters on the site, Carlos thought they'd be behind one of the warehouses—nearly impossible to get around, of course, unless he wanted to scale another stack of cars.

Not unless I have to, thank you very much. His earlier climb had been enough to last him the rest of his life. He'd banged the hell out of both his knees when he'd come down hard on the cab of a flatbed truck, and he'd limped most of the rest of the way to the facility.

He stood in a small and crowded yard, which he'd hopped a fence to get to, memorizing the compound's sprawling layout as best he could before moving toward the main building. He wanted to make sure Jill was okay before he went hunting for a 'copter. As soon as he reached the building, Carlos broke the first window he could reach with the M16's stock and boosted himself up.

He sat on the frame, looking into a long, narrow, bunkerlike room, dimly lit and littered with bodies. To the right was a set of doors with an exit sign overhead, probably leading out to the main warehouse; he'd have to try the doors when he went for the helicopters. To his left, though, was a metal ladder that went straight up to a hatch in the ceiling. He couldn't have asked for more.

Well, an elevator, maybe, he thought as he pulled himself through the window, his taped ribs protesting. *Although as long as I'm wishing, suddenly waking up and finding out this has all been a bad dream would be pretty nice, too.*

The room smelled like blood and rot, a smell that he had gotten used to, he realized. It smelled like Raccoon, and as he slowly climbed the ladder, he thought that he would die a happy man if he could just do it breathing fresh, untainted air.

The square metal hatch at the top lifted easily, swinging up and back on hinges to lean against a three-sided railing. Carlos ascended carefully into another dim room with a bunker feel, lined with consoles and cabinets, no bodies—

"*Caramba*," he breathed, stepping away from the ladder to the desk console against the front wall, set beneath large windows that looked out over the mostly dark yard. It was an old communications relay system, and even as he reached out to pick up the headset, a crackle of static hissed from a small speaker set into a side panel, followed by a woman's cool, clear voice.

"Attention. The Raccoon City project has been abandoned. Political maneuvering to delay federal plans has failed. All personnel must evacuate immediately to outside of the ten-mile blast radius. Missiles will be launched at daybreak. This message is being broadcast on all available channels, and will repeat in five minutes."

Stunned, Carlos looked at his watch and felt his stomach knot. It was half past four in the morning, which left them an hour, maybe a little more.

He snatched up the headset and started pushing buttons. "Hello? Does anybody read me, I'm still in the city, hello?"

Nothing. Carlos ran for the door at the back of the room, his thoughts repeating in an endless loop, *day break, Jill, helicopter, daybreak, Jill—*

—and the door, a metal shutter, was firmly locked. No keyhole, no nothing. He couldn't get into the building.

And I don't even know if she's here, maybe she started back already, maybe...

Maybe a lot of things, and as much as he wanted to find her, if he didn't secure a way for them to escape the city, they weren't going to make it.

He turned away from the door, not wanting to leave, knowing he didn't have a choice. He had to find one of those helicopters that Trent had told him about and make sure it was fueled up and working. Maybe he could buzz the facility, get her attention from outside, or find her on her way back to the clock tower.

And if I can't... He didn't finish the thought, well aware of Jill's fate if he failed.

Hardly noticing the pain in his side, Carlos ran for the ladder, his heart pounding and filled with dread.

TWENTY-SIX

When Nicholai saw Jill step hesitantly through the door into treatment operations, he immediately slipped back out of view, through the security side door and into a large, empty corridor that led to the chemical tank room. A fierce joy took hold of him as he eased the door closed, feelings of vindication and self-affirmation lifting his spirits high.

After he'd found Foster's data disk, he'd set up his laptop to combine files. That's when he'd seen the warning from H.Q. Not much of a surprise, it had been one of several possible outcomes projected, but it had further depressed him. A part of him had still wanted to get closure with Jill and Carlos, for what they had done to him, and he'd even been considering a final look around before calling for pickup. There was no time for that with missiles coming, and he'd been on his way to place the call when he'd heard footsteps.

She's here, I was right about her and now she's here!

He had to be right, or whatever fates were working in Raccoon wouldn't have sent her. He could see now that everything that had happened since he'd arrived in Raccoon had been predestined. Fate, testing him, sending him gifts and then pulling them away, to see what he would do. It all made perfect sense, and now there was a ticking clock, he had to get out, and here she was.

I won't fail. I've succeeded so far, and that's why this synchronicity has occurred. So that I can reestablish the control I command before I return to civilization. He could ask her about Carlos and Mikhail, he could question her thoroughly... and if there was time, he could dominate her in a more pleasurable fashion, a farewell that he could reflect back upon for years to come.

Nicholai quickly moved behind the door, his boot-steps echoing in the roomwide corridor, rifle ready. He'd earned this, and he was going to get exactly what he deserved.

* * *

Jill walked into some kind of operations room, her senses on high alert as she looked across the open space, decorated in classic Umbrella laboratory style—blank, cold, cement walls, metal railings that separated the bi-level room in an absolutely functional way, nothing bright or colorful in sight.

Unless blood counts... Dried splashes of it stained the floor all around the low worktable that dominated the room. Probably not Nicholai's work, unlike the corpse she'd found in the office next to the room with the broken steam pipes. A short man in his mid-30s, shot in the face, his body still warm. She had no doubt that Nicholai was close, and she found herself almost hoping she'd run into him soon, just so she could stand down, not have to look over her shoulder with every step.

She didn't see anything resembling a key card or a radio in the room, so she decided to move on— she could head through the side door in the nook to her left or go down. Side door, she decided, on the off chance that Nicholai had headed that way; so far, she'd been through every room she could get into on the second floor and didn't want to go downstairs and risk letting him get behind her.

She walked to the door, wondering again what had been done with the bodies of those who had died in the facility. She'd seen plenty of blood and fluid stains, but only a handful of corpses.

Maybe they were dumped downstairs... she thought, pulling the security door open and sweeping left to right with the Beretta. A corridor as big as a room, with a small offshoot at the back wall that headed right. Totally empty. She stepped inside... *or Umbrella ordered everything cleaned up so their employees didn't have to spend the crisis stepping over their dead coworkers—*

"Freeze, bitch," Nicholai said from behind her, roughly jamming the barrel of his rifle into her lower back. "But drop your weapon first, *if* you wouldn't mind."

A sarcastic rephrasing of what she'd said to him in the park, and she couldn't miss the thread of almost hysterical glee in his voice. She'd been careless, and she was going to die for it.

"Okay, okay," she said, letting the 9mm slip from her fingers and clatter to the floor. She still had the grenade gun on her back, but it was useless—in the time it would take her to unstrap the thing, he could empty a mag into her and have a chance to reload.

"Turn around slowly and back away, hands clasped in front of you. Like you're praying."

Jill did what he wanted, backing across the room until her back touched the wall, more afraid than she wanted to admit when she saw the constantly twitching smile, and the way his eyes rolled from side to side.

He's gone over. Whatever was wrong with him to start, being in Raccoon sparked it into a full-blown psychosis. The way he looked her up and down filled her with a different kind of fear. She knew of several effective ways to stop a rapist's attack—but that was assuming she was still able-bodied enough to fight, and she doubted very much that Nicholai would approach her without firing a few well-placed shots first.

She glanced to her left, down a narrow hall that

dead ended at a closed door. *Won't make it, try to talk to him.*

"I thought you just wanted to get out of the city," she said neutrally, not sure what tack to use. She'd always heard that crazy people should be humored, but she couldn't see that it was going to make much of a difference; Nicholai meant to kill her, period.

He casually walked toward her, smiling his trembling smile. Thunder rumbled overhead, a distant sound. "I want to get out *now*, now that I have all the information. I killed all of the others for theirs, the Watchdogs. Umbrella is going to have to deal with me, and only me, and I'm going to be extremely wealthy. It's all balanced out, and now that you're here, my success is assured."

In spite of herself, Jill was curious. "Why me?"

Nicholai moved closer but stayed a safe distance away. "Because you took the antidote," he said in a matter-of-fact tone. "Carlos stole it at your bidding, don't try to deny it. Tell me, are you working on your own initiative, or were you sent to interfere with my plans? How much do Carlos and Mikhail know?"

Christ, what do I say to that? Again thunder muttered overhead, and Jill found herself distracted by it, too confused by Nicholai's bizarre reasoning to answer him right away. Strange, that they could hear it through the heavily insulated ceiling...

...*not as strange as thinking about the weather at a time like this.* She had to say something, to at least try and prolong her life; as long as she was breathing, there was a chance.

"Why should I tell you anything? You're going to kill me anyway," she said, as though there was something to tell.

Nicholai's smile faltered, and then he brightened again, nodding. "You're right, I am." He aimed the rifle at her left knee and licked his lips. "But not before we get to know each other a little better, I think we have enough time—"

Crash!

Jill fell backwards, sure she'd been hit, *but he didn't fire, it was thunder—*

—and the ceiling was falling, part of it, chunks of drywall and concrete raining down as Nicholai screamed, firing wildly—

—and disappeared.

* * *

Nicholai had her within his control, she was going to bleed and cry and he would be victorious, he had won—

—and then the ceiling gave way, debris crashing over him and something giant and cold and hard wrapped around the back of his neck. Nicholai fired, screaming, *A witch, she's—*

—and he was yanked up into the dark by the massive, icy thing, a hand, Jill's shocked face the last thing he saw before the fingers tightened, before a cold and living rope coiled around his waist. The hand

and rope pulled in opposite directions, and Nicholai felt his bones crack, skin and muscle stretching as blood filled his mouth, screaming—

—*this is wrong I control stop*—

—and he was torn in half, and he knew no more.

* * *

Jill could only see part of what happened, but it was enough. As a river of blood poured over the hole's ragged edge, splashing to the floor, she heard the rumbling growl of the Nemesis and saw a tentacle snake down through the steaming red gush, searching—

She didn't dare run beneath it. She turned and ran down the offshoot, scrabbling for the grenade gun, her only weapon—

—*bam*, she hit the heavy door and was through, into a dark and echoing abyss, a wave of stench hitting her like a slap. She slammed the door closed and reached for the only light she could see, a glowing red square in a panel next to the entrance.

It was a light switch, and as rows of fluorescent bars fluttered on, she saw and understood two things simultaneously. The dead Umbrella workers had been dumped here in a huge pile, the source of the incredible odor—and there were no other doors. She was trapped and had a single load of buckshot with which to defend herself.

Oh man, think, think—

Outside, she heard the Nemesis howl the only word it knew, the terrible cry encouraging her to move, to do something. She ran for the tremendous mound of corpses, the only thing in the giant U-shaped chamber that wasn't bolted to the floor. Maybe one of them had a weapon.

The segmented metal floor rang hollowly beneath her feet, telling her where she was—some kind of garbage dumping room, the floor obviously capable of opening up to drop waste into some unknown below, vats of chemicals, a Dumpster, the sewers. Didn't matter, because she had no idea how to operate such a system; all she cared about at the moment was finding something she could use against the Nemesis.

The dead people were all in advanced stages of decay, thick, hot, gaseous waves of stink radiating from the darkening, bloated bodies, the pile almost as high as her chin. Jill couldn't afford to be particular; she dropped the grenade gun and immediately started to paw at the corpses, lifting sticky lab coats, jamming her hands into pockets that squished beneath her flying fingers. Pens and pencils, soggy packs of cigarettes, loose change—a key card, probably the very one she'd been looking for. *Wonderful, isn't that just—*

BOOM! BOOM!

Giant fists hammered at the door, echoing in the large chamber. The door was going to give in seconds, she'd have to go with what she had. No way she could kill it, but she could try to get around it.

Tucking the key card into the top of her left boot,

she grabbed the gun and ran back toward the door, thinking that Nicholai had at least left her with a good idea, *least he could do, the crazy bastard—*

Jill took a position next to the door, close to where it would swing back upon opening. She didn't stand directly behind it, the plan kind of fell to shit if she ended up crushed.

BOOM, and the door flew open, slamming into the wall inches from where she stood, the Nemesis storming in, arms and tentacles spread wide as it howled for blood.

It's changing, getting bigger—

Jill aimed at its already mangled lower back and fired, the load tearing into its flesh from less than ten feet away.

Screaming, the creature stumbled forward, and before it could stand up straight again, Jill was through the door and gone, praying that she'd have time to call for help and get away before it found her again. She pounded through the corridor, snatched up the Beretta, and sped into the next room, out into the hallway.

At least time to call; she may not survive to meet rescue, but Carlos still could, God willing.

* * *

There was only one helicopter, but it was in excellent shape, fueled and ready to fly. If he could find Jill, Carlos thought they might make it after all.

He sat in the pilot's seat, looking over the controls, running over the basics as best he could remember. He'd been taught by another merc with no formal training, and it had been a while, but he was pretty sure he could pull it off. The 'copter was an older two seater with a hover ceiling of about 4,000 feet, range, maybe 200 miles. He still didn't know what some of the switches and buttons did on the control panels, but he didn't need to, to get the thing airborne. The cyclic control stick moved the bird forward, back, and sideways. The collective control altered the thrust, controlling height.

Carlos checked his watch and was unhappily startled to see that twenty minutes had passed since he'd heard the announcement about the missiles. He'd spent a few minutes checking the helicopter, and there'd been a couple of zombies roaming around in the yard he'd had to shoot...

Didn't matter. They now had between twenty and forty minutes, tops. The facility compound was too big, he'd never be able to cover it all in time—

—so use the goddamn radio, dumbass!

Carlos reached for the headset, amazed that he hadn't thought of it, promising himself that he would smack himself silly for the oversight later, when he had time. Assuming there was a later.

"Hello, this is Carlos Oliveira with Umbrella, I am in Raccoon City, copy? There are still people alive here. If you can hear me, you have to stop the missile launch. Hello? Copy?"

No way to know if someone was getting his signal. Umbrella probably had a block on all outgoing transmissions, he'd just have to try and—

"Carlos? Is that you, over?"

Jill!

He felt weak with relief as her voice crackled into his ear, perhaps the sweetest sound he'd ever heard. "Yes! Jill, I found a helicopter, we have to get out of here, now! Where are you, over?"

"In a radio room, at the Umbrella facility—what did you say about a missile launch, over?"

She was so close! Carlos laughed, *We're outta here, it's over!* "The feds are gonna blow up the city in like half an hour, at dawn, but it's okay, we're ready to fly—do you see that ladder in the middle of the room? Over."

"Yeah, it's—they're going to blow up Raccoon, are you sure?" She sounded totally bewildered and forgot to use radio protocol.

We don't have time for this!

"Jill, I'm positive. Listen to me—go down the ladder and start running, you'll end up where I am, there's nowhere else to go. Through a cement room to the exit sign, then outside, then through this huge warehouse—there's some kind of a power generator in there, you'll have to run around some equipment. The back door will be at about... eleven o'clock from the front, got it? I'll be on the other side. And you better bust ass to get here, no dicking around."

There was the slightest pause, and Carlos could

hear the tight smile in her voice when she responded. "Dicking around you *wish*. On my way, over and out."

Grinning, Carlos powered up the 'copter as the deep, navy blue sky began to lighten, preparing for dawn.

TWENTY-SEVEN

Jill slid down the ladder and started running, her mind reeling with the news about Raccoon. She couldn't imagine what had been going on outside of the city in past days that the conclusion had been reached to blast a quarantine site out of existence.

Of course it has to be blown up, they would have wanted that once they'd collected their data, to make sure all the evidence is destroyed—

Jill leaped over a sprawled body, then another, and was at the doors with the exit sign overhead, just as Carlos had said. She barreled through and was greeted by wonderfully fresh, cool air, heavy with dew.

Dawn, he said they were launching at dawn. Half an hour was a generous estimate. Jill ran faster, through a winding corridor of stacked cars and junk metal, and there was the warehouse, straight ahead. It was big, low, and wide, and she was already thinking in hours when she hit the heavy, steel-reinforced front doors.

Eleven o'clock... She couldn't see the back door for the giant wall of unidentifiable machinery in the way, all thick pipes and metal shielding, but Carlos had said she'd have to run around some equipment. She veered right—

—and stopped in her tracks, staring at the monstrous apparatus that Carlos had mistaken for a generator. It was some kind of a laser cannon, huge, cylindrical, she'd seen them before but not even half the size—it was at least ten feet high and twenty long, and as big around as a table for six. Dozens of cables led from various outlets to the wall of machinery she stood next to, and it was aimed approximately at the front door, making her wonder what the hell they'd tested it on...

The back door slammed open. Jill reflexively pointed the Beretta and saw Carlos standing there, the whining sound of a revving helicopter outside.

"Jill, come on!"

He was obviously glad to see her, but she could read the urgency in his face, a reminder of what was coming as the door closed behind him.

She jogged toward him in the sudden silence, shaking her head. "Sorry, I was surprised is all, that's a laser cannon, biggest I ever—"

Ka-rash!

Near the ceiling by the front door, a giant mass exploded out of the wall, disappearing from their sight as it fell to the floor behind the wall of machinery. Jill had just an impression of a swollen, bulbous body surrounded by claws and tentacles, and she knew that she'd been right about the Nemesis. It was evolving.

A beat later there was another crash. Sparks crackled and flew from a tall panel next to the entrance, and a gurgling, warped howl erupted into the room, the cry of the Nemesis, but horribly mutated, deeper, rougher—

"Come on!" Carlos shouted, and Jill ran to him as he jerked at the handle on the back door—

—and it didn't open, and Jill noticed the small blinking lights on the panel next to it and understood that the Nemesis had shorted out the locking mechanisms.

They were locked in the warehouse with the thing that had been the S.T.A.R.S. killer, and it was screaming for blood.

TWENTY-EIGHT

Carlos heard the thing howl and knew what it was. He'd only caught a glimpse of the monster on its way down, but it was big and badass, and he suspected that they were screwed.

Jill raised her voice to a shout, and Carlos could only barely hear her over the Nemesis's seemingly endless scream.

"Where's the .357?"

Carlos shook his head. He had the M16, but he'd stowed the heavy revolver and the rest of the rifle's magazines on the helicopter.

"Grenade gun?" he shouted back, and it was Jill's turn to shake her head.

A 9mm and maybe twenty rounds left for the rifle. *We'll have to blow open the door, it's our only chance—*

Carlos knew better even as he thought it. The front and back doors were heavy-duty, they'd have better luck blowing a hole in the wall—

—and the answer hit him, and he saw that Jill already had it from the way she was staring at him, eyes wide and blinking.

The Nemesis-monster's howl was winding down, but a horrible, wet slurping noise had begun, the sound of something vast and sticky moving slowly and steadily across concrete.

It's coming for her.

"Can you operate it?" Carlos asked, already steeling himself for a confrontation with whatever the Nemesis had become.

"Maybe, but—"

Carlos cut her off. "I'm going to distract it—get that thing running and let me know when to duck."

Before Jill could protest, Carlos hurried past her, determined to do whatever he could to keep it from getting to her, *at least it's slower than it was, if I can just slow it down a little more—*

He reached the end of the wall of equipment, took a deep breath, stepped around the corner—and cried out in involuntary disgust at the oozing, undulating mass that crept and crawled toward him, pulling it-self along with clawed, shapeless appendages the color of blisters. Fleshy lumps rose and fell like bubbles in a pot of stew along its twisted back, thin, black fluid trickling from dozens of tiny slits on its body, wetting the floor, lubricating its meaty passage.

Carlos picked a slightly raised lump on top of the giant, pulsing creature and opened fire, the rounds splashing into the fleshy surface like pebbles into a stream, *tat tat tat—*

—and lightning fast, one of the tentacles at the front of the body lashed out, slapping Carlos's legs hard enough to knock him down.

Carlos scrambled backwards through the pain in his side, awed by its incredible speed and not a little afraid. The bulk of it moved slowly, but its reflexes were insanely fast, and it had reached across three meters of open space to knock him down, seemingly without strain.

"*Puta madre*," he breathed, the worst curse he could think of as he rolled to his feet and backed away. It was already to the corner of the metal wall, ten meters or less from the cannon where Jill was wildly slapping at switches. He'd distracted it about as effectively as a fly distracted an airplane. *How much time do we have left before daybreak—*

Suddenly, it howled again, a chorus of sound, each small, leaking slit on its body gaping open, a thousand mouths screaming, creating a trumpeting, deafening roar.

It wasn't going to stop. Carlos backed further away and opened fire again, a waste of bullets, but there was nothing else he could do—

—and then he heard the powerful, rising hum of a mighty turbine spinning fast and faster, and Jill was screaming for him to move, and Carlos moved.

* * *

She hadn't been able to find the power main, no buttons or cords to connect, and she didn't know enough about machines to figure it out. She'd seen Carlos fall and her heart had stopped, but she'd forced herself to keep trying, knowing it was all they had.

After a second frantic, desperate search she'd found the power switches on its base, and the machine had thrummed to beautiful, wonderful life.

"*Move!*" Jill shouted, pushing the levers that slowly and precisely raised the cannon, its movements spelled out digitally on a small screen next to the base. She could feel the energy building, the air around her heating up, and as Carlos got out of the way and the Nemesis-entity slithered out into the open, she found herself positively thrilled, almost overcome with an intense and violent sense of self-satisfaction.

It had killed Brad Vickers and tracked her mercilessly through the city. It had murdered the rescue team and stranded them in Raccoon, it had infected her with disease, it had terrorized her and wounded Carlos— and that it had been programmed to do these things didn't matter; she hated it with everything inside of her, despised it more than anything she'd ever despised.

The mutated, aberrant thing inched forward on a wave of slime as the cannon's hum reached an explosive crescendo, the sound drowning out everything. Jill's words went unheard, even by her.

"*You want S.T.A.R.S., I'll give you S.T.A.R.S., you piece of shit,*" she said, and slammed her hand down on the activation switch.

TWENTY-NINE

A brilliant light, white but shaded with electrically searing orange and blue, burst from the end of the laser cannon in a beam of concentrated fury. Arcs of heat and light stormed over the body of the cannon like miniature bolts of lightning, and the laser found the once-Nemesis's writhing, pulsating body and began to eat.

The creature that had once been the pride of Umbrella's development section whined and thrashed, flailing its multiple limbs in a frenzy of agonized confusion. The tight beam of light bored into its flesh, as relentless as it had proved, melting layers of tissue and soldering harder materials—bone and cartilage and pliable metal—into fused and useless lumps.

The creature began to smolder, then smoke, and as the brain stem inside of it withered and cooked, the Nemesis ceased to exist, its program wiped, its improbable heart finally bursting silently, deep inside.

A few seconds later, the cannon overheated and shut itself down.

THIRTY

The helicopter lifted up and away, a little jerky at first, but Carlos quickly found his balance. The first streaks of real light were swelling into the eastern sky as the doomed city fell behind them. It seemed so strange to finally be on their way, after days of wanting it so badly, of working toward nothing else.

"Nicholai's dead," Jill said, her voice cool and clear over the headset. It was the first thing she'd said since they'd taken off. "The Nemesis got him."

"No great loss," Carlos replied and meant it.

They fell into silence again, Carlos content to just fly for the moment, give himself a chance to be still. He was dog-tired and wanted only to get as far away from Raccoon as possible before the missiles hit.

After a moment, Jill reached across and placed her hand over his, and that was okay, too.

* * *

Jill held Carlos's hand as the sun inched slowly up over the horizon, turning the sky magnificent shades of pink and gray and lemon yellow. It was lovely, and Jill found that, as hard as she tried, she couldn't feel sorry that Raccoon was about to be dusted. It had been her home for a while, but it had become pain and death for thousands of people, and she thought that blasting it to hell and gone was probably the best thing that could happen to it.

Neither of them spoke as the sun continued to rise, as the miles flew beneath them, forests and farms and empty roads appearing fresh and bright in the gently warming light.

When the sky flashed white and the sound wave hit them a moment later, Jill didn't look back.

EPILOGUE

Trent had his hands full for most of the day, listening in on the spindoc meetings, arranging for media sympathy with a few of their bought networks, and explaining the difference between HARMs—the air to surface missiles that the army had used on Raccoon—and SRAMs to the three heads of White Umbrella. Jackson, in particular, was unhappy that the larger tactical missiles hadn't been used; he didn't seem to understand that a deliberate nuclear incident within the United States had to be kept as small and contained as possible. Ironic, that a man with so much wealth and power could be so oblivious to the reality he had helped create.

Trent finally had a few moments to himself in the early evening, after a final review of the Watchdog reports. He took a cup of coffee out onto the balcony of the rooms he used when he was at the DC offices. The brisk twilight was refreshing after a day of recycled air and fluorescent lights.

From twenty stories up, the city below seemed unreal, sounds distant and features blurred. Gazing out at nothing in particular, Trent sipped his coffee and thought about all he'd witnessed in the past few days from the shielded privacy of his home. Umbrella's few dozen stationary remotes in Raccoon had had nothing on the satellite pirate that piped information to his private screening room; he'd been able to follow several dramas that had unfolded in the last hours of the city.

There had been the rookie policeman, Kennedy, and Chris Redfield's sister—the two of them had barely escaped the lab explosion, managing to save Sherry Birkin, the young daughter of one of Umbrella's top research scientists, of all people. Trent hadn't had contact with any of them, but he knew that Leon Kennedy and Claire Redfield had become part of the fight. They were young, determined, and filled with a hatred for Umbrella; he couldn't have asked for better.

Trent's high hopes for Carlos Oliveira had been well met, and that he had joined forces with Jill Valentine... Trent had been utterly transfixed by their escape, pleased that two of his unwitting soldiers had worked so well together, surviving in spite of Jill's infection, the lunatic Russian, and the S.T.A.R.S. seeker. Use of the experimental Tyrant-like units was still in question by many of the White Umbrella researchers; for as deadly efficient as they usually were, they were also very expensive, and Trent knew that the debates would go on, fueled by the loss of two units in the destruction of the city.

Ada Wong, though...

Trent sighed, wishing that she had survived. The tall, beautiful Asian-American agent he had sent in had been as brilliant as she was competent. He hadn't actually seen her die, but the chances that she had escaped both the lab explosion and the complete obliteration of Raccoon were slim to none. Unfortunate, to say the least.

Overall, though, Trent was satisfied with how things were progressing. As far as he could tell, no one in the company had the slightest inkling of who he really was or what he was doing. The three most powerful men in Umbrella relied on him more and more every day, completely unaware of his agenda— to destroy the organization, from without and within, to devastate its leaders' lives and deliver them to justice; to organize an elite army of men and women committed to Umbrella's downfall, and to guide them as much as he was able in their quest.

If his methods were complicated, the reason was simple: to avenge the death of his parents, both scientists, murdered when he was a child so that Umbrella could profit from their research.

Trent smiled to himself, taking another sip from his mug. It sounded so melodramatic, so grandiose. It had been almost thirty years since his parents had been burned alive in the alleged laboratory accident. He'd left the pain behind long ago—his resolve, however, had never faltered. He'd changed his name, his background, given up any hope of ever having a normal life—and regretted nothing, even now that he shared responsibility for the deaths of so many.

It was getting dark. Far below, streetlights were flickering on, sending up a soft glow that would radiate out into the night sky like a halo above the city. In its own way, it was quite beautiful.

Trent finished his coffee and absently traced the Umbrella logo on the side of the cup with his fingers, thinking about darkness and light, good and evil, and the shades of gray that existed in between everything. He needed to be very careful, and not just to avoid being discovered; it was those shades of gray that worried him.

After a few moments, Trent turned his back on the gathering dark and went inside. He still had a lot to do before he could go home.

ABOUT THE AUTHOR

S.D. Perry is the author of several tie-in novels to popular series such as *Aliens*, *Alien vs. Predator*, *Star Trek* and *Star Trek: Deep Space Nine*. Perry also wrote the movie novelizations for *Timecop* and *Virus*. She is the daughter of bestselling sci-fi author Steve Perry and lives in Portland, Oregon with her husband and two children.

For more fantastic fiction from Titan Books in the areas of sci-fi, fantasy, steampunk, alternate history, mystery and crime, as well as tie-ins to hit movies, TV shows and videogames:

VISIT OUR WEBSITE
TITANBOOKS.COM

FOLLOW US ON TWITTER
@TITANBOOKS